TIME
OF THE
UNICORN

TIME OF THE UNICORN

by Barbara Jefferis

William Morrow & Company, Inc.
New York 1974

N

Fiction

Book design by Helen Roberts

Printed in the United States of America.

1 2 3 4 5   78 77 76 75 74

Library of Congress Cataloging in Publication Data

Jefferis, Barbara.
  Time of the unicorn.

  I. Title.
PZ4.J45Ti3 [PR9619.3.J3] 823   73–20468
ISBN 0-688-00249-8

He is self-armed, for a radiant horn rises from his forehead to the distance of four feet. The nature of this wondrous animal is that he is both fierce and meek, like to a scapegoat.

His virtue is no less famous than his strength inasmuch that the wild beasts do not drink from the deep pools until he has stirred them with his horn, and thus he purifies the means of life for those who have no virtue to do it of themselves.

TIME OF THE UNICORN

On the sixteenth day it seemed that a witch had knotted a black wind and tied it to the mast. Since early morning the tormented ship had lain pitching, bow into the wind, and at each new gust she snubbed to her sea anchor. Two men were needed to hold the steering oar, and a quarter hour at it was the most they could manage before it overpowered them.

Sea and sky were of one colour, and to the passengers, wrapped in coarse blankets Walter Faber had broken out from the stores he was carrying, it seemed that they were caught on a monstrous treadmill made of wind and water, and that they had been climbing up and sliding down the same set of waves for an infinity of time. In fact they had been drifting backwards and sideways a little every minute of the awful day.

At intervals the sea and the sky darkened, and icy rain blew in on them horizontally, rattling along the deck. They didn't notice it, for it was indistinguishable from the constant rain of sea spray that had soaked them all, turning the waist of the ship into a stinking puddle of sea-diluted vomit.

The passengers felt themselves totally divided from the crew of the ship. The good humour and the jokes they had shared with them when they left Dartmouth were forgotten now, and the sailors seemed alien people —brutish and self-absorbed. Those on deck worked stripped and sweating in the freezing wind and spray, and when they were relieved for a few minutes at the steerboard they planted their feet and rode the ship's movement upright, working each shoulder in turn under a clasping hand to free the painful locking of their muscles.

The passengers could do nothing—nothing except find a confined corner, wedge themselves in, kneel down and pray and promise things to God. Many hours before they had leaned precariously over, dipped their beads and their relics in the sea and nailed them to the mast of the *Grace Dieu*. Walter Faber had watched them sourly. He disliked nail holes in his mast, and he felt that naviga-tion was not God's business, but the captain's. He said as much to one of his own people and the man crossed him-self and spat, forgetting to turn downwind, so that his piety was flung quickly back in his face to frighten him. The priest, too, had seen the people nailing their holy objects to the mast. He thought it a wise move if it went no further, but frightened travellers sometimes found the dipping of their relics not enough, and were moved to dip their spiritual masters too. Father Nicholas was an old man, and time had burned away a good deal of his zeal.

In the late afternoon Walter Faber decided to set his sail again, and a great clamour of fear and protest rose from the passengers. It seemed to them that they had already been caught for an immeasurable time in the fury of the storm and that, under sail and under cover of darkness, they might well be blown beyond the known limits of the world and over the edge into the black maelstrom of the sea. Faber was patient with them. Some had paid their fares. Some would not pay until they made a safe landing at the other end of the voyage. He tried to explain to them that, though they seemed to be stationary, they were being blown sideways, that he dare not try to hold that station through the hours of darkness, on a lee shore. They looked wildly around them. The thought of a shore, any shore, was happiness; but there was nothing to be seen through the grey curtains of the storm. "What shore?" they said. "How far? Make for it!"

"Five miles," Faber said, "six miles," and he was thinking perhaps two, perhaps one, perhaps twenty. "The wind is set from the northwest, and it will blow all night."

"We are, each one of us, like ships blown out of port by God's bitter wind into God's bitter dark," Father Nicholas said, comforting nobody.

In the meantime all of Faber's crew had come on deck for the raising of the mast, which for many hours had lain canted out over the roof of the forward fighting-castle, with its square sail bundled to the yard. While two men worked at the windlass in the bow, bringing up the sea anchor they'd been trailing through the long day, four others climbed in the bitter wind to the forecastle roof to manhandle the heavy mast high enough to give the stern windlass a purchase on it. Four others worked there, driving long handspikes into the holes of the windlass log, heaving down, moving the spikes to holes freshly exposed, heaving down again. The mast came up with agonizing slowness, and as it caught the wind it seemed that the shocked little ship stood still for a moment, and then slid sickeningly backwards down a wave. Slowly the mast was dragged groaning higher and higher, while the lashed sail fought its wrappings and the holy relics jangled soundlessly in the wind. As the foot of the mast came upright in its tabernacle Faber himself drove home the wooden pins that would hold it there. The lashings were let go to free the sail from the yard and the *Grace Dieu* began to twist and slew. As she came sharply about, bow to stern, her aftercastle caught the wind like the tail of a weathercock and brought her up again, stopping the spin.

Now she had forward motion at last, and the deck communicated it to the passengers through their aching feet. It seemed to warm and cheer them a little, though soon their anguished stomachs began a new protest against the hardened rhythm of the ship's pitching. Faber set men to the braces again to fight the wind in the sail's great leather belly, and slewed the yard around as far to the steerboard side as it could be set. His object now was to beat out to sea and put as many miles of wild wind and water as he could between the shore and his ship. Most of the passengers were crowded into the meager cover under the ship's forward fighting-castle, reluctant to go down into the holds while the light lasted. There was no sign of the sun, but the clouds to the west were darkly streaked with orange. They watched that way, bearing the spray in their faces for the comfort the last of the light could give them.

Clodagh had kept a distance between herself and the other passengers throughout the storm, as she had on the preceding days of the voyage. From the dock, as she had watched the loading of the horses and the caulking up of the big door which had let them into the hold, she had also watched the women who came aboard, and found no good reason for striking up acquaintance with them. All but one of them were her inferiors, and that one she took to be some sort of nun. The voyage would soon be over, and nothing about them suggested that she would meet any of them again. Her better clothing, the fact that the captain spoke to her by name and that she had been given a few boarded-in feet of private space against the wall of the stable in the stern hold, stopped them making any approach to her. The three knights who had come aboard were not, she thought, from her part of the country, and the rest of the men, as far as she could see, were only common soldiers.

She had spent most of the day of the storm wrapped in a blanket and wedged between the larboard-side bollard and the rail, in the comparative shelter underneath the aftercastle.

Certainly it would have been warmer in her refuge in the hold, but she'd been driven out of there by the stench of horse piss, and of blood. The horses, strung by their girths from ringbolts in the underside of the decking so that their hooves just brushed and scraped the floor, had interested her enough to take her down there two or three times each day to watch them feed and physicked against the seasickness that attacked them long before the storm began. She liked the clamour and excitement of their exercise time, when, with whip-crackings and excited cries, the men who looked after them drove the poor swinging beasts to gallop in midair, whinnying and straining to get a purchase with hooves that barely grazed the flooring boards. But in the morning, after the storm began, one of the horses had broken free from its girth-cradle and run crazed with fear on the tilting floor of the hold, smashing down the timber partition between the stable hold and the passenger hold and demolishing Clodagh's private retreat. It had been clubbed down, and its throat cut, among the bedding and the clothing bundles of the passengers.

She had been in the hold at the time, had barely escaped the thrashing forelegs of the horse as it reared crazily up and came through the hold partition, and she was determined not to go down again during the night.

Half an hour after the sail was set the last of the light had faded from the western sky and most of the passengers had gone belowdeck to escape the cold, some to the stern hold where they belonged, others, after argument, to the partitioned-off end of the forward hold, where the sailors slept among the cargo.

Time passed. She watched with wide eyes, seeing nothing in the darkness, hearing nothing but the sound of water and the drumming of the wind in the spars and against the leather sail. At short intervals the two steersmen were relieved by two others, and the two that were relieved dropped down out of the wind below rail level a few feet away from her to rest before they took another turn at the oar. Then a light appeared in the waist of the ship, giving her eyes something to focus on, and she could see that the captain was there, and that a man was slowly climbing the mast with a great lantern. He hung it from a hook below the level of the yard so that the leather sail acted as a reflector for it, throwing a thin light into the waist and back into the recess under the aftercastle where Clodagh was crouched. It showed her that there were two other people there besides the steersmen. One was a crouched bundle—someone apparently already asleep with his blanket pulled over his head in tent fashion. The other was a young man who stood, holding the deck rail with both hands and staring out over the port side of the ship. "It's worse," he shouted to her, "putting the lantern on makes it worse out there." She didn't answer him but she craned up so that her eyes were above rail level and looked out into the storm and indeed it *was* worse, for though the wind seemed to be dropping, the blackness had closed in on the ship like solid walls. She stood then, clutching the blanket around her, leaning out and searching the darkness for the moon or stars. Nothing. It could be the clouds, of course, or it could be, as she had heard other passengers suggest, that the storm had driven them so far off their course that they were now in a part of the sea not covered by a sky.

The young man beside her turned his back to the sea and slid to his haunches, in the shelter of the rail. "Down," he said, pulling roughly on a fold of her blanket, "down, or your neckbone will break and fall into your gullet."

She turned and dropped down to the deck beside him, pulling the blanket more tightly around her shoulders, suddenly glad, after a day of fear and sickness, to have a few minutes of talk with somebody. His voice told her that he came from her part of the country, but the blanket into which he'd cut a head hole covered him from his neck down to mid-shin, so that she couldn't place him by his clothes. He wore his hair a little longer than was customary, and his tanned face made her wonder whether his time in the fields was spent in hunting or in drudgery. He moved a little closer to shelter her and then he turned to look at her in what light there was and said, "Spine of God, but you've got beautiful eyes!" It was a remark that had served him well in his own village.

She looked at him coldly. That branded him a soldier,

since soldiers commonly had a pressing need and a high disdain for women. But when she found that he dropped his eyes uncomfortably under her cool glance she thought perhaps if he was a soldier he was a raw one, and merely apeing others. "Have you taken the Cross?" she asked.

He looked up again, and grinned. "Had it thrust upon me," he said.

"Where do you come from?" she asked uneasily.

"Dittisham," he said, naming a village only a few miles from her own.

"You were one of those mad ones, marching and shouting," she said. "You should have prayed instead."

The boy laughed. "We prayed," he said, "but our prayers were thwarted by the prayers of priests asking for battle-axes."

"Never mind," Clodagh said. "Think of your reward— Jerusalem!"

"My grandfather was there, fifty years ago, in the first war. 'Fighting will make a man of you,' he says. Make a corpse of me, more like. Are you going there?"

"Porto," she said. "I'm not going beyond Porto," and turned the talk quickly back to his affairs. She wanted very much to know whose conscript he was.

"These knights?" she asked. "Are you with them?"

"They're Porto reinforcements," he said. "I've to go all the long and bloody way."

"Under whose banner?"

"Robert Apelfourde's," he said. "A bloody foreigner."

"No foreigner," she said. "English-born, the same as you are."

"Small likeness," he said. "A Norman, a landlord and a captain." Then he looked at her a little anxiously. "You're not a Norman?" he said.

She shook her head. An untruth by gesture was only partly an untruth, and she was only partly Norman—though she was married to one. Against all sense she shared some of the antiwar feeling of the Dittisham men, that reluctance to go to somebody else's war that had made them wear their hawks on their right wrists as a sign of peace, and oppose the Second Crusade by marching backwards and forwards through their village while it was preached there, chanting the name of the Saracen leader, Nur-ad-din, Nur-ad-din, in time with their marching feet. But Robert Apelfourde had bound himself to go with two hundred men, and his lieutenants had known how to bring pressure on his reluctant people.

The captain had come back from his place near the mast, and was standing in front of her, looking down. "You'd do better in the hold, Lady," he said. She shook her head. "Here," he said, holding a leather bottle out to her. "Drink. It'll warm your stomach."

She shook her head again but he pressed it on her, leaning below the level of wind and rail so that she could hear him. "A mouthful," he said. "You could wash the dead with this, and they'd resurrect themselves." She smiled and drank a mouthful of the wine, and found it did warm her pleasantly. "The wind's dropping, isn't it?" she said. "Aye, dropping," he said, and took the bottle back, and turned away. She noticed that he didn't offer it to the young man, which confirmed what she already knew—he was a common soldier, a landless man, a nobody, a tenant of her husband, Robert Apelfourde.

"*He* sees some reason for the expedition," she said, pointing at the captain's back. "He thinks it *is* a just and holy cause."

"Just and holy profits," the young man said. "Land the troops, unload the stores, and fill your empty holds with all that rich stuff the camel caravans bring in from further east. He's another Norman."

She laughed, though her laugh made no real sound in the wind. "Why do you hate them so much?" she said, leaning closer to him to make her question heard.

"They're backward-looking," he said. "Always over their shoulders, looking into Europe. They don't understand what an island is. They want to drag us all into Europe, so they can be cosy with their cousins. Twopence a day, and pull down my house over my head if I won't go."

"Someone has to go," she said. "D'you want the Saracens just a jump away, on the other side of the channel?"

"All I want's to be back on the other side of the channel," he said, and his words brought the cold wind back to her, and the nearness of the black sky and sea.

"Save us, Holy Sepulchre," she said automatically, and pulled the blanket more tightly around her shoulders, clenching her teeth to stop their chattering.

"Here," he said, "you're freezing," and startled her by pulling the blanket roughly away from her. He bunched the middle of it, hacked it quickly through with his knife to make a neck hole, and knelt on the deck beside her to pull it over her head. Then he pulled his own blanket off and dropped it over her head, so that she was warmly encased in two. "Don't," she said. "You mustn't, you'll be cold," but the added warmth was so comforting that she knew it would take more strength than she had to give it up. He was wearing a knee-length gambeson of boiled leather—all that he would have to protect him in coming battles, though his superiors would wear chain mail over theirs.

"How old are you?" she asked suddenly, but he didn't hear her.

"I'll filch another blanket, and come back," he said.

"Don't," she said sharply. "Don't come back. I want to sleep."

He looked at her for a moment, and then he stooped to a free end of rope lying slack on the deck beyond the bollard and passed it behind her and around her waist and swiftly knotted it again to the bollard. "Sleep," he said. "They'll have to wake you if they want to alter sail." He moved a step or two away and looked back and said something that she couldn't hear clearly because the wind took his words and whipped them off into the fizzing darkness, but it seemed to her that what he had said was, "I hope I figure in any dreams you have."

It was a long time before she slept. Now that he was gone she seemed quite alone on the ship as the hours passed. She saw the movements of the others—the waiting steersmen relieving those at the oar, the four of them at last relieved by four others who came up in the darkness from the hold, the panicky seamen whom the captain had sent, uselessly as lookouts, to the bow and to the fighting top at the head of the mast. But the crew had been fighting more than sixteen hours already against the storm; they were too tired to shout above the wind unless shouting was really necessary, and they took no notice of Clodagh, nor of the tented blanket where some other passenger slept a few feet away. She felt entirely alone, except for the comfort of the rope the Dittisham man had secured around her waist. She knew that she would have been a little warmer if she had gone down with the other passengers into the ship's hold, but for her there was a sort of comfort in the night's wild air, and the wildly swinging lantern on the mast. Down

there, she knew, there would be very little light, but perhaps enough for them to see her fear. On the first day
out she had lain awake through the twelve parts of the
night, holding herself rigidly with her head pressed
against one wall of her compartment and her feet braced
against the other, hearing the working of the timbers
and the slap of water against the hull and fearing that
there were icthyocentaurs there, upward men and downward fish, separated from her only by the thickness of
the planking. On the succeeding nights she had slept and
woken and slept and woken again, dreaming that hordes
of creatures were encircling the keel, since every creature
on the earth, she knew, had its counterpart underneath
the ocean. If she were to go down into the hold tonight
there would be no concealment for her fear, since the
maddened horse had broken down her shelter. On deck
she was less afraid, since the more frightful of the ocean's
creatures were known to swim always in the depths.

Robert Apelfourde had sent for her because he had
elected now to delay going on to Jerusalem. Or she
thought he had—it was not entirely clear to her from the
word-of-mouth message which had ordered that she and
her servants and any of his men still awaiting transport
should be put aboard the *Grace Dieu* at Dartmouth in
the care of his factor, Richard Orm. When he had taken
the Cross, with a ferocious yearning to spill Turkish
blood, she had been not much averse to the prospect of
his absence on a campaign that was to last two years.
Now it seemed that he had changed his mind and joined
the Portugallers. She didn't know his purpose or his reason. She thought there were no Saracens there, and certainly no holy places to be liberated; but a man who
loves fighting can find something to fight in any country
where he finds himself. The news that he might stay

there for a season before going to Jerusalem had not surprised her. What had surprised her was his summoning of her. Perhaps he had found the Iberian women not as sultry as returning servicemen had said. In fact she would have been glad enough to go, had it not been for the sea voyage that was necessary. She still hoped to have a child, and when she discovered after his departure that she was not yet carrying one, two years had seemed a long time to wait for another chance. Thinking of him kindly, for he was a good enough man and had not yet reproached her for five years of childlessness, she was glad enough to be going, in spite of the discomforts of the journey.

It had begun so differently for her, with bright sun and sparkling water, a crowded dock, and her restless mother's envy to sweep away any fears she had about the voyage. A number of small ships were in the port, and the air was full of the sound of shipwrights' hammers, patching up the damage of old voyages. The docks were crammed with soldiers and their bundles, knights in fur-edged cloaks and oiled chain mail, sailors in drink, captains who dared not take their eyes off conscripts for fear of losing them, horses and stores and bedding waiting to be loaded, small domestic encampments of worn-out women and children who were going along to the war, as part of the baggage.

"By my life, I envy you," Blanchefleur said, turning all the time to watch what was going on close to her, in the distance, on the docks, on the decks.

"You're welcome to my place," Clodagh said, smiling a little wanly at her mother. She had been lit with excitement at the proper time, but the long delay and the bleak thought of separation from her mother had worn her down.

"You're not sick?" Blanchefleur said, peering at her through eyes narrowed against the sun.

"Not yet."

"You won't be sick at all if you don't eat." Blanchefleur reached into the basket at Clodagh's feet, chose a cold dumpling, took a big bite from it and passed what was left to her daughter. "Eat now and pad your stomach, while there's firm ground under your feet," she said.

They had come down to the dock at the appointed sailing time, followed by Clodagh's girl and by two servants carrying her clothes and baskets of food for the voyage. Richard Orm had met them, shaking his head and grumbling about delays. "The carpenters are still in the hold," he said. "They've hours of work yet, and Faber must stand guard on them himself, or they'll skimp the work and be off to the next ship."

"A proper place was promised for your mistress," Blanchefleur said. She didn't like her daughter going so poorly accompanied, but places on ships were now almost as hard to get as places in Heaven.

"It's done," Orm said. "No bigger than a kennel, but it's private."

By early afternoon, when it was clear the *Grace Dieu* would not sail that day, Blanchefleur and Clodagh sent the servants home and feasted from the baskets, giving some of what was left to the hungry wives and children of the common soldiers.

"I'll take your place, Clo," Blanchefleur had said a dozen times, and each time they laughed together because it was an old joke between them that she could have had Robert Apelfourde if she'd wanted. She had been tired of widowhood by the time Clodagh was ready

for marriage, and she was no more than four years his
senior. But her land was secured to her only until she
remarried, and in the end it had been better politics to
protect Clodagh by letting Apelfourde have her. If he
died, or if he got tired of her and trumped up an annul-
ment, Blanchefleur would still be mistress of her own
land, with a roof to offer her returning daughter. Clodagh had been thirteen at the time, too young to be con-
sulted in the matter. When she was safely married to
Apelfourde, Blanchefleur had explained the reasons to
her. Apelfourde had seemed put out when she passed
the information on to him. She didn't know whether it
was because he had been outthought in the matter of the
land, or because he would have preferred her mother in
his bed. She supposed it was that. For herself she liked
him well enough, but a man who was more than double
her age would not have been her choice. It seemed natural that he had more to say to her mother than to her
when they were all together.

"Still to be going, still to be moving!" Blanchefleur
said on the second day of waiting on the dock, stretching
her arms as though she would embrace the port and the
ships. "Clo, Clo, d'you remember the ship, and the wild
night, crossing to Ireland, and nobody knew where it
was we'd landed, and the people's talk so thick and singing the devil himself couldn't tell what they were
saying?"

"And the horses," Clodagh said, "little and rough.
And my father, with his beard and his great dog . . ."

"*There* was a man," Blanchefleur said, and began to
mourn.

Clodagh didn't really remember her father. She played
at remembering him because of the pleasure it gave her
mother. Blanchefleur had run off with him, a wild Irish

thane who'd been sent to England to parley some sort of peace while the other wild Irish chiefs went on fighting despite the parley. Blanchefleur's father had sent all the men he could gather to bring her back, but Diarmid O'Fan had come well-guarded into England, and by the time they were found and taken Blanchefleur was big with child. Her father had been pleasantly surprised to find the man was a proper Christian, though he didn't believe his claim that he owned wide lands and houses. He wept while his household chaplain married them, but he rejoiced piously when their unborn child was promised to God in expiation of the irregularities of their marriage. When Diarmid went back to his lands in Ireland, Blanchefleur's father saw reason to hope that his daughter would stay in the world until the child was ready to take its vows, and that she would then go into a convent herself. Instead Blanchefleur had stayed in his household until her daughter was two, and had then taken her child and her servants and her belongings, and embarked for Ireland. That was the journey Blanche-fleur was now reminding her of.

"I wish this ship was going to *Ireland*," Clodagh said.

"Ah—I too," Blanchefleur said. For three or four years, until he was clubbed down and ridden over in battle, she and the child had roamed about after Diarmid, never quite certain where they were or where they were going, but always with him, and happy, and well served, and in better houses than she'd known in England. "Portugal is nothing," she said. "But you'll go to Jerusalem after a while, where the streets are lined with fruit trees, and paved with emeralds and gold."

"Is that *true*?"

Blanchefleur laughed. "It's what everyone believes," she said. "Could even the *infidels* be so shuttle-witted?"

A disturbance had started at the other end of the dock, and the people waiting beside the *Grace Dieu* pressed forward to see what was happening. The captain, Walter Faber, came down onto the wharf and joined Blanchefleur and her daughter. He had come to speak to them several times in the last two days, timing his visits so that they coincided with the uncovering of the food baskets. Blanchefleur thought it was a fair enough bargain, and fed him generously, since she expected him to pay Clodagh special attentions on the voyage. "What's happening?" they asked him. "What's the noise about?"

"Marching, shouting, broken heads," Faber said, and spat his disgust.

A dozen youths broke away from the others and ran towards the *Grace Dieu*, chanting over and over again "Nur-ad-din, we won't win." Those waiting on the wharf jeered at them, pelted them with dirt, tried to trip them.

"What do they mean?" Clodagh said, turning to Faber.

"They're against the war," Faber said. "They don't want to go. They support the Saracen leader, Nur-ad-din."

"But he's the enemy," Clodagh said. Her mother laughed. "Well, isn't he?" she said uncertainly.

"The archenemy," Faber said. "The Defiler. He follows Mahomet, who says all are equal before God, and the rich should share all they have with the poor."

"Others have said the same," Blanchefleur said. "Our Saviour said it."

"Not the same thing" Faber said. He didn't want to enter any arguments. He wanted to get his ship away before the last of his men absconded. He didn't like carrying conscripts, or women, or children, or civilians. He liked his deck filled with knights and his hold with knights' horses, all of which could be emptied out at Antioch to make room for good cargoes of stuff that had been brought overland from Cathay and India. He knew a great deal about sailing and trading, a little cosmography, a lot of dirty stories, and almost nothing of how people lived on shore, or the uncertainty and poverty of their lives since Stephen had had the throne. He thought that things had taken a very poor turn in Portugal, but he had to go there, since he couldn't carry enough drinking water unless he put into the Duoro, the last friendly port, to replenish it. Half his passengers would be landless soldiers and their families, persuaded to fight there by the promise that everything captured would be divided among them afterwards according to rank. He'd be hard put to it to get their passage money from them before they landed, and his passenger hold would be half empty for the rest of the journey to the Holy Land. "There's no discipline now," he said. "People go where they like, say what they like, and everyone's equal to his master. A strong king, like the old one, that's what we need. Build ships. Send all this rabble to fight the Saracen."

"And prevent the sea captains trading with the enemy?" Blanchefleur said.

Faber frowned. "You don't understand the business, Lady. It's the surest way on earth of weakening him." He leaned, uninvited, and took an apple from their food basket. "Go home," he said. "The wharf's no place for you, with these ruffians. We'll be off tomorrow. I can promise you that, if I can find enough hands to help get the horses loaded."

Blanchefleur laughed at his back, as he walked away.

"What a fool," she said. "The sort that would set fire to
his own hair, to get rid of the nits in it. No matter.
Richard Orm is loyal and sensible. He'll look after you."

They took Faber's advice, going back through the
town to the house where they were lodging. When they
got there they found that Clodagh's girl had run off.
They'd missed her at the wharf, but had thought she had
gone back to the house with the other servants when it
was clear that the ship would not sail that day. The
others knew, or pretended to know, nothing. They were
sent out by Blanchefleur to look for her and bring her
back.

"They won't find her," Blanchefleur said. "Poor silly
girl, she had a black fear of going on the water."

"She's not to be beaten when she's found," Clodagh
said. The girl had served her for five or six years, and
she was fond of her.

"She'll not be beaten," Blanchefleur said. "And she'll
not be found. The port is full of Freiesans and Scots and
Flemings and runaway serfs and dispossessed freemen
and unemployed soldiers looking for bread and trouble,
and women. Now you'll have no one." They had
brought no other female servant with them, and if the
Grace Dieu was to sail next day, there was no time to
send for a replacement.

"I'll need no one," Clodagh said. "I'm not so grand,
suddenly, that I can't comb my own hair. There'll be
other women. And besides, I have a partitioned place to
myself."

"But without her you'll forget everything I've said,"
Blanchefleur complained.

"I'll forget nothing," Clodagh said, and laughed.
"How could I? You've told me all of it so many times."

"Perhaps there is no real harm," Blanchefleur said.

"Apelfourde will have foreign servants for you. Be on your guard. No frolicking. None of the easy ways of England, remember. The foreign Normans don't live and mix as we do."

"The more fools," Clodagh said idly. She'd had the difference explained a dozen times.

"And remember, you'll be watched and noticed. Apelfourde is Hervey's vassal, and Hervey is the King's so you'll live grander and less jovial than we do here. Confess only to priests that come from England, remember to have cucumbers brought for your hands, pray every day to Our Lady to bring us back together, don't eat any foreign foods that you haven't seen eaten here, keep your mulberry gown always wrapped so the silver on it won't tarnish, don't overheat your spleen by sleeping during the day, and above all keep your head covered against the sun, for it can let the madness in," Blanchefleur said. She burst into laughter at the boredom on her daughter's face.

There seemed good hope of sailing, when they went back to the dock early the next morning. This time Clodagh's clothing bundles and her bedding were taken aboard for her by one of the crew. Horses were being led and pushed up a plank from the wharf through a big doorway opened in the hull. They were followed by a line of men carrying their fodder, and when these men came out again the last to go in were three knights, who preferred the plank into the hold rather than the ladder to the deck, because of their armour.

"So young," Blanchefleur said regretfully, looking at them. "Far better suited for beds than for battlefields."

The big door in the hull was swung to and barred into its place, and half a dozen men began caulking the closures to keep the sea out. The captain was everywhere now, checking the tow and the sails, cursing the latecomers cluttering his ladder, feeling the beginnings of the loud and cheerful mood that would come to him as soon as his deck moved under his feet. He came over the side and down the ladder again to see that the caulking had been done to his liking, and saw that Clodagh was still standing there with her mother. "Best go up, Lady, if you've not changed your mind," he said, giving her a little push towards the ladder. "We'll be away now, in a dozen heartbeats."

Blanchefleur threw her arms around the girl, hugging her so that she lost her breath. "Be safe. Be happy," she said. "And pray for us both—pray specially." Widowed, she had loved her only daughter too dearly to honour her promise of dedicating her to God, and the dishonoured promise made a special bond between them.

The captain followed Clodagh up, and the ladder was pulled inboard as the mooring ropes were thrown off. The *Grace Dieu* began to move at once, and Clodagh ran up under the forward fighting-castle to look down on the rowers in the boat that was pulling them out into the wind. Then she ran back again to the waist of the ship to wave to her mother. Already there were many yards of green water between them, dappled with sunlight and flecked with bubbles from the oars and the ship's wake. Her mother had cupped her hands to her mouth and was shouting a last message. Clodagh leaned far out, straining to hear the words. "Clo," she heard. "Don't forget . . . cover your . . . against the madness." She laughed and waved with both arms and then folded her extended arms so that they wrapped her head, to show that she understood. It was not this gentle sun that her mother warned her against, but the fierce sun of the strange places where she was going.

Now, on the *Grace Dieu*'s deck, in the bitter cold, she threw up one arm to protect her head against the wet black madness of the night and, with her other hand clasped over the restraining rope the Dittisham man had knotted around her waist, she slept at last.

She woke at a loud cry from the helmsman, as the *Grace Dieu* heeled over in a fresh squall of wind. She clutched at the bollard to which she was roped and looked up for reassurance at the lantern on the mast with the great straining belly of the sail beyond it. Above it, in the dimmer light, she could see the lookout craning down from the fighting-top with a moving mouth from which the wind expunged every word. Then, as she watched, the windward shrouds parted with a crack, the sail blew out with a thunderous bang and the lantern swung away high over the side of the ship as the mast bent in a great bow. She scrabbled at the rope that held her so that she could free herself and move quickly out from underneath the menace of the mast, but she couldn't find the knot and, in panic, she covered her head with her folded arms and shrank small and tight against the canting bulwarks. There was a sound like the splintering of a great tree, and when she looked up part of the sail was struggling like a live thing on the deck, and the only light came to them eerily from somewhere over the side. Men climbed out from the hatchway to join those of the crew on deck, and she heard Faber shouting orders to them to let go the ground tackle. She felt the ship begin to swing broadside to the waves, but she had her head down again, searching frantically for the knot that held her while there was still light to master it by. She found it, unknotted it and stood up, holding to the bulwarks against the sickening wallow of the ship, and as the *Grace Dieu* turned head to wind and buried her larboard rail in the dark water she heard axes cutting away the fallen rigging, the end of the sail blew overboard and the light was doused.

In the darkness she stood perfectly still, straining to hear above the wind the shouted orders about ground tackle and cable, Faber's orders to the steersmen, his blasphemous appeals for light. Seconds passed and a third squall hit the ship, pushing her backwards like a giant hand, before two small rush lanterns were brought up to be hand-held where they were wanted at bow and stern.

She looked quickly behind her, and saw that the tent-like bundle that had kept her company all night had been covering the priest. He stood now, with his arms locked around a supporting post of the aftercastle and his hands devoutly clasped in prayer. She let go the rail and rushed to him, sliding on the deck, and locked her arms over his, beating at him with her fists, saying, "There was a man, there was a man up there . . ." He opened his eyes and looked at her, and she pointed wildly up, into the vacant darkness, and said, "Up there, up there . . . at the top of the mast, a man, I saw him, there, save him, save him." The priest made the sign of the cross with his thumb without unclasping his hands and said, "Pray for him, pray for him," and she heard him take up his prayer where she had interrupted him, ". . . *peccatis tuis perducat te ad vitam aeternam Sacerdos dicit. . . .*"

She turned away from him, sick with the fear that she too, at any moment now, would follow that man she had last seen with gaping, voiceless mouth, into the greedy waves. She would have liked to pray but she could remember no prayers. In any case it seemed pointless to pray now when there was a professional beside her who could do it for her. She edged forward a little where she could watch the paying out of the great twisted ropes that were the ship's cable. When the last of it had gone she made her way carefully along the streaming deck to the shelter underneath the forecastle. The wind squalls had been the forerunners of more rain, and the aftercastle offered no shelter now that the ship had turned. She took up a position alongside the captain on the larboard side, feeling there was some protection in being near to him. The dim light held at knee level by one of his crew showed her only the left side of his face. He seemed to be leaning out, listening. "What can you hear?" she called, and he turned, startled by her voice.

"Go below," he said impatiently, but she shook her head. He shrugged. "You'll do as well here . . ." he said, and went back to listening.

"What can you hear?" she said again.

"Nothing yet, praise Mary Virgin. Listen," he said, "and pray."

"Listen for *what*?" she said, thinking nothing could be heard above the sound of wind and water.

"The cries of seabirds, and of breaking water. If we're getting close to land, we'll hear them."

"But we're anchored," she said. "Aren't we anchored?"

"All the ground tackle's down, and all our cable's out. There's no more we can do, except to listen."

She listened for a long time after he had left her side, straining eyes and ears out in the darkness for sight or sound that would break the monotony of the black disorder. She could hear the thump of the waterlogged gear against the side of the ship; later she heard again the sound of axes as Faber's men cut the broken mast and its tangled gear free from the ship for fear its steady pounding might knock holes in the hull. She stayed at the rail an hour or more after that was done, but the only sounds she could hear were the sounds of water, the sounds of wind gusts and a strange high squealing overhead in the dark that she knew was the noise of sirens laughing and jeering at the *Grace Dieu*'s people.

When the ship struck she had been crouched again, half dozing, for an hour or more, worn out by listening and watching and by a new bout of unprofitable retching due to the changed motion of the crippled ship. A few others had come up, preferring the open deck to the imprisoning hold, and they were crouched there too, hoping, complaining, praying and vomiting. She had been dreaming of water of a different sort—bright water, clear water, shallow water, water that ran in sunlight between green banks, where bare-legged servants beat the house linens on the wet brown stones. She woke to a vile uproar of breaking water and of breaking timbers. The stern of the ship was canted hideously above her, and she had been flung right into the forepeak under the fightingcastle. The next wave smashed the *Grace Dieu*'s flimsy forecastle down on top of her, and she was in the water, with the deck still under her feet, and with broken planking boxing her in at chest level. She fought it, hoisting herself by her arms to climb above it, hearing the screams of those trapped below— the screams of people and the screams of horses. As she pulled herself to the top of the pile of broken timbers the next wave hit the ship and she was washed off and sucked out and away into pounding water and the black

doom of night. She tried to scream and the water filled
her mouth and she went under, and she had lost herself and felt she was being pulled away from the direction where the land must lie, and when her head at last
broke free of the water she flailed and turned so that she
faced the next wave, and it turned her savagely over and
drove her down to a great depth. She could feel her
soul battering at her eardrums in its efforts to get out
of her dying body, and she stopped struggling and found
that she had surfaced again, and drew a breath before
the next toppling torrent bore her down.

And now, away from the ship and whatever it had
struck on, the waves took a longer and a gentler way
with her and she had time to breathe adequately between submersions and even time to fight against the
enveloping blankets she wore, struggling to lift one side
from her shoulder over her head. She went down again
with her head muffled in the wet wool, but her struggles
and the wash of the water cleared it, and she surfaced
free of its crippling drag. Now she could keep afloat a
little better by using her arms, and she could see a line
of lightness ahead of her, and beyond it a darker darkness that must be land. Gradually she was washed closer
and closer to the line of lightness, and she thought it
might be breaking water with sand and safety beyond,
and she prayed to the Virgin, not moving her lips but
praying in her mind, which the Virgin would surely
understand in her circumstances, and then some tower-
ing thing went past her in the water with a high squeal
and a flying mane and slashing iron forelegs, and she
thought it was Fastitocalon come to take over her empty
body and she remembered all the myriad creatures of
the water who needed a land body before they could
bring themselves ashore, and she gulped water again

and went down, and was caught in the breaking waves close to the shore, and her soul took up again its frenzied battering to escape her tortured body, which was being dragged helplessly backwards and forwards through thick weed and abrading sand.

Slowly she became aware that all the noises were diminishing—the noises of the storm and the sound of the panic beating of her blood within her veins. She opened her eyes and found that she was lying at the water's edge, her cheek pressed heavily against the sand and her hips and legs still washed by the last little rushes of each incoming wave. For a time she lay still, breathing for the pleasure breathing gave her. It seemed to her possible that she was in the same world, that she was still alive. The thought of the sea behind her, and of the soul-hungry things that it contained, forced her to make the effort to pull herself forward by her arms until her body was clear of anything that might reach up out of the water to get her. In moving she became aware of something standing at the water's edge some distance away, something that seemed, in the dim light, to have the shape and stature of a man. She pulled herself to her hands and knees and watched it for a little while, afraid that its appearance might be only a trick of the light. Then she got to her feet and found that she could walk, and broke from a walk into a shambling run. She didn't know what shore she was on, or what people inhabited it, but any human thing was better company than the creatures she had just come through.

The figure turned when she was a few yards away from it, and watched as she stumbled on. She ran to it, clutching at its arm to steady herself, and looked into a face that was on a level with her own. She recognized him. She had seen him on the ship, where he had mucked out in the hold after the horses, grinned, pulled at the lobe of his ear and spoken no word of English. His hair was so fair that it appeared white against his pink skin, and his pale blue eyes were naked-looking, and lashless. Father Nicholas had told her he was a Hyperborean, of a race who lived in sunshine and plenty beyond the north wind, and spoke a language no one understood. No matter. He must have a soul of his own. He would not want hers.

Half a mile away, beyond the next headland, they had lit a fire at first light and warmed and dried themselves and filled their bellies. They sat close to each other for comfort, keeping their eyes turned towards the cliff and away from the beach where some of their drowned companions lay, white and wide-eyed, in the seaweed at the water's edge.

Leadership of the small group had fallen inevitably to the twin soldiers Godwin and Edwin. They had, in any case, reinforced their claim by providing both fire and food for the survivors. The six of them had huddled in a silent group throughout the remaining hours of darkness after each had waded ashore and found the others, not daring to make fire for fear it might bring some enemy down on them from the cliffs above. But when dawn and a careful watch suggested that the cliffs were empty, Edwin had found the flint and tinder still safe in the leather pouch at his waist, and had made a fire while Godwin dared to go back past the corpses into the sea and salvage a floating baulk of timber on which the captain's monkey had come safely almost to the shore. As Godwin pushed the baulk ashore the monkey escaped from him and rushed gibbering and pleading up the beach, raising his skinny arms to Godwin's stout mother, Godda, as a child might do. There was some argument then, about the propriety of eating him, but Father Nicholas, pressed by the others, sketched a blessing in the air above the little monkey's head, and it was quickly dispatched and skinned by Godwin, roasted on the coals of the fire and divided into six roughly equal portions. Joice, the young wife of a soldier who had been aboard the ship, refused the first portion that was given to her because it came from the lower belly and the loins, and it was known that people who ate outlandish things took on their characteristics. It was passed first to Godwin and then to his brother Edwin, and both refused it boastfully. It seemed an unsuitable portion to be given to the priest, so it was passed to Gyll, the young conscript soldier who had come from Dittisham.

When they had eaten the little meat the monkey provided, they gathered up the drowned who lay on the beach—three men, one woman and a little child—and threw their bodies back into the receding tide. Father Nicholas had wanted to give them proper burial at the cliff foot, but Godda's desperate arguments had prevented this. The bodies of the drowned belonged to the spirits of the sea. If they were robbed of them they would take other, living, bodies to replace them. Father Nicholas gave in. He prayed long and fervently over his poor drowned people before they were dragged into waist-high water and pushed out into the hungry tide. Then he prayed silently and fervently for himself. He was the only Norman among five English peasants. By every right he should have assumed leadership of the little group, and he knew that no one would have challenged his right. But he felt old and ill and unable to argue with them and to make decisions. He prayed that

God would forgive him this last dereliction of his proper duty.

To the other five, the beach seemed a better place when the dead bodies were gone, and they began to argue about their next move. They stayed close to the fire, and they kept their backs to the sea. The sea had had its turn with them, and they had beaten it. The only dangers they feared now would come from the low cliffs above them. They were suffering from thirst and they knew that, before long, they would have to move inland in search of water, but it seemed a chancy thing to do before they knew what country they were in. No one could remember exactly how many days it was since they had sailed from Dartmouth, nor how many long hours they had run before the wind on the last night before the ship had been dismasted and brought up into the wind again to drift steadily sternwards with her anchor trailing ineffectually.

To the twin brothers, who had sailed before into the Duoro, it seemed likely that they were many hundreds of miles beyond Porto and beyond the entrance to the Mediterranean. "We were caught in the current that races out from Cape Bocandur and drops over the edge of the world into the slime," Godwin said. "If this is any known place, then it's Africa," he said, causing the two women to look fearfully up to the cliff top, expecting to see ill-coloured monocle men, or great snails with shells large enough to make a house for five or six people.

But to his brother, Edwin, it seemed more likely that they had been borne along by the cold, circular Canaries current. "We are on the shore of some other country, on the other side," he said.

"But that's not possible. The sun rose *there* today,"

Gyll said apprehensively, waving his arm in the direction of the cliffs, "and it rose there every day that we were sailing south. If we've crossed the sea, as Edwin says, then today the sun would háve risen on the other side."

They stared at each other, uncertain of the logic behind his words. "No," the priest said firmly, with the authority of an educated man. "God has so arranged it that, no matter where you find yourself, the sun will always rise to the east of you."

"That's cod," Godwin said. "How if you travel east and east, to the very end of the earth? The sun would rise to the west of you then, for sure."

Edwin and Gyll saw the force of this, and nodded their agreement, but the priest was firm. "Only on the day when Jesus Christ comes again will the sun be seen to rise in the west," he said. "That is the east," he said, nodding towards it. "Whether we have landed on this side of the ocean, or on that, makes no difference to the sun's position."

Gradually, by argument and by long reconstructions of the turns and the times their ship had seemed to make, they came to believe they were on the western seaboard of some Atlantic country. Whether it was in fact part of Iberia or part of Africa made very little difference to their next decision for plainly, in either case, they would do best to walk towards the north. "Unless," Godwin said, and he was only half joking, "it happens to be the day on which Sir Jesus has come back, and we'll be walking south and never know it."

Once the decision was made, it was clear to everyone that the party was not really ready to move. Godda was willing enough, since she was stout and broad and in any case had been supported through the worst of the

water by one of her twin sons. But the priest was weak
and pale and coughed continuously, and Joice wanted
time to pray for her lost husband's soul before they began what all believed might be a very long march. In
the end it was decided that the twin soldiers should
climb the cliffs in search of birds' eggs and of water and
a means of carrying it, and that Gyll and Father Nicholas should stay on the beach to protect the women, and
join them in their prayers for the souls of the dead.

"Watch Gyll," Edwin called to Joice as the brothers
moved off. "Remember he's the one that's eaten the
monkey's pizzle." But already the girl was on her knees
and soon Godda and Gyll and the priest had joined
her, and as they prayed together for the dead Gyll remembered, with the others, the face and the voice of the
girl to whom he'd given his blanket on the *Grace Dieu*'s
deck.

On the southern side of the headland the balance was
heavily Norman, the more so since Walter Faber had
survived the wreck of his ship and got ashore with the
others. It seemed natural to them that he who had com-
manded the ship should command them now that they
were cast ashore, and at first it seemed to him, too, that
this was a natural thing.

Clodagh and the Hyperborean had not discovered the
presence of the others until morning. They had spent
the hours of darkness crouched close together in a cleft
of rock beyond the high-water mark and at times, for
comfort, each had talked aloud, though each knew the
other had no understanding. As the dawn began to
water down the darkness they had seen that there were
other people on the beach, but at first they had been
afraid to go out. As the light increased they would see

that the people were people from the ship, and that the
bodies and the blankets at the water's edge were bodies
and blankets from the *Grace Dieu.*

The blankets drew them out, for the night had been
an agony of cold and darkness, and they ran seaward
first to gather a wet blanket each before they joined the
five figures at the farther end of the beach.

They found Walter Faber there, and the young
knight Simon de Baude and his brother Geoffrey, and
Eleanor of Canterbury who had taken the Cross in her
own right, and Magnus, a common soldier, who was
dragging driftwood down to the fire he had just lighted.

Faber, mourning his lost ship and his lost profits and
even, a little, the loss of his pet monkey, was pleased
enough to see the Hyperborean since, until he had appeared, Magnus had been the only man he could put to
manual labour. There was the fire to be tended, food to
be found and graves to be dug for eight beached bodies
which would be buried below the tidemark, with whatever Faber could remember of the burial service.

Of the fifteen-man crew there was no one left but the
Hyperborean and himself, and he had not yet learned
any way of speaking to the boy he had pressed into
service on the Dartmouth docks. He could, however,
be ordered with a gesture and hastened with a blow,
and he was a useful addition to the party.

Of the thirty passengers the *Grace Dieu* had carried,
there were five with him now on this desolate beach,
and two of them were women and would be a burden.
To Walter Faber the sea and the shore were two different worlds. At sea his authority came from the deck
underneath him, and the rank and experience of any
passengers he carried didn't affect *his* overriding authority. He had been alarmed at first to find there was

one of the Crusader Knights of God among the survivors, since he outranked the captain anywhere but aboard the captain's ship. But Simon de Baude had quickly deferred to him, confessing himself less experienced even than other knights of his age, since God had sent him into the world left-handed. This debarred him from tournaments, and would keep him an untried fighter till he fought in earnest in the Holy Land.

The two women of his party pleased him much less than did the deferential de Baude and his young brother, Geoffrey, who acted as his squire. Whenever he had been at sea Faber's first move ashore was to find female company, but not from high-toned bitches like these two. He cursed the luck of the storm that had brought them ashore, instead of a couple of the wives of common soldiers he'd been carrying, who could have pulled their weight by day and borne someone else's at night. One of these, he knew, was the wife of Robert Apelfourde, a promising captain among the Crusaders. The other, Eleanor, was young and desirable enough, but plainly strong-willed, and there was nothing he disliked more in a woman. There was a cross embroidered in red silk on the left breast of her water-bedraggled cloak, and she carried her valuables in a scrotum-like pouch of soft leather, instead of in the embroidered purse most women wore at their belts.

The storm had died overnight and the sky was clear. A stiff wind from the sea was throwing up curtains of sea spray from which the rising sun struck myriads of rainbows. Each wave that came flooding in carried its burden of night foam, weed and flotsam from the ship. Even the sand seemed foreign, because of its whiteness and its powdery fineness. Above them the headlands seemed to have no trees—only tussocks of grass and

bubiallas and spiky thickets of salt-loving bushes. Faber
set the Hyperborean to picking up the things that had
been thrown ashore. There were sodden blankets, oars,
a few horn plates and cups and water bottles, leather
buckets, odd shoes and sandals, articles of clothing from
the Crusaders' stores which had floated free as the hold
broke open. When those had been gathered he set the
boy to stripping the clothing from the dead, while Magnus worked at digging, with a piece of plank, a sand
trench deep enough to take their bodies. Dried out, the
clothing would be useful to his party, and unless the
Resurrection Day came very soon the clothes would
have rotted beyond the point where they'd be useful to
their owners.

When the trench was dug he left Magnus and the boy
to put the bodies into it, and went up the beach again
to gather the rest of the group. Personally, he believed
in nothing higher than his mast, but he knew the disci-
plinary value of religious services, and he wanted all
his party at the trench-side. When he returned with
them, he was surprised to find that Magnus had laid the
eight bodies with their faces hidden and their bare backs
and buttocks uppermost in the trench.

"They'll have enough to do finding their right places,
being as they're buried in foreign sand. We'll give them
a head start, for the world will turn itself upside down
when the Last Trumpet blows," Magnus said, and
crossed himself and dropped to his knees. He was a
good-humoured rogue, made temporarily devout by a
bad night.

The others knelt, and Clodagh tugged at the piece of
rope with which the Hyperborean's short gown was
belted, bringing him down onto his knees in the sand
beside her. The captain sketched the sign of the cross

over the trench, and intoned bits and pieces he remembered from different church rituals. Then they left the boy and Magnus to pile the sand back over the bodies in the trench, and walked up the beach again to the comfort of the fire. They built it up with driftwood Magnus had collected. The sun was higher now. They turned their back on the sea. There was no comfort to be had from its chilly blue under the light blue shine of a cold sky.

Until this time there had been no discussion of their whereabouts, or their future plans. Now Eleanor of Canterbury began it, standing pale and proud with her light hair loosened to dry and her eyes narrowed against the sunlight, so that it found no colour about her except for the scarlet cross on her somber cloak.

"We can't stay here without food or shelter or water," she said. "We have to decide in which direction to walk."

"We'll keep close to the coast," Faber said, because the thought of going inland frightened him.

"You may walk on the water for all I care," Eleanor said. "I walk *nowhere* until I know where I'm going. What country are we in?"

"Iberia," Faber said. "We are somewhere on the Iberian peninsula."

"It has a long coastline," Simon de Baude said. "D'you suppose our friends are to the north of us, or to the south?"

Faber hesitated. He had thought that his would be the decision as to which direction they should take, and he had not yet been able to make up his mind. "They should be in the south," he said, "but how far south . . ."

"North," Eleanor said. "Surely in the north? Porto's the gathering place for all the English and the Flemings and the Germans."

"True," Faber said. "But is Porto to the north of us, or the south?" They stared at him, and he felt more confidence. "By my reckoning," he said, "we were two days out from Porto when the storm struck. We are therefore driven ashore north of our port. If we walk south we'll come to it. And any people we meet will be friendly people."

"And if you are wrong and we've been blown south of it?" the young knight said. "What then? We'll walk a long way, and we'll find no friends."

"Blackamoors," his brother said, with an uneasy laugh.

"Not so," Faber said. "The Crusading Armies have gone south. They set out on the march a month or more ago."

"To *march*," Clodagh said. "To Jerusalem?"

"No, Lady," Faber said with a smile. "That would be a march longer than most of them have signed for. They've made a bargain with Alphonso Henrique to drive the Moors out of the country for him. Those who take the cities have the right to sack them before they hand them over to the king. They're marching south for Lisbon now, if they're not there already, and your husband among them," he said, nodding to Clodagh.

"Not he," she said. "His were solemn vows, made publicly, at the hands of a bishop who was preaching the voyage of God. There are no exemptions granted from solemn vows."

"He's gone south to Lisbon," Faber said. "These are matters for the Supreme Command. The Pope has ruled that the Moors in Portugal are as obnoxious to God as the Saracens in Palestine. Besides, they are closer to home."

"We should walk *north*," Eleanor said, and Simon de Baude nodded his agreement. "If we have been blown

south of the entrance to the Porto harbour, then by
going south we may walk into the enemy's hands."

"And if we are north, and we walk to the north?"
Faber said.

"What lies there?"

"The sea."

"Then we walk into the sea," Eleanor said. "I've no
mind to go south and meet the infidels with only a
handful of us to protect ourselves."

Magnus and the Hyperborean boy had finished their
work and come to stand behind the others as they talked.
The boy, perhaps sensing what the argument was about,
kept gesturing and grimacing, throwing his arm in the
direction of the north and muttering the same few
words over and over. "Monkey see, monkey do," Magnus said, and hit him a great blow in the stomach, which
made him double up and roar with laughter.

"Is that his name?" young Geoffrey said. "Monkey?"

"As good as any other," Faber said, "for it's common
knowledge monkeys don't speak for fear that if they do
they'll be put to work." He spoke peremptorily, to hide
his satisfaction that a sensible decision had been made
for him, and he could now put it into effect. "We will
walk north," he said, "keeping close to the coast, and
making a start tomorrow. Today we will rest, searching
the beach after each tide for anything else of value that
may come ashore." The *Grace Dieu* had disappeared
during the night, sliding down into the depths of the
waters while they were getting ashore, they supposed.
A half mile out there were jagged towers of rocks in
islanded groups, and in daylight it wasn't possible for
them to be certain where the ship had hit.

Clodagh looked up and down the small beach on
which they were camped. "Before we leave," she said,

"shouldn't we search beyond the two headlands? There may be other bodies there. There may even," she added on a note of hope, "be others, like us, who've survived the storm."

"That beach," Faber said, pointing to the north. "The other one's unlikely, because of the set of the tide and the current." This was his territory, and he felt confident about it. "We will search the beaches to the north as we go. You must rest today," he said to the women. "Sir Simon and Geoffrey and I will make a shelter for you, for the night. Magnus and the Monkey will take the leather buckets and go inland a little, till they find water and something we can eat." They were, after all, the most expendable, and nobody could say what horrors might lie inland from the beach.

Eight days were to pass before the two groups found each other. In those eight days the people of Faber's party had grown dispirited and thin. Often they were without water, and what little they could find was dipped from rock basins streaked with the excretions of seabirds.

Faber kept them close to the sea—in sight of the sea except when they were driven inland to round the steep gullies of rock that so wasted their strength. At night he led them down again to the beaches. At first they had been inclined to argue about this, or at least to lend their support to the arguments of the headstrong Eleanor that proper food was only to be found by going inland. But the captain's fear of losing touch with the sea was great, and he overbore them.

As the days passed even Eleanor argued less, and the others spoke hardly at all except at night, when they huddled together in soft sand at the base of some cliff. To each of them it seemed a sort of madness that they should climb up the cliffs and climb down again so often, that they should walk long hours through each day at the edge of the cliffs where the walking was most difficult, that they should walk every day instead of devoting proper time to the search for proper food. But someone had to lead them, and it was unthinkable that it should be a woman.

Though Faber insisted that they should stay close to the sea, he would give them neither time nor instruction in how to get a living from it by fishing. They lived on messes of plants and berries, on lizards, shellfish broken from the rocks and things they found washed up at the tide line—starfish and small crabs and the dead bodies of seabirds. At night they dreamed of food, of fat bacon and brown ale and bread with thick crusts, until they were woken by dry mouths and stomach cramps and painful diarrhea. Nobody slept for very long at a time because of the movement and the stir of the others, the exhausted groans, the whimpering of the fourteen-year-old Geoffrey, who followed behind the others without complaint during the day, but cried for his mother every night in his sleep. Faber himself was suffering as much as any of them. He was troubled by his legs and by piles, by his responsibilities, by a disturbance in his vision, by his fears and by the discovery that his urine was ruddy-coloured, which told him that his liver was seriously overheated. He swallowed a potion Eleanor made for him by squeezing the ooze from leaves she claimed to recognize, but its only effect was to spread the fire from his liver to his bowels, so that both boiled endlessly.

✿   ✿   ✿

The other party, led by the brothers who thought and acted as one, had fared very much better. Their spirits were high. They had struck inland on the second day, and from there had moved northward only when they had food in their bellies. They were hungry often, but what food they found was of better quality. Twice they had had hares brought down by the brothers with stones, and to those they had added birds' eggs, trout taken by Gyll of Dittisham by methods he'd learned on the overhanging banks of Robert Apelfourde's streams, bustards caught in the brushwood and small birds taken in the thickets with snares they had made by the patient unravelling and retwisting of some of the blankets salvaged from the beach.

Father Nicholas had recovered a little from his water ordeal and was strong enough now to walk when the brothers decreed walking, and to pray every day at the seven prescribed hours. He thought he would, when he had more strength, try to bring the other five back to some sort of daily observance, but for the time being he was satisfied if they gave him an amen for his Misereatur, or even with the *nominedomini* which Edwin and Godwin would obligingly supply where any gap in a Latin prayer seemed to invite their response. It worried Father Nicholas that he might not, when the time came, have enough spiritual and physical strength to give Joice the protection she would need. He had watched the brothers watching her, and he feared there was nothing in their looks that suggested that they considered themselves to be in competition. And he found nothing in the girl's looks which suggested that she would long withstand them. Her sun-browned face was strained by hardship and uncertainty about her husband, but her young plump body had a look of ripeness and easiness that made him fear the future. Her sort had always troubled him in the confessional, and it troubled him here. At present her virtue was protected by her mourning, but he didn't think that would save her for very long. Godda, he thought, would be no help to him in protecting her, since she seemed to regard her twin sons as twin miracles of her making. And he could scarcely hope to enlist Gyll of Dittisham's aid since fear of the two had already taught Gyll to keep a proper distance from her at their fire.

They had been camped for three days in a half-cave made by overhanging rocks on the bank of a stream when they found the others. The brothers had called a halt because fish were plentiful there, and if they could find some way of catching more than they needed to satisfy their immediate hunger, they would have something to carry with them when they moved on. They had found the stream by following a lagoon, and on the second day Gyll and the brothers had gone back to collect armloads of lagoon reeds and bring them back to the camp. Gyll's plan was to make a big round withy basket to catch fish in, so they could smoke a supply. On the third afternoon Gyll had stayed weaving his basket on the bank of the river, while the twin brothers went back a second time to the lagoon to get more rushes.

Faber's party had been forced inland by the mouth of the lagoon, and had followed close to its edge through mists and seaweed heaps and across marshes that turned to slop under their weight. They had been following its twisting shoreline now for three days, and it had begun to seem that the lagoon stretched east across the very center of the world. Each time they found ground firm enough to support little bits of pasture grass and bushes they thought they had at last reached the lagoon's end, but each time they found another arm of it, forcing them further inland, further eastward. The birds that cried in the air over their heads were seabirds, and gave them no indication of where better water than the brackish stuff in the lagoon might be. Mussels chipped from the stones at the edge of the water were the only food they could find. They had left the mists behind them now, but the smell of rotting seaweed came to them like a foul breath on the wind that blew from the sea, and their eyes were hurt by the dazzle of the sun on the glittering salt basins close to the shores.

It was Clodagh who first saw the two men waist-deep in water, gathering rushes from an islanded clump fifty feet out from the shore. She had seen them without really noticing them at first, and as Faber's party drew closer to them she kept her eyes on them, but without much interest. She had seen other things during this day's march—houses and water pumps and grazing cattle —and these two figures seemed no more real to her than the others that had retreated and faded as she walked towards them. But then Magnus, walking behind her, saw the men and shouted, and the figures became real and she saw them turn and reach down into the reeds and come up armed with heavy clubs of wood.

And then the men were wading towards them and it was clear that Faber and Magnus knew them, and she sat down and waited as the others did. She knew that the unreality must be in her own eyes, because the wading men appeared to her to be exact images of each other.

She sat with her eyes closed, listening to the talk and understanding very little of it, except when she heard it said that four miles away there was clear water, shelter from a cave and perhaps a little food. It seemed to her that four miles was too great a distance for her, but someone pulled at her and she opened her eyes and stood. Then she was walking again as it seemed she had been walking since the beginning of the world, and she knew that her eyes had indeed been tricking her, for there was only one man where before she thought that she had seen two.

Godwin had left his brother to make the slow journey with the people of Faber's party, and after going back into the water to gather up the bundles of pulled reeds, had headed back at his own pace to their camp on the river. He found his mother and the priest and Joice there with Gyll, who was working still on the weaving of his fish basket.

"We've found them," Godwin said. "Seven more of them, from the ship." He was not well pleased by it, since they looked a poor lot, and would have to be fed.

"Seven," Father Nicholas said. "From the ship. Who?" And Joice echoed the "Who?", shrieking the word as she scrambled to her feet. They stared at her, knowing she was the only one for whom the answer had any real importance.

Godwin, even less pleased, looked at her without speaking.

"Who, Godwin?" Father Nicholas said. "Tell us who?"

"Seven," Godwin said. "Captain Faber, a couple of nobs, a couple of women, a soldier and some sort of a foreign boy who worked in the holds."

At the words "a soldier," Gyll had turned towards the girl. She was down on her knees on the ground trying with closed eyes and clasped hands to pierce heaven with a paternoster.

An hour later, while Godda and the priest got together what food they had to offer, Cyll went out with
Joice towards the lagoon. He wanted to say to her,
"Don't hope, there's only one, it's silly to hope," and he
wanted to say, "And don't give up hope either—we've
found seven today, we may find ten more tomorrow,"
but there was no point in speaking. She couldn't listen
to him, she couldn't stop talking. She was walking
quickly, shaking her tangled red hair from her eyes,
smiling widely so that he saw the gaps left by two lost
teeth. She knew he was found, he was safe, God was
good, she would fast every Thursday of her life in order
to thank Him, and when they got home she would take
her mother-in-law into her house, the old bitch, and
treat her as kindly as if she was the Mother of God herself.

A mile or so from their camp they came upon the
party straggling through low bushes and small trees, Edwin leading the way, then a tall woman, then a boy and
the captain. Joice was gone from his side, running back
beyond these to those who must be following behind.
He started to run, wanting to be with her when she got
to the seventh, but then he was stopped in his tracks by
the sight of the girl from the deck of the *Grace Dieu*.
She stumbled a little, and he thought she hadn't seen
him. He went to her side and touched her, and she
looked up at him, and he noticed how dirty and pale
her face was as she smiled, but she didn't speak. He took
her arm, and put his other arm around her shoulders
to support her. He was afraid that this might offend her,
that she might shake him off. But in fact she leaned
heavily against him, and somehow the fact that her feet
were bare narrowed the gulf between them.

Finding her again had so excited him that for the

time he had forgotten about Joice. On the *Grace Dieu*
he had gone to sleep thinking of this girl, and had
woken in the water. He had thought of her often since,
gone to sleep thinking of her, because he had found
Joice often in his thoughts during the day, and knew
that it was dangerous to think too much of her when
he could read just how she figured in the thoughts of
the brothers. "If the other girl was here," he had thought
often enough, and gone to sleep thinking it, only to
wake and remember that she was a long way above him,
and, in any case, almost certainly dead. Still supporting
her, he looked around, searching behind him to find
where Joice had gone. A man who looked like a soldier
brought up the rear of the file, but he was walking
alone. Gyll stopped, pulling Clodagh to a halt beside
him. He thought that Joice might have run on and on,
searching for her lost husband after the last of the seven
had passed her. But as he turned again to explain to
Clodagh why he must leave her and why she must wait
for him, he saw that Joice had come back past him again
while he was not watching. Now she walked at the head
of the file. She was holding Edwin's arm with both
hands, walking sideways so that she could look directly
at him as she spoke. Gyll heard her laugh. The laugh
was shaky, with a note of hysteria in it.

That was the first night on which they didn't douse
the fire and huddle closely together for warmth and
comfort as soon as the light was gone. Both parties, in
the time since they had come ashore, had been afraid to
use fire at night for fear it might draw hostile attention
to them. But now their augmented numbers gave them
confidence, and there were in any case questions of
leadership and direction that would have to be settled,

though as yet nobody had mentioned any of these things.

"It's an empty country," Godwin said. "Never a man have we seen, never a farm beast. . . ."

"Nor never the mark of a foot of any of them," Edwin said.

"In some countries," Faber said, "in some countries I have sailed to, there are men that go on all fours like a goat, and they nest in trees."

"Mother of tortoises!" Godda said, and looked apprehensively up.

"And they leave no footprints behind them. When they hunt they launch themselves from among the branches, and pin their prey to the ground by falling head first and impaling it on their horns."

"All men are made in God's image," the priest said.

"But nobody has seen God," Faber said. He knew that the goat-men existed somewhere. He thought they had not sailed far enough to be among them yet. But inland country, and tree country where you could no longer smell the sea's breath, robbed him of what little courage he had. He had to get them back to the coast as soon as he could. "We are now beyond the end of the lagoon," he said. "Tomorrow we start walking north again, and west of north and always west and west, till we're back on the edge of the sea."

There was a long silence. Most were quiet because of the utter weariness of the thought of walking again. The Monkey and Clodagh and young Geoffrey de Baude were quiet because they were asleep. The priest was the first to speak. "Your people need to rest," he said. "These ladies . . ."

The brothers had been leaning together, talking across Joice, whom they'd placed between them. They had had a taste of independence in the last eight days, and they had no mind to come automatically to heel at the sound of a Norman voice. "Best to stay inland, where there's food," Godwin said.

"There's food at the coast," Faber said. "We've done well enough."

The brothers laughed. "Well enough!" Edwin said. "You're shit-starved. Two days, three days, and the crows'd've had your eyeballs for their dinner."

"We'll do well enough now," Faber said, counting around, "with six . . . with seven young men, and the Father and me as well to order things. You shall be divided into two parties," he said, momentarily feeling a deck under his feet again, "and one will forage while the other does guard duty."

"We'll be divided into two parties, like we were before," Godwin said, "and the priest can go with whichever one he likes."

Gyll had been following all this carefully, looking from face to face in the flickering light. He knew that the twin brothers were right. He knew, too, that it wasn't possible for the brothers to command a party that had five nobs in it—six really, since the girl sleeping close to Eleanor seemed Norman in spite of what she had said to him on the ship. He also knew that if the party divided, he would go with whichever group she chose.

"We will travel together to whatever our destiny is," Father Nicholas said. "We are Christian people, and God has sent us together on a strange pilgrimage. We lift up our hearts to Him. We humbly pray that the Creature and His Mother will protect us, and that God, who gives the cattle their food and also the chickens and the ravens, will do the same for us."

They were silent. All this, they felt, was very well, but it didn't solve any questions of leadership.

"But not here," Faber said, after a pause. "It seems God let the cattle and the chickens get too hungry, and they've gone off."

"So must we," Godda said. She had been going to say more in support of her sons, but she found that Eleanor was looking at her. She would argue with Faber, and even argue with the priest if she had to, but Eleanor, with the red silk cross stitched to her bedraggled cloak, seemed to her neither woman nor nun, and a little awe-inspiring.

"I doubt whether the people are safe in any of your hands," Eleanor said. "You are not skilled in leading people on the land. And perhaps you were not too skilled at sea either," she said, speaking to Faber, "or we might not be where we are. Father Nicholas may look after our souls. It's not sensible to ask him to look after our bodies as well. And for myself, I do not choose," she said, looking at the brothers, "to be guided anywhere by bumpkins."

"By the four hands of Satan, you go too far," Faber said. The words spilled out of him. He had stood too much. His party had been handicapped by two useless women, and this breastless one had argued with him on every day of the march. "A woman without wit enough to get a husband into her bed is not to be listened to. Are we oxen?"

"I have wondered," Eleanor said.

"We gain nothing by being unkind," Father Nicholas said. "If the lady wishes to speak, it is a courtesy to hear her."

"God's spine, what she wants is to lead the party!"

"The party could do worse," Eleanor said. "But all

I've asked for yet is the right to be heard. My life is precious to me. I don't put it willingly into the hands of fools."

"Speak then," Faber said, "and then let those who have the knowledge to do it decide what is to be done."

"I have that knowledge," Eleanor said. "The chances that we'll survive are very small, and survival is as much the businses of the women here as of the men." She looked around her. Two of the women were now asleep, as though satisfied to leave all decisions about their lives to others. The slattern Godda was listening, though heaven knew how much she could understand. It seemed to Eleanor that the only useful members of the party were the four common soldiers—Magnus and Gyll and the brothers. But they could not be trusted with the leadership. "The group must not divide," she said, "for we don't know yet how far we have to go, nor what horrible chances we may have to face. If we stay together, some may survive. If we divide, none will." She noticed that those who crossed themselves at her words were Faber and Godda and Gyll and the young knight. "Also," she said, "we must not go back to the sea. Let the experience of the lagoon teach you. We will get little food there, and no water. If, later, we find the means of making nets, then we can move closer, staying where there is water, and sending men down to get fish when they can." They were listening to her now. "There's food here," she said. "We should not leave this place until everyone is strong enough to walk well, and to run when running becomes necessary. Before we leave here we must be armed. The women as well as the men. Pikes can be made from timber, lances, clubs. We are a company of people. We need a leader, as any company does."

"Jesus has said that wives are subservient to husbands, women to men," Father Nicholas said.

Eleanor smiled at him. "He put it to no personal test," she said. "But it is the way the world works."

Faber saw responsibility for the party slipping away from him, and he was not sorry. Let the priest have nominal leadership, just as the church had nominal leadership of this Crusade, which Bernard of Clairvaux had preached. Neither Bernard nor God, he thought, was much concerned with practical details. They would leave matters of troops and equipment and decisions on where to strike to those who had experience in the field. The priest would do the same. Let him lead the people with his eyes on heaven, while the captain walked behind, watching the strategy. "I make no objection," he said. "It is altogether fit that the priest should lead us."

Father Nicholas took no notice, having abstracted himself again to pray. But in any case everyone's eyes were on Eleanor, who shook her head violently, and struck the ground in front of her with her fist. "We are taught that, next to a priest, a knight is the man most worthy of our respect."

This confused them. It didn't seem a useful contribution, unless perhaps she supposed that by taking the Cross she had somehow transmogrified herself into a Knight of God. Then Simon de Baude spoke for the first time, and they turned to look at him.

"I am unworthy," he said. "And I am unskilled."

"But not without conscience," Eleanor said. "Not without liability. And eggs today are better than chickens tomorrow." He was the right sort of knight, she thought. Chivalrous, malleable, a fool.

Simon stirred his brother, Geoffrey, with his foot, thinking it only right that his squire should be awake if knightly responsibilities were to be thrust upon him. "I do not know . . ." he said, hesitantly. "It's true my sword is dedicated to the king's service, and to the protection of the poor and the weak and the needy. . . ."

"Of which there are a good number here," Eleanor said.

The boy at his feet stretched himself and yawned loudly, and Simon kicked him sharply again, stiffening his own determination by the action. He stood up. "Under God," he said, "and with the help of His saints, I will take charge." The boy came to his knees beside his brother, ready for whatever duties a squire might have at so solemn a moment. The others' lack of response seemed to suggest that the solemnity had passed them by. Faber watched Simon, withholding the angry arguments that occurred to him. It was true that this kek-handed stripling who had never fought an action did outrank him. It was possible, too, that his lack of experience would make him manageable. He could fire Faber's missiles, and interpose his knightly person between Faber and any that might chance to ricochet. Looking at Eleanor, the captain nodded his considered agreement.

Eleanor looked quickly around the group, from Faber's face to the priest's, to Simon's, Geoffrey's and the still-sleeping Clodagh's. She didn't look at the faces of the other seven, because all except the Monkey were English, and they would have to do what they were told. For the first time she saw that there were thirteen people in the party, and crossed herself quickly as she realized it. "Well, *tara, tantaro, teino*," she said lightly. "That's settled, and we can sleep."

"In a moment," the priest said, thinking the refrain from a popular song hardly a sufficient blessing before a night that could hold so many hazards for them. He stood up and spread his arms widely, to include all of them, waking and sleeping, in his prayer. *"Attendite, popule meus, legem meam: inclinate aurem vestram in verba oris mei. Aperiam in parabolis os meum: loquar propositiones ab initio* . . . Give ear, O my people, to my law: incline your ears to the words of my mouth. I will open my mouth in a parable: I will utter dark sayings of old . . ." It was a very long Psalm, and one of the few in which he was word-perfect. As he repeated in Latin the dark sayings of old, those who were schooled caught the words for bread and flesh and corn and manna and angels' food, and were comforted by them. At the end Edwin and Godwin withheld their *nomine-domini*, as they were withholding judgment on the leadership of Sir Simon, until they would talk about it outside the nobs' hearing. The others let the priest lead them through an ave, a kyrie and a paternoster, and were glad that God had seen fit to save the priest when He drowned the rest.

They stayed three more days on the bank of the small river, resting, fishing, arming themselves, feeling their way towards alliances with others in the group. Simon de Baude's leadership impressed none of them, and to find themselves in this situation without anyone of exalted rank to take responsibility was like finding themselves walking around without a head.

But in spite of this feeling, rest and food and being in a larger group had given them reserves of cheer and confidence. The brothers often had their heads together, and no one knew whether they were talking about Joice or against Sir Simon. Godda had been the one most troubled by the joining up of the two parties, because she was the one least used to dealing with well-born women. She had half expected them to insist on being waited on, spared, deferred to. Eleanor's often repeated statement that "we are all equal, under Sir Simon and the priest" hadn't impressed her much at the beginning. It reminded her of church, where the priests said God loved everyone equally, but the rich got the places away from the drafts and were served first at the mass. But when she saw Eleanor divide up the food and wait for the last portion, she was impressed by it. The Lady Clodagh seemed to hold the same views. She noticed that neither stopped their conversation when she or Joice interrupted them, but widened it to include them. She saw that they didn't expect anyone to yield them places at the fire, and that they shared the search for wood suitable for making weapons. It surprised her and it pleased her, giving her a motherly regard for the two young women. "Here," she would say roughly, seeing them at something they were unaccustomed to, "let me—I'm more used."

Clodagh was glad of Eleanor's example. She would have hesitated to act in that way herself, would have hung back, remembered Blanchefleur's warnings against the free and easy ways of her home. Eleanor's attitude surprised her, but it pleased her, too, since she was an active girl, brought up in the freedoms of a manor where the only gentlefolk had been women.

The situation was not an easy one for Simon de Baude. He leaned heavily on the advice of Eleanor, he prayed often, he avoided contact with Faber as much as he could, for fear that Faber would find out his deficiencies. His brother, Geoffrey, still served him as his squire insofar as there were any squire's duties to be done, but the bulk of Geoffrey's attention was on Eleanor, for whom he had developed a boy's burning passion. He lived in her light, wanted to serve her kneeling at the equal distributions of available food which were their meals, no longer cried for his mother at night if he could sleep at Eleanor's feet and if her hand had rested a couple of times on his head during the day. These three made one trinity.

Joice and the twin brothers made another. At some time during the first night on which the two groups had come together she had turned to one or the other of them less to seek consolation for the loss of her husband than to escape for a few minutes the blackness of the unwalled night. Since the brothers seemed to all intents interchangeable, she had found them so. The alliance seemed reasonable enough to all the others except the priest, who knew it to be base and unholy. He prayed for their souls. He prayed also for the soul of Joice's lost husband, and he prayed that it might indeed now be separated from his body, so that Joice's sin would be reduced from the vileness of adultery to the lesser infirmity of fornication. He reminded himself of the popular belief that God does not punish the same sin here and hereafter. He wished there was some way of knowing whether it was true. He thought that perhaps their unlawful nights would be adequately punished by the miserable days which must lie ahead. He hoped so. He tried to put out of his mind the thought that the gates of heaven might ultimately be closed against a faithless shepherd who had run from the wolf instead of facing him in defense of his helpless sheep.

Gyll and Clodagh and the priest formed another trinity of sorts, a loose one that grew from their liking for each other's company. The old man liked to look at them because they were young and strong and had recovered quickly from the walking and the ordeal of the wreck. They were absorbed in each other's doings—Gyll would watch Clodagh as she moved about the fire. She was the only one of the women who went into the water to help with the basket-fishing Gyll controlled, going not because she was needed but because she enjoyed the splashing and the wading. The priest thought of them as beautiful and uncomplicated children, and was flattered that they attached themselves to him. Their attachment to him came from the fact that they were not children, and that what troubled them was too complicated to go easily into words, even between them. They hung about the priest because they liked him and because they hoped that he could help them, though there was no way that they could ask him for his help. It was not moral guidance that they wanted from the priest. The barrier between them was social, and therefore higher than any the church could raise.

The fourth group of three had been formed by default, and consisted of Faber, Magnus and the foreign boy. The boy stuck close to Magnus, who had the sort of liking for him he might have had for a bothersome dog, cuffing and pummelling him, but making sure he got his share of food. Faber treated the Monkey in the same way, but without any liking. He'd been set to work on the ship by being kicked, he could be set to work in the same way on land; and after all there was no other way of communicating with him. To have the boy and Magnus close at hand gave him back a morsel of the authority he had been forced to surrender to Sir Simon, and he made a mouthful of directing these two in the work of collecting wood and making a shelter and keeping the camping place shipshape by his own high standards. Magnus disliked him and his orders, but there was no niche for him anywhere else. Godwin and Edwin kept him at a safe distance from Joice; he wasn't much at home with priests or nobs or nobs' women, and the old duck, Godda, was too old for him by twenty years. He amused himself by teaching the boy a few words of English. A kick from Magnus would now make him say "amen" at the end of a prayer, "piss" when he wanted something and "bugger you" when it was given to him—a joke that never lost its charm for young Geoffrey.

Godda's days, while they remained at the side of the river, were devoted to admiration of her sons, approval of Eleanor, supervision of the smoking of the surplus fish and, making a virtue of necessity, to a piety she'd never pretended to before. Several times a day she begged Father Nicholas to find some way of celebrating the mass. "We can't go out from here without it," she said. "We need it for a shelter over our heads and a poultice on our hearts."

"We have no bread," Father Nicholas said, unconscious that he was disapproving her vision of the sacrament as therapeutic. "Nor have we any wine," he added hastily.

"If Sir Jesus can turn fishes into bread, He can turn them back again," Godda said, "and we have fish enough."

It was something to which Father Nicholas was giving a great deal of thought. Whether as plaster or poultice or as propitiation or atonement, his people needed the sacrament before they moved out again on what might be for all a last and difficult journey. He began to collect a few large mussel shells, cleaning and recleaning them with sand and with the ball of his thumb rubbed repeatedly along their inner surfaces. He found they had a dark and pearly beauty, cleaned and kept moist, which fitted them to be used as altar vessels. But the provision of housel vessels was the smaller part of his problem. Some substitute had to be found for the bread and wine normally offered by his congregation. Most of it went, as was proper, to the church's kitchen and its poor-tables, but a part of it, blessed, came back to the altar at the next mass. "Believe, and you have eaten," he said to them repeatedly while he tried to find a solution to the problem. "Believe, and you have eaten." But their belief was weak. They needed substance. It was a matter on which he prayed continually for guidance, and over which he felt a certain resentment against those priests who had trained him in the long years of his novitiate half a century ago. They had not prepared him for the need to improvise, they had let him believe that the normal materials for the miracle that would flow through him would be always at hand. He knew that the bread he needed was wheaten bread, and that though it could be made from the meal of almonds or the meal of chestnuts, its integrity declined disastrously. In any case, they had neither chestnuts nor almonds. And the wine, fermented or unfermented, needed to be the pure juice of the grape. He knew that the Aquarians commonly used water instead of wine at the sacrament, but they were a wicked people, and iconoclasts, who questioned all truths, sanctioned many wickednesses and tried to reduce the majesty of God to a comfortable coziness. Much prayer and thought, though, had more than half convinced him that the Aquarians' error was to use water when wine was freely available to them. Perhaps there would be no error, or very little, in blessing water in a place where God had chosen that they should be without wine. The problem of the bread, however, remained to tease him. "Believe," he told them repeatedly.

"Believe, and you have eaten." But the words made no sense at all to Godda, and even Eleanor and Sir Simon seemed troubled by them, and shook their heads, which influenced the more ignorant to suspect that the priest was deliberately withholding something due to them.

Sir Simon, schooled by Eleanor, had decreed that they should eat twice a day when the food was available, in the morning and again at evening. She had also, with an egalitarianism which surprised him, spoken strongly against allowing the party to fall into the two groups that came naturally to it. She wanted all to eat together, with the women served, or helping themselves, first. In practice he found it not a bad plan, since it allowed him to oversee a fair division of what food there was.

Gyll's withy basket was providing them with a good supply of fish, and all of this except for any edible innards, which were stirred in with the masses of small game and birds Magnus and the twins provided for their meals, was smoked to be carried with them when their march began. The basket, having proved its worth, was to go with them too. They used it only in the warmest part of the day, in clear pools where the sun struck down onto the water, driving the fish into the shadows of the overhanging banks. They laced waterweeds and fronds of fern into the wicker of the basket to make a weedy refuge for the frightened fish, and then Gyll would lower himself quietly into the water with it, wade to midstream, and hold it there, submerged, until the ripples of his passage had subsided. Then two or three of the others would jump noisily into the water lower down and wade towards him following the line of the banks, and it was a poor drive when they didn't frighten three or four good fish away from the banks and into the shelter of the basket.

The rest of the day they spent hunting, making weapons and searching for roots and berries that were edible. Not many berries got back to their common meals, since they were scarce, and were usually eaten at once by whichever of the party found them. They were hungry all the time, but not painfully so, and at least they were digesting what they got quite comfortably. Anyone suffering from painful stomach cramps and diarrhea learned to keep quiet about it, because to admit it was to be greeted with jeers and accusations of greedy secret eating. Most of the hunting was being done by the twins and Geoffrey de Baude and Magnus, who was followed everywhere he went by the foreign boy. They found little except rabbits, an occasional hare, small birds, birds' eggs for which they sent the Monkey up into the trees, lizards and snakes. Any snakes they killed were skinned and thrown into the river to attract fish, since Satan inhabited their bodies, making them inedible.

Faber and Eleanor and Simon de Baude spent their time making arms for the party, patiently shaping club heads at the end of short branches, and sharpening lance-like points on the ends of long staves. The total armoury that they had brought with them consisted of the daggers the de Baudes had worn at their belts and a skinning knife Magnus had found on the beach among the things washed ashore from the ship. Geoffrey's dagger was a poor, toylike thing, but at least it gave Eleanor something with which to cut a cross into the haft of each weapon, so that the priest could bless it.

At midday on the last day of their stay by the river, the twins and Magnus and the Monkey came back with very little meat, but they brought birds' eggs, and one of the blanket pouches they used for carrying game brimming with brown pods that contained beans. Godda took a handful of the beans to Captain Faber who, being travelled, was the one to pronounce on whether or not the food they found was edible. He broke a pod open and sniffed at the inside of it, and then he bit an edge off one of the beans to taste it. "They're carob beans," he said. "Safe to eat. Some people call them locust beans."

At this Father Nicholas, who had been watching him, fell to his knees, clasping his hands in the position of prayer. "*Sursum corda*," he said. "Lift up your hearts. It is St. John's Bread. We can celebrate the mass. These are the locusts John the Baptist lived on when he was crying in the wilderness, even as we are."

While the four women husked the beans and began the task of grinding them between stones to make a flour, all the young men went back, with blanket pouches, to gather all the carob beans they could find. They could be used for daily bread as well as for the mass, and they would be easy to carry with them when they set out to walk towards the north.

Godda had supervised the grinding of the flour, but when it came to mixing and baking the bread, she refused to go on with the work. "Let *her* do it," she said in an undertone to Clodagh, indicating Eleanor. "Nuns ought to do it. She's next best. She's never galloped under any man."

Clodagh took the wooden platter in which they'd collected the flour to Eleanor, and watched her as she made a dough of it by breaking in a couple of the small mottled eggs the men had brought, adding a few drops of river water. One of the eggs had been fertile and blood-streaked, and the flour had picked up specks of dirt from the stones with which they'd pounded it. She noticed

that Eleanor's thin fingers were whiter than the dough,
but she supposed God's miracle would work on it as
well, or almost as well, as it would work on clean bread.
Now Eleanor was shaping the smirched dough into small
flat cakes, and when that was done she crossed herself
with her streaked right hand, and knelt to lay them on
the hot stones of their fire.

Father Nicholas celebrated his mass in the last half
hour of light in the small clearing on the bank of the
river. He had ordained that there should be only a general confession. The sin of his decision lay heavily on
him, but there were three confessions he did not wish to
hear. He had made the altar himself, clearing the ground
around it on his hands and knees, and setting up a timber crosspiece between tripod legs made from boughs
and bound together with some of Gyll's withy rushes.
Under the altar, kneeling, he had buried the few sacred
things that his congregation could muster. Most of their
relics had gone down into the sea, nailed to the broken
mast of the *Grace Dieu*. But Eleanor had given him,
from between her breasts, a small crystal phial that contained three of the Virgin's tears, and Faber had lent
him a piece of the sail of James Zebedee's fishing boat
and Geoffrey de Baude had contributed a little pyx that
held some of the clay from which Adam had been made.

The mass frightened them. Silence inhabited the
place. The clearing, as the light faded, seemed to be peopled by anathemas. They were used to hearing mass
under a roof, where they could prop their backs against
a wall and say Paternosters while the priest did his part
up at the east end, or where they could walk about and
talk with their friends until the server signalled to them
that the priest was done with his Latin and was almost
ready for the Elevation. Here these things seemed im-

possible. They listened in silence, casting quick glances into the bushes behind them. Eleanor and the two de Baude brothers made what Latin responses were called for, but Father Nicholas did what he could for them in words they could understand, making a prayer for them out of the book of Jonah of how they had gone down into the water and the foul stinking weeds of the sea had covered their heads. He made a litany of their own troubles—"Jesu that was laid on a hard crib, give us patience in our pain and adversity; Jesu that was wrapped in simple cloth, help us to bear the cold; Jesu that lived forty days without food, help us to bear hunger; Jesu which raised diverse dead bodies, arise us, Lord, from slugging in deadly sin."

Each one of them, as they came forward to the altar, laid on the ground underneath it, as offering, one of the precious locust beans the men had gathered during the afternoon. These would be kept separately, and ground into flour so that mass could be celebrated again on their journey north. As they came forward one by one, the English hanging back as was customary until those of Norman blood had made their Communion, Father Nicholas found his concentration disturbed by worry over what should be done if the Hyperborean boy should present himself before him on his knees. But the Monkey did not come. He stayed on the edge of the group, watching curiously, grinning to himself and pulling at the lobe of his left ear in the habitual gesture he used when he was puzzled. Father Nicholas made a mental note to baptize him in the river's water before they left it on the following morning. Since he spoke no language they could recognize, then he could be baptized as an infant that spoke none. He would give him, he thought, the Christian name of Jonah.

They ate well after the mass, portions almost large enough to fill them of a stew of fish entrails and bony small birds satisfyingly thickened with locust beans. The last of the light had faded with the last of the priest's prayers, but the mass seemed temporarily to have sanctified their camp and made it safer, and they kept the fire alight and ate more slowly than usual. There was cheerful talk from the twins and the other loudmouths about the buckets of ale with which they would soon be washing away the reek of fish and dung. Simon de Baude had, after consultation with Eleanor, decreed that the party should move off to the north next day, and though there was more argument about where they were, those with enough knowledge of the world to be listened to were still of the view that they were somewhere a long way south in the Iberian peninsula. De Baude still thought privately that by walking south they might find themselves in Lusitania, where the mares conceived by the west wind and bore colts that were faster than any other horses on earth. Since he was happier ahorse than afoot, he would have chosen to lead his party south. But the homing instinct of most of the others made them prefer the idea of going north, and Captain Faber now seemed to feel sure that in this direction, if they kept walking long enough, they should come at last to Porto and the Crusading Armies of God.

When the food was finished Magnus kicked open the fire and covered the coals with soil. The companionable talk gradually stopped, and they settled themselves to sleep. Because their prayers had pushed back the fears of the night, they spread themselves, in their chosen groups, a little further apart than had been their custom. The priest stretched himself on the ground on the spot where he had been sitting, beside the buried fire. Clodagh had moved a few feet away, to the far side of a tus-sock of grass that supported her head and screened her from the others without putting any dangerous distance between them. Gyll took his usual place, less than a foot away from her, but slightly further from the fire, so that his head rested on a patch of ground on a level with her waist. He lay on his back for a long time, staring at the night sky and wondering how to bridge the gap between them. The foot of ground was not the problem that bothered him; it was simply that he suspected holiday and lady terms were called for, and he knew none. Even if I knew them they wouldn't do me any good, he thought. It was common knowledge that Norman women were fine and false and pernickety in bed, and set more store on fancy words than action. They were not to be taken by the fierce frontal attack that was every man's stock in trade in the villages. But she was only half Nor-man, and therefore perhaps English enough to need an-other sort of shriving before they went out on a march that none of them really thought could bring them any-thing but heavy difficulties. The stirrings and grum-blings of the others, trying to find some comfort on the hard ground, had gradually stopped while he lay worry-ing and watching the sky, and he thought now that the rest were all asleep. Perhaps she was asleep too. She had made no sound or stir for a long time. As he watched the sky he saw an ill-omened thing—a star falling to-wards the east—and he turned quickly on his side to avoid the bad luck of seeing its extinction. He was even closer to her now, and he saw that she, too, was lying on her side, and that she was watching him.

"We have to walk a long way tomorrow," she said, whispering. "You should sleep."

"My wank won't let me," he said.

"*Wank,*" she said scornfully. "That's a ploughman's word."

"It's a ploughman's wank," he said, edging closer so his whisper would carry. "Made for digging furrows." He heard a little sound of laughter caught quietly in her throat, and he thought that perhaps this high-toned Norman courting talk wasn't so difficult after all, since he seemed to be doing it successfully. But he couldn't think of anything more to say, he couldn't see how they kept it up for long. Instead he used the time to inch even closer, so that now his head and shoulders were on a level with hers. He felt her breath on his face for a few seconds, but then she turned on her back, and lay staring up into the night sky.

He heard a sound a few feet away, beyond the tussock of grass, and turned to look, but he couldn't see anything in the darkness. Joice was there, he thought, with Edwin or with Godwin or with both, and he mourned after her for a moment or two. She would have suited him better. He would have known how to deal with her and preferred the dealing, but the brothers had no mind to share her with anyone else. He looked back at Clodagh, propping himself on his elbow so that he was looking down into her face. She had folded her arms back so that her head rested on her hands, and she was staring up wide-eyed into the sky. Her position pulled the stained stuff of her gown tightly across her breasts. He didn't really want to touch them, he was afraid of touching them, but he cupped one of them tentatively with his right hand, remembering how one of the girls in his village had said to him angrily, "Tits first—where's the manners!" when he'd tried to go to work too hastily with her. The touch of his hand on Clodagh's breast seemed to have no effect on her beyond bringing her

eyelids down from their wide stare to half cover her eyes.
He thought his caress might have a little more effect if
he slipped his hand through the neck opening and
under the stuff of her gown. But he didn't do it. She
was, after all, a *married* woman, which seemed to alter
things.

A long time passed while he stroked her, hating her.
He was not really thinking of her now; he was thinking,
with envy, of Edwin and Godwin probably sleeping now,
and of Joice, also sleeping, having done twice the good
this cold bitch could do even if she were to try, which
didn't seem likely. Suddenly she turned her head towards him. "I'm cold," she said. "Put your leg over me.
I'm cold."

He turned, bringing his right leg across her body and
his mouth close to her ear. "Ready?" he said. "You're
ready?" She didn't answer him, she didn't appear to have
heard, and since he'd already talked a great deal more
than he thought desirable, he could think of nothing to
do beyond thrusting his tongue wetly into her ear. She
began to move then, sighing, pushing against him, moving her head on the ground so that he thought the others
might wake and hear them. The more he tried to
quieten her, the more restless she became, so that in the
end he thought there was no way to tame her but by
lying on her. She began to fight him then, but half-
heartedly, he thought, and he was beyond trying to understand her or to master any more of the conventions of
her class. She seemed to be saying, "Not yet, not yet.
Keep still. Let me sleep first," but that was ridiculous, it
made no sense, and after a moment or two her movements became obliging instead of defensive. When he
withdrew himself, depriving her of his seed, she struck
at him with the edge of her hand, catching him painfully

at the base of his throat so that he forgot where he was, and yelped aloud. "Never do that again," she said in a fierce whisper, and in the midst of his anger he noticed the promise in the last word. He rolled away from her and sat up with his back half turned. When he looked back she was lying with her eyes tightly closed and her praying hands held against her face. He forgot his anger then and leaned over and put a finger to her cheek, and found it wet with tears. "Don't," he said, bringing his mouth close to her ear again. "Don't do that. It's all right. It'll be all right."

"For you," she said. "You're not married. I'm married. You made me commit adultery."

"I didn't make you do anything," he said. "You were as ready as I was."

"You wouldn't wait," she said. "I begged you. Adultery's *mortal*. Why wouldn't you let me go to sleep first? What happens when you're asleep is only venial."

"Go to sleep now," he said, sorry and bored. "It'll be all right. You go to sleep now." He lay beside her, holding her in his arms, and thinking of Joice. He was asleep a long time before she was.

He woke in the false dawn, before any of the others were stirring, and in the instant in which he first opened his eyes, he thought that she was looking at him. He propped himself on his elbow and craned up to look around at the shivery bundles of sleeping people just discernible in the quarter light. Then he rolled quickly over her, sliding an arm beneath her to raise her hips. She seemed to be sleeping quietly, breathing softly through partly opened lips. This time her body accommodated itself to his easily and happily. "Stay with me, this time stay with me," she said, from the depths of her sleep. He had forgotten his anger, he had forgotten Joice.

he had forgotten the night and the march of the coming day, he was happy to stay with her. For him, it was baptism. And an immoral thing. He was used to quick couplings with wanton girls at the back of barns. Honour demanded that he should not impregnate anyone until he was ready for marriage, when he would do it deliberately to test her desirability as a, wife. Childlessness was all right for rich people when God willed it, but He mustn't be allowed to will it for the poor. He thought perhaps that he was being cozened with the oldest trick, until he remembered that this girl had a husband already, and horrid fears about the fires of hell. This made it harder for him to understand, and more confusing; he didn't think about it for very long, but slept again, until he was woken by the dawn stirrings of the others.

Twice during the third week of their walk, the earth shook under them, while they were camped at night. It frightened all of them except the priest, who said that it moved at God's will. The rains seemed to have gone now, and the stars shone with unnatural brightness in the dry air.

Only the captain, and Magnus, who had been to war before, had ever grown accustomed to the unnaturalness of sleeping under the sky. And perhaps the Monkey, because no one knew what he had done and seen. But the others' nights had been roofed and walled, and only a fool ventured out unless his thatch were alight. They had grown accustomed to their camp at the head of the lagoon, and sleeping had become a little easier as each night passed without external alarms. Now that they were walking again each night's camping place had its own perils.

Father Nicholas blessed each for them before they settled for the night, but they had no knowledge of the places where they slept, and so they could know nothing of the afrites that might inhabit it. Water, when they came to it, had its special dangers for, let the priest deny it as he would, there were a host of water places in sweet safe England that claimed a life a year, and who could tell how much hungrier the water bogles might be here. Godda, behind the priest's back, took the precaution of throwing a share of whatever food they were carrying into any stream they crossed, saying, "Eat hearty, good devil, sweet devil, we'll bring you more if you let us hunt tomorrow." Not that they came to many streams. With the carob beans and the smoked fish and what the hunters could find they were getting enough food, but they suffered a good deal from thirst on most days' marches, and often they had to sleep at night without drinking.

This raised, again, questions of their whereabouts. In their familiar places water was everywhere; you'd be hard put to find a place where you could walk two hours without crossing it, and it misted down through the soft air in the mornings and seeped slowly into any hole dug in low ground. But this was a hard place, bright, with sharp shadows, and the light was so strange to their eyes that it brought back again the fear that they had been swept beyond the known limits of the world. Certainly the land seemed uninhabited, for in three weeks they had found no men and no structures that could have been used as shelters by men. Nor had they seen any large animals—no cattle, no deer, no pigs, though they had heard night noises which suggested the prowling presence of fearsome things. The nights when the earth shifted under them, as though it were some great creature that twitched in its sleep, caused Simon de Baude to ask Captain Faber, privately, about the existence of the Behemoth.

"Certainly he exists," Faber said. "But not here. He's in the ocean."

"As we were, don't forget," Simon said. "Isn't it true that he looks like an island, seaweed, sand and all?"

"How else would sailors be persuaded to moor their ships and go ashore?" Faber said.

"And then he waits till they are settled, with their fire alight and camp made for the night, before he plunges down into the sea again, taking them with him?"

"It's happened so to hundreds," Faber said.

"Then how can you be so sure that we are on land, and not on Behemoth?" Simon said. "Even a monster has to sleep. What were those movements that we felt? He may be getting ready to dive at any time."

"Use your wits," Faber said scornfully. "Behemoth lives by eating the people he drowns. How could thirteen people feed a creature so great that we have walked three weeks on him, without reaching his further edge?" It annoyed him still that the party's fortunes should be in the hands of a man so little capable of logical thought that he could not see that a great sea beast that appeared to be an island would appear to be a *small* island, if he were not to need half the world's population for his dinner. At the same time, much as he resented de Baude and his assumption of leadership, he could not help being a little sorry for the young man. In the end they would walk into populated territory again, and Faber would get a new ship, with all the opportunities of trade and profit that it offered. All young de Baude would get would be a passage to the Holy Land and the war, perhaps on Faber's new ship. The life expectation of young lieutenants like him had been roughly seventeen days in the First War, and he didn't think it would be any longer in the Second. And the Moors had nasty habits with their prisoners.

For the first few days after they had moved from their camp at the lagoon head, they had walked for the greater part of each day without making any great progress because of the rough gullies that had to be crossed and because, after the first hour or two, their pace had to be slowed for the sake of the priest and Godda, who tired easily. In the beginning Simon had chivvied them to keep walking because it seemed to him that another mile, another ten miles, might end their trek. Soon he realized that they could not keep walking if proper time was not given every day to the hunt for food. At the end of ten days all the smoked fish was gone. They would have nothing now but what they could find during the day. It was then that Simon de Baude decided that the march should begin later and end earlier, so that the first two hours of light, and the last two before darkness, could be spent in hunting. This eased things a little for the women, who spent these hours close to the place where they had camped, looking for edible nuts and berries and grass. The seven younger men spent those hours in hunting for meat of any sort they could find. Godwin and Edwin usually hunted alone, but took the Monkey with them to fetch and carry. Simon de Baude and his brother, Geoffrey, went with Magnus and Gyll, learning from them their poachers' watchfulness and silence. Faber stayed in camp, though he was free enough to them, and to the women, with advice about how food was to be got. The younger men resented his inactivity, but couldn't see how his presence would be useful on their hunting parties. In camp he was loud with orders which Magnus and the Monkey obeyed quickly, Gyll slowly and the twin brothers not at all, turning away with half smiles as though they hadn't heard. On the march he was quiet, for though he was a great deal younger than the priest he was unused to walking, quickly became short of breath and in any case felt that his Norman blood excused him from carrying water or weapons while there were peasants there to do the work.

The food that they could get was still the same poor stuff—birds' eggs, small birds, an occasional hare, lizards, a snipe or two patiently snared with knotted vines when they came to marshy areas. Sometimes they managed to take a few fish with Gyll's withy basket, and Eleanor rationed out the stock of locust beans, allowing Godda to make a little of her heathen-tasting bread every second day. Because they were on the move all the time, they were hungry all the time. The bright sun bothered them, and though it was already October they wove head coverings for themselves, fearing, as Blanchefleur had feared for Clodagh, that madness might creep in with the heat of the sun. At sundown the temperature dropped with startling suddenness, and they ached with the cold throughout the hours of night. They had been walking for several days before they realized that they had kept no count of time. After much argument about how many days they had been at sea, how many days ashore, they agreed at last that their planned walk had begun on the first of October, and the priest now carried a notched stick in his belt, and recorded the passing of each day with his last prayers at night. October reminded them of the coming winter, and of their hunger. At home it was the livestock month, the time of killings for the brine barrels, when the farmyards would be loud with the cries of beasts, and the kitchens full of basins of blood for the puddings. Here there were no stores to be laid in, and the best they could hope for was enough food for one good meal each day. They had stopped

questioning what went into the common pot, had long since stopped asking the hunters whether they had killed what they had brought in, or whether they had found it lying dead. Only Eleanor seemed more willing to go hungry than to eat some of the messes that the others ate. Often, after praying over her food, she would eat a bare mouthful of it and give the rest to Geoffrey. Even God's blessing, it seemed, could not sweeten the stuff for her. "Eat it," the others would urge, handing her her share of flesh morsels clinging to stewed bones. "All flesh is grass. Eat it."

"I'll take the grass before it's spoiled," she'd say, and make her meal of any vegetable roots they'd found and a few locust beans, broken and moistened with ooze wrung from the leaves of trees. She was growing thinner even more quickly than the others, but she could still match them in walking and scavenging.

Though Sir Simon de Baude had nominal charge of the party, the real control still lay in Eleanor's hands. Simon could ask her advice where it would have shamed him to ask Faber's, and she would give it to him in such a malleable form that the final phrasing was his, as the final decision seemed to be. She was, unrecognized by any of them, the one person who kept them unified, because only in regard to her was there any deep respect unshaken by the increasingly uncomfortable contingencies of their daily lives. Father Nicholas loved her for her piety, and used his abundant charity to suppress the feeling that piety in a woman would have been more God-pleasing had it been less noticeable. The twin brothers and Magnus had a surprised respect for her as one who was above them as a woman and a Cross-taker and was yet not squeamish about rough language and rough living conditions. Young Geoffrey de Baude was usually close to her and the Monkey, surprisingly, was often there a little behind him and a little after him, grinning and pulling at his earlobe and watching her as though the understanding he needed might light on him from her. Faber was afraid of her as he was afraid of all women of his own and higher ranks. But she embodied all the superiorities that had to be preserved in a situation where the better people were dependent on the labours of the lower, and he commonly deferred to her, telling himself that the deference was due to her femaleness alone.

But it was her attitude to the other women which did most to keep peace and solidarity. She made no distinction of rank between Clodagh and Joice, but bound both firmly to her by an open friendliness that seemed to conspire against the natural domination of the men. Any tendency their concupiscence might have had to give rise to tensions and divisions in the group she disciplined by ignoring both the tendency and the cause. For Eleanor it was as if their nightly couplings were too small an irrelevance to engage her interest.

But if the concupiscence of the two younger women was a matter of indifference to Eleanor, it was a major cause of pain to Father Nicholas. Each night, after prolonged prayer, he determined that exomologesis—public denunciation, public confession, public penance—was the only possible plan for their salvation, but by the end of each day he was so wearied by walking that he had no strength left except for further prayer. He didn't, himself, blame the walking and his age, he blamed himself for spiritual apathy and cowardice. These two young women endangered not only their souls but the immortal souls of Gyll, Godwin, Edwin—and his own. He seemed to hear the voice of his long-dead novice master saying, "The first faults are theirs that commit them; the second faults are theirs that permit them." Sometimes at night it was very difficult to silence the voice so that he could sleep.

Mass was celebrated whenever the priest's notched stick affirmed a Sabbath, and each time a new altar was set up, with the same relics buried underneath to sanctify it. Each time he waited hoping that the five, or one of the five, would stay away from the improvised altar, giving him the opportunity to open publicly the question of their sin. But each time each of them took the sacrament, and each time he knew that the sin was his. If they, in ignorance, believed that a general confession could absolve them without particular penance and their promise not to sin again, then the blasphemy was his in not instructing them. He had begun to add to that blasphemy now, by resenting the burden God had laid on him in his old age. He preached often against the sins of blasphemy and lechery and infamy and perjury, and at each mass he told them again that nothing so estranges the heart from the love of God as women's faces.

At night, by the fire, when the mass was over, Eleanor raised the question. She had begun to tire of this constant preaching against women. "It must often seem," she said in her firm voice, "that woman is to be preferred to man, because of the better material she was made from." They listened to her, as they always did, but they were not certain what she meant by it.

"Better material, and in a better place," Eleanor said. "We know that Adam was made from a handful of dirt, and that Eve was made from a piece of Adam's side."

"Used dirt. Secondhand," Captain Faber said.

Eleanor smiled at him. "Perhaps," she said. "But dirt into which God had already breathed. And besides, Eve was made in Paradise and Adam somewhere outside, before the Garden existed. Isn't that so, Father Nicholas?"

"So we are taught," the priest said patiently. "But we are taught, too, that woman and Satan came into the world together, the Devil entering it by the hole God made in Adam's side."

"So the Devil came out of the hole *whole*," Eleanor said. "No part of him was incorporated in Eve."

"No, Lady, that's not the way it is written," Father Nicholas said. His bones ached and his conscience was troubled. He longed for sleep, not argument.

"Written by men," Eleanor said softly.

"By *God*," Father Nicholas said severely.

"But no clay man could conceive God. He had to use a woman to work His miracle."

It seemed to Father Nicholas that he had heard this said before, and that there was some proper form by which to counter it, but his utter weariness prevented him from remembering it. He contented himself with saying "God loved Mary Virgin, as He loves all virgins, for Her purity."

"And exalted Her even above the choir of angels," Eleanor said, smiling the smile the Virgin's name always brought to her lips. They had extra food that night, a handful each of water snails they'd found climbing the weeds by their mouths in a shallow pond. She leaned forward, and ignoring Geoffrey, to whom she usually gave food, divided her snails into three small heaps before Joice, Clodagh and Godda, as though in celebration of their link with Mary.

"In Cathay there are snails as big as a house," Faber said. "So big that after the meat is taken their shells can shelter a whole family."

"And besides," Eleanor said, "it was to women that our brother Christ appeared, after His death."

"I wish we had some of them here," Godwin said. "One snail like that would feed us all half a week."

"And there are birds, too, who have no legs and no need of legs, because they fly all their lives and never settle to the ground."

"There can't be many of them," Magnus said. "It must be a powerfully difficult thing for the cock to do his trick while they're both flying."

"God provides for all things," Faber said. "In the back of the male bird He provides a snug hole, lined with feathers, where the hen lays her egg and where the hatchling stays till it is ready to fly."

"The pelican is the most wonderful of all God's birds," the priest said, "for the pelican hen caresses her young so savagely with her claws that she kills them. And then, after three days, the father comes to the nest. In his despair he rips at his own breast with his bill, and the blood that spills from his wounds revives his dead children. So Christ does for us, at the Eucharist, and will do, till we all rise at the Day of Judgment."

"Except the Irish," Edwin said with a grin at Clodagh. The brothers and Magnus had accepted her more easily when they found her name was not a sign of exalted Norman blood, but of a heritage more outlandish than their own. "They're to be judged by St. Patrick, not by God."

"I expect he'll hear the Last Trump, like anyone else," Clodagh said, pleased by the teasing.

"He'll be late, like all the Irish," Edwin said. "Or he'll miss it, out snake catching at Armagh."

"We'll catch nothing in the morning if we don't sleep," Simon de Baude said. He was troubled when the talk led them back to matters of religion. The last weeks had hatched in him a fear that God was dead, or else that they had strayed into a dominion which He didn't overlook. He was worried, too, by the need to find meat, and quickly, if they were to continue walking even at their present pace. Although he had no certain way of measuring it, he was sure that his people were taking longer to walk shorter distances each day. The country seemed to get rougher and more barren as they walked. He had begun to wonder whether Faber had been right in his insistence that the sensible course would have been to stay close to the coast. It would have meant more walking, steeper climbing, longer detours in order to get around the gullies and the chasms that let water down to the sea. But there would have been water, and perhaps fish as well, and what would detours have mattered after all, since walking without them got them to no useful place in this rainless country that seemed forsaken by God and man? Meat was their prime need, to keep up their strength. What he feared now was that the time would soon come when one of the women would fall ill, or when the old priest could walk no longer, and might have to be carried. "How many more cakes can you make from the locust beans?" he asked Godda.

"Few enough," she said, pushing at Godwin to get the blanket bag of beans he was using as a pillow. She shook it, so that all could hear how small their supply was. "A small cake each, on two more days," she said.

"Father Nicholas has some," Joice said.

"A handful," said the priest. "They must be kept for the mass."

"We could go back—three or four of us," Magnus said. "We could bring a big supply—and it'd be a chance for the others to rest."

They thought about it, but the carob beans were many days' walk behind them. Perhaps Magnus and the twins and Gyll could walk in a day three times as far as the whole party could manage, and if they could find them again were strong enough to bring a good supply, but each of them was frightened at the thought of splitting the party.

"It is too far," Simon said. "And we have no surety that we would find them again."

"There'd be too few left to hunt for the people here," Faber said.

"We should turn back, all of us," Godda said. "We know there's food of a sort back there."

"And spend the rest of our lives sucking birds' eggs?" one of her sons said impatiently.

"We must go on while we have strength," the priest said. "We may find more carob trees. We may come to soft country, where there is meat to be had." He had a sort of vision, for a moment, of land that flowed with milk and honey, but he knew that that was a long way off, near Jerusalem, and that in any case God would not let him see it, since he had failed his people.

"We should get back to the coast, and quickly," Faber said. He thought of how he would set the men to fish there, and the women to gather shellfish from the rocks, and of how much closer England would be when there was only water between them, and of the possibility that they would be found by a ship. "We should go back to the seashore, walking due west until we reach it."

"Sir Simon leads," Eleanor said, "and he thinks we have more chance of finding human habitation by walking north and keeping a little inland."

Simon was glad of her support, though no longer sure that he agreed with her. "There is no country on the earth that hasn't men and animals," he said hopefully. "If we keep going, we must find them in the end."

"What sort of men and animals?" Godda said fearfully.

"No country is limitless," Simon said. "We have walked already perhaps a hundred miles, perhaps more."

They were silent, thinking about it. Then Clodagh spoke. "That's twice the distance from my home to Glastonbury, and I didn't make the pilgrimage, because I thought it was too far."

The others were silent, thinking of prayers scamped, promises broken, pilgrimages not made. But the priest brought them sharply back to their present omissions. "Perhaps God is angry with us because we have not kept the Sabbath," he said. He had argued it with them when their march began, but he had been overborne by Simon and Eleanor, whose view it was that they should walk every day, and make restitution when they came to a safer place. "If our Sabbaths were spent in prayer, then God would put us in the way of his lesser creatures, to supply our wants." He thought, too, of what a whole day's rest might do for the pains that bedevilled him with every step.

"We will keep the next Sabbath," Simon said after a moment's thought, and felt the power of command descend on him. This was the first decision he had made, the first order he had given, without first being prompted to it by Eleanor.

"It's seven nights away," Father Nicholas said, but the thought of it was still a comfort to him.

"And in the meantime we will stop our walk in midafternoon, to give those who are to hunt a little time of rest first, and a longer time to hunt before the light goes.

If we do not soon find meat . . ." Simon said, and left the end of his sentence in the air.

"We will be forced to eat someone who's young and relatively plump," Eleanor said, making one of her rare jokes. "How glad I am to be thin and unattractive to cooks."

"I'll be the one for the pot," Magnus said.

"You!" Godda said with a cook's scorn. "You'd be gristle and a thin gravy."

"I'm a penitential lamb," Magnus said, "and they eat sweet."

"More of a sacrificial goat, from the look," Gyll said.

"A lamb," Magnus said with a grin. "A penitential lamb. I go for my master, Alain Hugolin, who had his pilgrimage penance commuted to the equipping of another man to fight."

"And if you're killed?" Gyll said.

"A man can be killed in his own backyard," Magnus said. "And this way, I'd get more for my death. I get a rose noble every month I'm away, more than most common soldiers get . . ."

"Twice what I get," Gyll said. "I'm on tuppence a day."

"Well, there you are . . ."

"But I'd rather be on tuppence, and have my credits to myself. This way, even if you're first into the Holy Sepulchre and take it with your own hands, St. Peter will mark the credits up to Sir Hugolin."

"Is that right?" Magnus said, turning to the priest. He had not thought of it like that before. The pay, and the promises that his wife would not be turned off their land if he died, nor forced to remarry if she didn't care to, but allowed tenant rights for herself and her children, had seemed to him such a good deal that he hadn't thought of the chance that anything he suffered might not earn him any remissions of his purgatory time.

"They'll be credited to your account, my son," Father Nicholas said. "Just be careful that you don't exhaust your credit with your sins on the way."

Magnus grinned with relief. "Small chance of sinning in this company," he said.

And so the priest, in trying to bring counsel and comfort to Magnus, was faced again with his own dilemma. Five of his small flock were open fornicators: the Lady Clodagh was certainly and Joice was very probably, since it was not yet certain that her husband had drowned, living in adultery before his eyes. He thought of the penances he should impose upon them—fasting, prostration, the wearing of sackcloth, lying in ashes, mortification in food and drink, exclusion from the sacrament—and he knew that there was no point to the penances, and that in any case he lacked the indignation to impose them. None of his people had enough to eat, and there was mortification enough in their disgusting diet; they were cold at night, and they went in rags, and very soon even the rags they had would fall off them; they lay in dirt at night, and to make them lie in ashes would be to give them special privileges, since those who got closest to the ashes of their fire were the ones who suffered least from the cruel nights. Exclusion from the sacrament was the one penance that he could properly impose, and for this decision he prayed continually to God for strength. God didn't seem to hear his prayer, for each day he found it a little easier to postpone the decision, to hope that they would end their sin of their own accord, or that weariness and a low diet would end it for them. He was not a worldly priest. He had been used to hearing the voluntary confessions of those who

sought him out, who listened to his exhortations humbly
and then removed themselves from his sight so that he
didn't have to bear witness to their obedience or the lack
of it. Clodagh's rank bothered him. He had never been
a great-house chaplain, but he'd heard enough to know
that even the Church agreed that circumstances, sometimes, could alter cases. Perhaps because of her youth,
perhaps because of her mixed blood, there was little in
her behaviour now to remind him that her rank, though
not equal to that of Eleanor and the de Baudes, was
higher than the rank of those he customarily confessed.
But he reminded himself that she was the wife of Robert Apelfourde, and that it must be repugnant both to
God and man that she should couple on the ground with
one of Apelfourde's humbler tenants. As yet he had not
opened the question with her, and he could not bring
himself to refuse her the Host. He thought of himself as
a man of no courage and without steadfastness, and
knew that the greater share of God's punishment would
be his.

The differences of rank still bothered Clodagh, though
they had ceased to matter to Gyll after a few days. It was
not that he forgot her difference. In fact it was at the
heart of his feeling for her. This feeling was to him very
remarkable, outside the ordinary run of things, most
surprising, too delicate to last him very long, and full of
laughter. It was as though, through contact with her,
some of the fancy feelings that the goliards sang about
had rubbed off on him. He was in love, and it wasn't
after all a made-up thing to help pass the time for people who spent their days making it pass. It was a prick-
ing delight, an itch under his skin, with no likeness at all
to the feelings he'd had in the past for various sensible
and obliging parish girls. The thought of Robert Apel-

fourde troubled him a little, though it wouldn't have bothered him at all if he'd been some other man's tenant. But when at last they reached Porto, as they would, he would disappear into the crowds of English and Flemish soldiers said to be there, and even if there were blabmouths in de Baude's party, Apelfourde would scarcely take their word against his wife's. In any case one or both of them might be dead before they came back from Jerusalem, and that would put paid to Gyll's tenancy anyway.

Their social differences rankled more with Clodagh, making her sometimes peck at him in a scolding way in front of the others and waste his time and hers by an assumption of superiority when they managed to be alone together. Her capriciousness, never prolonged, and her faultfinding became part of her charm for him, as evidence that there was some unnamed thing about him that could engage her attention endlessly. It didn't escape him, too, that though she was critical of certain crudities in his lovemaking, and though she mocked him for the farmyard words he used, his virility surprised and flattered her. "I dub you nine times a knight," she would say, "for tireless tilting," flattering him, in his turn, by using the courtly terms of the tournament.

What bothered her as much as his lower rank was the suspicion that he was younger than she was. He couldn't see any sense in this objection, and earned himself half a day's angry displeasure by telling her what every farmer knew—that the only way to get twin calves was to put a young bull over an old cow.

When she had first asked his age he hadn't realized how important the question was, and he'd said "about seventeen."

"About?" Clodagh said. "Don't you *know*?"

"There are a lot of us. People forget."

It presented to her a frightening picture of poverty, births in crowded huts where the older children played under the bed, brutal upbringing.

"Are you a freeman?" she said apprehensively.

"Of course I am, you silly girl," Gyll said on a burst of laughter. "Do I look like a serf, do I act like one, make love like one?"

"Then if you're a franklin, why don't you know when you were born?"

"I've told you. There were a lot of us. My father was as good a man as I am. He didn't have to crusade in the hope that God would give him sons," he said, taking a dig at Apelfourde that made her smile. "I was born not too long after Michaelmas," he said, "that's all I know."

"You haven't got a yearday!" she said, remembering how hers had always been celebrated with presents and feasts and dancing—and with costly presents since she became Apelfourde's wife.

"So what?" he said, tired of the topic. "I've got every day in the year for myself."

"What's the very first thing you can remember?" she said, hoping to get nearer to his beginnings through his memories.

"Falling into the water when the *Grace Dieu* went down," Gyll said. "I didn't begin to live till I first saw you."

"No, *really*," she said. "What do you remember when you were very little—some great event that stuck itself in your mind?"

"Getting my thumb stuck between the rope and the roller over the well in the yard. My thumb's never looked the same since," he said, showing it to her.

"Poor thumb," she said, putting her lips to it. "But

not your thumb, stupid, something that everyone re-
members."

"I don't remember anything that everyone remem-
bers. Yes, I do," he said, after a moment's thought. "I
remember the great bonfire we had in the village, when
King Stephen was crowned. There were pigs roasting
there, and whole sheep. I burned my hand fishing my
leather ball out of the fire."

"You made a habit of putting your hands in foolish
places," Clodagh said.

"And still do," he said, one hand now at her thigh, the
other at her navel. She was not to be sidetracked. "How
old were you," she said, "that day when you burned your
hand, when Stephen was crowned?"

He had been, he thought, about four, because about
that time his mother had borne her eighth child and first
daughter, his little sister, Hoby, whom he still loved. He
added a couple of judicious years. "I was six," he said.
"I remember it perfectly."

"That was in 1135," Clodagh said. "I remember it too.
I went with my mother to Winchester to see the corona-
tion. You must have been born in 1129. You're eighteen."

"Then I'm the same age as you."

"But I've been married five years."

"What difference does that make?"

"And anyway, I was born on Lady Day."

"A few months—nothing."

"You should have a yearday," she said. "Everyone
should have a yearday. We'll choose one for you."

"I'll share yours," Gyll said.

"No," she said, not wanting to share it. "Yours is near
Michaelmas, you said. You can have the very first Sun-
day after we reach the crusading people in Porto."

"All right," he said, "that's my yearday." But in fact it'll be my disappear day, he thought, because he knew that he would not see Clodagh again after they reached the town. He thought that she must know it equally well, though there were times when she refused to remember it.

There were other things that entranced him, apart from her gentle ways. The smallness of her wrists and her waist, and the fact that he could span the first with one of his hands, and the second with two. The thinness of her arms was pleasing to him, too, because he was used to arms browned and bulged by haying and bucket carrying. So were the heavy dark lashes that shadowed her cheeks and made her eyes seem dark until she lifted them to look directly at him with her sea-green gaze. But the thing about her that gave him the greatest gratification was the blue veining of her white breasts. He had seen only the swollen breasts of farm women feeding their children; the breasts he had handled had been briefly exposed to him in the twilight of barns where the light had discovered no veining to him, and he thought that the blue veins in the downward curves of her breasts were the positive proof that she carried Norman blood. To put his lips to those veins made him feel holy, almost as though heaven somehow approved of him.

He was used to proper standards of exchange between temporary lovers—presents like cheap rings and brooches expected and brought when beasts were taken to market, and handfuls of flowers plucked from the nearest hedgerow on his way to the barn. With Clodagh he could never be sure how his gifts or his words would be accepted, but though he was often surprised, he was never offended. Once, while out hunting, he had picked for her a posy of spiky mauve flowers with long curling white stamens for which he knew no name, braving the teasing of the twins to carry them back to her. She had looked at them, sniffed them briefly and flung them behind her into the bushes beyond their campfire, saying "They're no good, they're foreign flowers." The others had roared with laughter at his expense, but he hadn't minded. He knew she was thinking of the flowers at home—proper flowers, breezeblossoms and speedwell, lady's-smock and primroses and hedgeball—and he admired her choosiness. It seemed that she would approve only of things that were familiar, and for him it marked her difference from peasant people, who were used to making the best of what was offered. One morning she had woken him before the others were stirring, shaking his shoulder and whispering fiercely in his ear, "Listen, listen!"

"It's only a bird," he said sleepily.

"But it's singing in *English*," she said.

He propped himself on his elbow and listened for a moment. "It's a throstle," he said.

"It's beautiful," Clodagh said. "Don't let them hurt it. I hate these Iberian birds. They're very little better than Captain Faber's stupid bird with no legs, and their taste is vile." He listened a little longer and turned to look at her, but the sound of the thrush's song had sent her contentedly back to sleep.

Her marriage, her better clothes, her outlandish name and her certainty of her own worth had seemed to set her apart at first from Godda and Joice and the peasants in the party. But her name (and half of her blood) had proved to be Irish, her clothes were now dirty and torn and had lost their distinction, and since she'd been tamed by one of their own sort her marriage could hardly set her apart any longer. For all that, Godda and Joice were still faintly uneasy with her. They had given up calling her "Lady" when they spoke to her, and now called her "you" since they didn't yet feel right about using her name. If they wanted to speak about her they called her "her" to the men, which distinguished her from Eleanor, to whom they still gave her due title. The men were easier with her, even teasing her a little about her origins and her fine ways, but they were careful not to show that they felt some contempt. Things would alter, they knew, when they got to Porto; things would go back to their old form again, and who knew when a common soldier might not be under the hand of Robert Apelfourde and his lady? If they despised Clodagh a little, they had nothing but admiration for Gyll of Dittisham. Though they gave him much good and ribald advice because he was young, they had a proper respect for his manhood and prowess.

The fifth week of their walk was hard and long, and seemed to them to contain more than the proper number of days. On some of those days the men who hunted brought back almost nothing at all, and their one meal, eaten at night, was little better than warmed water with the miserable flesh of small birds in it, a handful of nameless tough roots and the brittle bodies of grasshoppers. Hunger undermined their optimism. Because the hunters still had the strength to hunt even though their hunting was unproductive, it seemed to the others that they must draw their strength from stolen food, and they accused them angrily when they came back empty-handed. Their nights were an agony because of the cold; hunger and coughing and the itching of their broken and inflamed skin kept them short of sleep. It seemed to them that St. Roque had turned his face away from them, for their prayers to him went unanswered. When they cut their feet on stones or scratched themselves in the foodless thickets through which they had to fight their way, the devil got in through every break and infected their blood. A great lopsidedness of his face bore witness to the agonies of Simon de Baude's toothache and he chewed bark endlessly, wincing against the pain, in the hope of curing his teeth by giving them proper employment. Toothache had bothered Edwin for a day or two as well, but Godwin had punched the tooth out of his mouth for him with a pointed stone, and the pain had drained away in an hour or two with the blood. Most of them had some sort of soreness in the mouth—swollen and pulpy gums or lips split by the cold—so that there was no pleasure to be had from eating the harsh stuff that was all they got. They had begun to develop boils and blains on their bodies, and though Captain Faber argued that these were caused by lack of proper meat, it seemed more likely that they were being punished by God. Certainly the priest thought so, and since a bleariness of his sight and hot swellings of the joints at his knees and his elbows were added to his sufferings, it seemed to him that God had more reason for anger against him than against the others. "Every country has its animals," he told his hungry people. "They have been made invisible to us, because we are unrighteous."

"Put your hand up the arse of that invisible ox and pull out its liver for me," Faber said, amusing Magnus and the twins, but he kept his voice low, not wanting to upset the priest.

"Remember Moses, that was with the Lord, in thick darkness, forty days and forty nights, and did not eat bread nor drink water," the priest said. "And Moses told his people not to be afraid. He told them that God had come to prove them, and that He would put no diseases on them, but give them flesh to eat in the evening, and fill them with bread each morning." They were listening to him now, because the mention of food attracted their attention. "Do not be stiff-necked," Father Nicholas said, grateful for the pain of his stiffened elbow and for the power of prophecy that seemed to descend on him as he pulled the tally stick out of his belt and held it up before them. "The time has almost come," he said. "God has not forgotten us. He will lift us on eagles' wings. The invisible will be visible again. Do his commandments. Our forty days in the wilderness is almost over."

Three days later it began to seem that the priest's prophecy would be fulfilled. They came to a small river —the first they had found for a long time—and caught enough small fish in the withy basket to half fill their bellies.

That night there was argument again as to whether or not they should stay where they were, close to food, at least until they had built up a little strength. But Simon de Baude ruled against it, again without the need to refer his decision to Eleanor before he announced it publicly. The haul from two hours' fishing had been too small to promise anything spectacular for the next day, and he believed that the fact that they now found themselves in better country argued that there was still better ahead. The priest supported him. Their forty days of hardship were not yet up. It seemed to him that he had been in the spirit when he spoke about God lifting them on eagles' wings. Canaan, he thought, lay two days' march ahead.

The following day they found themselves moving away from the sandy soil, the thickets and the barren trees that had marched with them for so many weeks. The soil was sandy still, but streaked with dark particles of loam that lifted their country spirits, and there were pine trees growing there that yielded satisfactory handfuls of pine nuts for those who could chew them. Bigger birds flew between the trees, and though it was harder to snare them there than it had been to snare little birds in their thickets of bush, there was a bird apiece to go into the stew by nightfall. They had seen no animals on their first day in the better country—no rabbits or hares or deer or wild pigs—but they went to sleep with their hopes reasonably high. Hadn't Father Nicholas said that every country had its own animals, and wasn't it borne out by the myriad stories Captain Faber had of the strange beasts that inhabited places he'd seen?

When the second day passed without their seeing any hot-blooded thing that went on four legs, it began to seem to them that there might be some truth in Father Nicholas's story that God, in his anger, had caused all the animals of the place to be invisible to them. "At night there are noises," Joice said, "that sound like huge beasts moving around our camp."

"Once I woke and I saw two flashes of green, and I heard a sound like sixteen cats purring, and what was that if it wasn't a panther?" Godda said.

"It's true it has a melodious voice," Faber said judicially, "and its breath is so sweet that it smells to us of spices. But it must eat to live. I don't think it was a panther you heard. There's nothing here for it. Why should it purr sweetly, on an empty belly?"

"Why should its belly be empty, if the place is full of good fresh meat made invisible to us by the sins of some?" Magnus said. He didn't believe in the invisibility of the animals, but something was preventing the hunters having much success, and the sinfulness of Gyll and the twin brothers was a constant source of jealous irritation to him. He looked hard into Joice's face as he spoke, and she mistook the meaning of his look for piety. She was with the other three women and Magnus and Faber, and Magnus was digging, under Faber's direction, to enlarge a soak at the base of a wall of rock. The priest was sleeping in a pale sun a little way off, having moistened his mouth with the first half-cupful of water which Clodagh had brought to him as he prayed. In his sleep it seemed that his mother came to him, but she was not his mother really; at one glance she was Clodagh and at another God's Blessed Lady, and her blue cloak swept a swathe of ground close to him and at once there sprang up a miniature paradise of tiny animals, all that Noah took with him in the ark. He fell to his knees to thank her for this bounty, but she laughed in his face, with teeth that were broken and horrible. And when she swept her cloak back over the ground, she erased all the gambolling beasts.

"Would the game come back—the small beasts good for the pot—if no one in the party sinned any more?" Joice asked, speaking to Eleanor.

"I don't know," Eleanor said, after a long pause. The behaviour of Joice and Clodagh gave her some pain, but she was not sure of the purity of her reasons, and in any case they were different from the priest's. "It's possible. The First War was lost because those who fought it were unclean."

Faber laughed. "The First War was lost because of stupidity," he said, "as this one will be. You don't win a war by keeping promises made by carpet knights who stay safely at home, issuing orders. Nor by trying to baptize a prisoner who, if he's taken *you* prisoner, would make a hole in your stomach and tie your guts to a stake, and flog you around and around it in a circle until all your innards were spilled across your feet."

"Our people do as bad, and worse," Magnus said surprisingly. "*Worse,* because it's done in the name of piety, and often enough to women."

"I'm not interested in the war," Joice said. "It's food that interests me. It's for the Lady Eleanor to say. If I sleep with my legs crossed, and *her*," she said with a quick side glance at Clodagh, "will that make God better pleased with all of us?"

"It's worth a try," Eleanor said. "You waste too much of your strength with your double play."

"If one man gives a woman strength, two should double the amount," Godda said tentatively. She would not normally have expressed such a view in front of a lady, but concern for her sons' well-being drove her to speak.

"You are wrong," Eleanor said. She preferred not to discuss such matters in front of Faber and Magnus, but Clodagh and Joice were each, in their way, worth saving, and her desire to help them overcame her reluctance. "A man is no more than a leech on a woman. He injects his poison to deaden her soul, and sucks it out of her body with his mouth."

"Leeches don't stick to empty veins," Faber said in an aside to Magnus. The woman's virginity irritated him— it was a commodity suited only to tender girls.

It had begun to irritate Godda equally, since it seemed to cast a reproach on plain, fecund women. "People should talk only of what they know," she said, bending so that she could look into Joice's face. "Empty

wombs make bad humours. I know what I'm talking
about. I have borne under my heart two heads, two
pairs of lungs, four ears, four eyes . . ."

"So has any bitch," Eleanor said carelessly.

". . . and I was more blessed then than I have been
since," Godda said, ignoring her.

"It's worth a try," Joice said, echoing Eleanor's words.
"I'll watch what *she* does. There's no point to one, if
not the other. If *she'll* stay by the fire, and not go off . . ."

Clodagh said nothing. It didn't seem to her likely
that God would deprive twelve other people of food
and shelter just because He wished to punish her, but
then so much of what He did was incomprehensible.
And if they were not, after all, in a Christian country,
if they were in a place beyond His sight? In front of
these people, and the sleeping priest, she wouldn't *refuse* to separate herself from Gyll at night, but she knew
that when night came she wouldn't do it. Gyll spoke
to the wild and loving streak in her that came to her
from her wild and loving mother. Not that Blanchefleur
would have approved her daughter's behaviour—she
might have been wild and loving when she was young,
but she'd been wise enough to take what she wanted and
then try to expiate it through her daughter's body and,
when that hope failed, to find an unexceptionable marriage for her. And if Robert Apelfourde hadn't taken it
into his head to go rampaging off over half the world
to fight God's battles for Him, the marriage would have
served them both well enough. His house was comfortable, and his manners pleasant. He knew the way women
set store by words, and he took pains to woo her play-
fully, salting his words with poets' phrases. "Coquerico
is knock-knocking with his staff," he would say. "Open
the gates of this little meadow and let him in." And,

once admitted, he would be decorous and undemanding, and soon sleep, leaving Clodagh to mumble her nightly prayer, "Get for me, O Mother Mary, a son before I go from this world. Do not delay to put his seed into my blood, O Womb in which the humanity of God was formed," before she, too, slept, satisfied with her lot. Gyll was another matter. Gyll didn't care a cock for conversation, as he told her when she protested at his urgent silences. And though she found this hard to accept and impossible to forgive, his potency in part made up for it. It made her shiver to think how tireless he would be, given proper food, a rest from walking and a good room with fresh, sweet herbs, every chair cushioned and a bolted door. The others, she found, were still watching her, waiting for some sort of reaction to the bargain Joice had proposed between them. She shook her head slowly. She was not sure herself whether she meant to imply doubt, or decision.

When the men came back they were almost empty-handed, once again, but they brought news of some unusual things. They had found the wheel ruts of an oxcart, long since bitten deep into damp clay, and now dried out so that they were filled with powdery dust. They had followed them for a long time, walking with the excitement of the hope that the tracks, though old, might lead towards other signs that people had been there and were close at hand. But the wheel ruts had ended as suddenly and senselessly as they had begun, coming from nowhere, going to no place. "What was at the end of them?" Faber said. "Woods? A river bank?"

"They ended where the ground grew stony," Simon de Baude said. "And on the other side, thirty long paces away . . . nothing. As though the cart and its beasts had gone down into the earth."

"Swept away," Father Nicholas said, remembering his dream.

"We found this," Geoffrey de Baude said, displaying on his palm a roundlet of dung, smooth and dark and about the size of a walnut.

"One?" Faber said.

"A scattering," Edwin said. "We brought one for a sample."

"Tracks?" Faber said. "There were hoofmarks near?"

"Nothing," Simon de Baude said, and crossed himself.

Clodagh bent to look at the pat of dung on the young squire's hand. "It's sheep's stuff," she said.

"Then it's a sheep of monstrous size," Gyll said, "and one of them would feed us for a sevennight."

"Panther dung," Joice said, remembering the green eyes Godda fancied she had seen in the dark.

"The panther's dung is pure white," Eleanor said, "and medicinal. This looks more like the turd of a deer, to me."

"And the cart tracks disappeared down into the ground?" Faber said.

Simon nodded. "Or so it appeared," he said.

"Let me look again," Faber said, putting his hand under the boy's as he bent to look at the dung. "In some places, so I have been told, there's a Celestial Stag that lives underground. When it escapes"—he withdrew his hand from underneath Geoffrey's—"it becomes a foul-smelling liquid that lies close to the ground, breeding death and pestilence." The boy jumped back and withdrew his hand, spilling the pat of dung onto the ground. As it hit, it split open, and they could see that it was the dropping of some grass-eating thing.

"Now you say it, it's like a stag turd," Godwin said, "and if there's stags about, there'll be does and kids."

"Save me the dropping," Eleanor said. "Stag dung, burned and mixed with the ooze of wild lettuce, is sovereign against these blains and boils we have."

Simon de Baude bent to pick up the two halves of the pat of dung, and put them into Eleanor's extended hand. "And if it should be nothing but goat dung?" he said.

"Then we'll all have more hair inside us than we have outside," Eleanor said with a broad smile. "For goat dung, treated the same way, is a strong charm against all sorts of baldness."

The other thing that the hunters had to report was a stand of trees, mysteriously scarred on their eastern sides. Each had been cut and seemed to have bled, and then the wide scar had scabbed over and healed itself. They were knotty trees, the men said, with a greyish foliage, and they had gathered from under them a handful of pods that looked like the mast of beech or oak trees. Faber broke one of them between two stones, but when he went to put a piece of it to his mouth, Simon de Baude said "Don't!" and knocked it from his hand. There had been something strange about the scars, something suggesting magic in the way they were all made at the same height and on the same side of the trees. Faber laughed uncertainly. He didn't believe many of the stories he told, and he wasn't much afraid of most magics, but he was glad that Simon had stopped him all the same. He picked one of the pieces up and, holding the Monkey by one shoulder, tried to force the stuff into his mouth. The Monkey pulled away, frightened, and struggled with him until Magnus took him by the other shoulder. They pushed the piece of mast between his teeth and the frightened Monkey chewed at it in his efforts to expel it from his mouth. The others watched, expecting he might die, or disappear. When finally he spat the chewed remnants of it out Faber and Magnus let him go, and he stood grinning foolishly, and pulling at the lobe of his left ear. It didn't seem to have had any poisonous effect, but time would show.

Their meal consisted of a mess of stewed frogs that Magnus and the women had found, eked out with edible leaves chosen by Eleanor, and the fat white-fleshed tail of a large lizard that Gyll had found sleeping torpidly in the sun. Then, earlier than was usual, Father Nicholas spread his customary prayer mantle over them, and they settled to sleep with fearful hopes of what the next day might bring. It was clear to them all that the hunters had been on the edge of new territory. What was not yet clear was whether they were coming to inhabited country, or to magic ground.

Clodagh had sought Gyll out and sat beside him while they ate, and when the others stretched themselves to sleep, he and she had moved a little way off, as was their custom. She had felt Eleanor's reproachful eye on her. Joice was avoiding the twin brothers, and had settled herself, in safety, between Eleanor and the priest. She didn't go to sleep for a long while, but lay thinking of her mother, of Apelfourde and of the cart tracks that disappeared underground. Later she heard a busyness by the dead ashes of the fire and, looking up, saw by the bright dry starlight that Edwin and Godwin had tired of each other's company, and gone to fetch Joice. She could see the smoke of their breath on the cold air. Godwin took hold of her by her feet and Edwin grasped her underneath her shoulders and quickly, while she struggled and protested silently, they lifted her clear of Eleanor's restraining arm and across the body of the sleeping priest, and carried her back between them to their sleeping place. After that, while Clodagh lay awake, there was silence except for the priest's coughing, the soft sounds Faber made getting up to ease his burning bladder and the scuffling the Monkey made climbing over the others to the safe spot beside the priest, to escape the marauding Faber, who had suddenly, in the cold night, conceived a longing for his pink Hyperborean flesh. Then there was silence for a long while, until young Geoffrey cried pitifully, in his sleep, for his mother. He hadn't done that for a long time, not for many nights.

The men led them, in the morning, straight to the limits of their journey of the previous day. They saw the old wheel tracks, and marvelled at their total disappearance; they saw the gashed trees, with their healing scars. It was Magnus's view that they were cork oaks, but Faber had a different theory for them. "All the cuts are on the same side," he said. "They face the rising sun. Do you notice that they have all been cut at exactly the same height?"

They nodded at him, expecting mysteries. "In Sweden or thereabouts," the captain said, "there is a giant elk with wondrously sweet flesh. He is a large, heavy animal, with a white coat and the black mane of a horse, and his legs are perfectly straight, and without joints in them."

"So how does he lie down?" Geoffrey asked.

"You've hit on it straightaway, m'boy," Faber said. "Without joints it's not possible for him to lie down. When he wants to rest he props himself against a convenient tree. He's too swift to be hunted on foot or by the fastest horse, but there's a way to take him all the same. The hunters make a cut in the tree, on the east

side because the great elk likes to wake with the sun on
him, and when he leans his great weight upon the tree
it breaks and lets him down. Having no joints to his
legs, he can't get up again, and the hunter takes him."

"As the stiff-necked man who dies unconfessed, and
can't rise up under the weight of his sins," the priest
said, improving the hour.

"If the elk sleeps in the sun, the cuts are made on
the wrong side of the trees," Gyll said. "Besides, we're
not in Sweden yet."

"I don't think it can be true," Joice said. "Not that I
doubt you, but I don't think it can be true. It couldn't
ever get out of its mother, with its stiff straight legs."

"Yes, that's a question," Faber said, appearing to consider it. "But remember that the greatest fool on earth
can ask questions that the wisest cannot answer."

They went on through this spread of strangely scarred
trees, still wondering about them, and when they came
to the end of them they were on the edge of a scarp.
There was a plain underneath them, sandy and reddish
where it was not clumped with bushes and trees, but
likelier-looking than the country they had travelled
through in the past weeks. In the distance they could
just make out a shallow chasm that they thought might
hold the bed of a river, and Simon de Baude agreed
with Eleanor's suggestion that it might be well to walk
a little east of north, in order to reach the chasm at its
nearest point. It took the women and the older members of the party a long time to find a safe way down the
scarp to the plain, but the young men went ahead without waiting for them, certain of good hunting in this
better place. When they rejoined the others late in the
morning, though, they had nothing with them but two
well-fleshed lizards, and the body of a scrawny broken-

winged bustard they'd been able to capture on the ground.

In midafternoon they came suddenly on a clearing in the trees, and it was plain to all of them that this had once been cultivated ground. There were small patches where the weeds now grew in a well-ordered way, there was a patch of hardened bare ground where a shed might have stood, or a hut, and there were small shards of hardened clay scattered about, as though something built of clay daub had been smashed by an angry giant's hand. Searching among the docks and thistles at the margin of it, Magnus found the remains of what must once have been a fireplace, and at the discovery they all crossed themselves, and looked carefully behind them. They had been out of touch with other human beings for so long, they had prayed incessantly to find them, but this evidence that they existed at once raised fears as to what sort of people they would be. Would they be Christian people or black heathens? Would they perhaps be the ill-coloured yellow and green men that Faber talked about? Would they have the acceptable number of limbs of acceptable shape, or might they be the huge-footed people who put one of their great feet over their heads to shelter them from the hot sun? They searched the whole area of the clearing very carefully, but they found nothing to tell them what sort of people had been there before them.

"God's going too far," Magnus said, checking first to see that the priest was not in earshot. "Invisibilizing the animals is one thing. Invisibilizing men is past a joke."

"He doesn't have a sense of humour," Faber said, and he was not speaking without reverence. "If it's jokes you want, Mahomet's more your man. He can take his heart out of his body to wash it, and he rides

some sort of an ass that has a woman's face and a pea-
cock's tail." Faber gave a great roar of laughter. "The
Moor's *believe* it," he said. "La ilaha illa Allah."

"Nominedomini," Edwin and Godwin said together,
as a counter to this heathen incantation.

Not very far from the remains of the fireplace, de
Baude had found a seedling olive tree, with a handful
of dried-out olives still hanging on it. It was clear that
this place had once carried crops of some sort, and while
the men went out to look for game and water, he set the
women to digging over the patches that had once been
cultivated. Two hours of labour netted them a bucketful of shrivelled, turnip-like roots—a useful addition to
anything the men might bring back for their night's
stew.

The men, when they came back, were empty-handed.
This was the first time they had failed to find anything
at all, and it frightened all of them. *"Pray,"* Father Nicholas said. "Confess yourselves. Tomorrow is the Sabbath, and the fortieth day." It had been agreed between
them earlier that the Sabbath should be their day of
rest, but nobody raised the question now and the priest
did not remind them of it, since plainly the next day
could not bring them out of their troubles if they stayed
in the same place.

The stew of withered turnips made a windy supper
that did little to satisfy their hunger, and for a long
time the cold kept them awake. The place frightened
them. They had moved a little way off from the hardened ground where they thought a hut had stood, but
who knew what sort of haunts these vanished people
might have left behind them, and what sort of charms
were powerful against them? "Something touched me!"
Joice said, suddenly sitting up. "I felt cold fingers moving along my arm."

"You're lucky if you can feel anything," Gyll said. "I'm as cold as a witch's tit myself, and have lost the power of feeling anything."

"There's something there," Joice said.

"There's nothing there," Simon said firmly. It was his job, as leader of the party, to speak with strength and confidence that would banish their fears, but it was a hard thing to do, in darkness and in cold, and with an empty stomach barking aloud for food.

"Could there be werewolves?" Clodagh asked. "I'm afraid to sleep, in case they get my soul." She knew that she could sleep if Gyll's arms sheltered her, but though he was close to her they lay untouching while the others were awake.

"Now it's touched me!" Godda said. "Fingers, dragging their cold nails up my throat to my ears."

"Be quiet, woman," Simon said. "There is nothing there. Be quiet." He crossed himself under cover of the darkness.

"God will protect us. We will say a prayer against the forces of darkness," Father Nicholas said, knowing that no one would sleep until the fears of the weakest had been quieted. "We will say 'Whatever manner of Evil.' That will knot a chain around us that no devil can break. You begin," he said to Eleanor, who was beside him.

"Whatever manner of Evil thou be," Eleanor said.

"In God's name I conjure thee," said Faber.

"I conjure thee with nails three," said Godwin.

"That Jesus was nailed upon the tree," Edwin said, finishing the verse.

"I conjure thee with the crown of thorn," said Magnus.

"That on Jesus's head was done with scorn," Godda said.

"I conjure thee with the precious Blood," Gyll said.

"That Jesus shed upon the rood," Clodagh said, lifting her hand to sign the air as she spoke, and letting it fall comfortingly onto Gyll's hand.

"I conjure thee, first as last," said Joice.

"With all the virtues of the Mass," said Sir Simon.

"And the holy prayers of St. Dorothy," Geoffrey de Baude said, leaving the last line to be spoken by the priest. *"In nomine patris et filii et spiritis sancti, Amen."* There were twelve lines in the charm, and twelve had spoken. That left the Monkey outside the charmed circle, since he couldn't speak. The morning would show whether werewolves had been prowling there.

They began their march in the morning at the usual time, but soon it was clear to Simon de Baude that they would not be able to walk even the small distance they had walked on other days. Several times he had seen Eleanor stumble and fall to her hands and knees, and though each time she had managed to get herself upright without help, she was having difficulty keeping up with the slow pace set by Geoffrey and Edwin. Joice, walking behind them, stumbled along in a continual tearful complaint about the pain in her cut and swollen feet, with a monotonous small shriek of protest every time Godwin pulled her forward when she stopped. Twice the priest had lagged far behind, and the last time, when Simon had gone back to get him, he had found him leaning his forehead against the trunk of a small tree. He seemed for a moment not to recognize Simon.

About the middle of the day de Baude called a halt. They shared the little water Magnus and the Monkey were carrying, and most of them drowsed at once where they had sat down. Young Geoffrey, ranging restlessly a little ahead of where the others were resting, saw something that at first he thought was due to weariness and hunger. He shook his head violently, rubbing the back of his hand across his smarting eyes to clear his vision. Then he went quickly back to his brother. He shook him. "There are houses," he said, whispering hoarsely. "Houses."

Simon went forward with him to look. Something in the way they moved alerted the others. Gyll and Magnus and the twins crowded forward with them to look where Geoffrey pointed. Perhaps half a mile away, beyond the bushes, there was a small village of half a dozen houses. They were low, and all their doors stood open. It was hard to tell at that distance what they were made of, but they had once been whitewashed, and their whitewash now was dirtied with thatch drippings and with damp stains from the earth. No one moved there—no men, no animals, no birds.

De Baude's party watched in silence for a long time. Then, "There's no one there," Godwin said.

"They'll be in the fields," Gyll suggested.

They let their eyes range over the whole expanse of land in front of them. They could see no activity of any sort.

"There'll be food," Magnus said.

"And better still, there'll be water," Simon said. "People don't build houses where there's no stream." Still they watched. There was something menacing about so silent a place. The others had come up to join them now, and the whole of de Baude's party was watching the place.

"In hot places, the people sleep for a long time during the day," Captain Faber said.

"True," Simon said. "And though this is far from being a hot place, they may have brought their customs with them from where they came." There was something unfamiliar about the shape of doorways and windows and eaves that made the houses more foreign-looking than anything that they had expected to find. "We will leave the women here, with Gyll and Magnus and the priest to watch over them. Stay out of sight," he said, "and stay quiet. The rest of us will go forward and see what's there."

"I will come with you," Father Nicholas said. He had taken the wooden cross from his belt and held it in front of him, at the level of his eyes. He seemed to have shaken off his weariness. "It is as God promised me," he said. "I will come with you."

The houses, when they got to them, seemed smaller and meaner than they had appeared from a distance, and the roofs of two of them had been fired, leaving them open to the sky except for a broken latticing of charred rafters. Geraniums grew among the weeds near the doors, scenting the dry air with their sardine smell. The little one-roomed houses were whitewashed inside, floored with hard-packed earth and completely bare except that there was a rough timber bench in one of them, and something that looked like a broken cradle in another. There were seven in all, with some low cow byres built against their rear walls, and small enclosures built of hurdles, some of them flattened and lying on the ground. The houses were built in two rows— four on one side of an open space and three on the other, and at one end, between the two rows, there was a well. The bucket had been cut away from the rope, but the rope itself had been left on the roller, and a pebble dropped in by Simon brought them back a pleasing sound from the depths. There was no sign of food in the houses, there were no animals, no crops, and though there were fruit trees—figs and apricots and olives—there was no fruit except for a few withered olives.

Simon stood, with Geoffrey beside him, trying to clear his mind so that he could decide what it would be best for them to do. There was something so comforting about the thought of sleep sheltered by walls, something so safe and domestic and familiar suggested by the fact that they were once more in a place where other men had been, that he was tempted to bring his people there at once. But at the same time there was something barbaric about the place. Why empty, why partly burned, why swept bare of every piece of broken rubbish and waste that would give some clue about the nature of those who had lived there? He stood irresolute for a long time, wishing that he had brought Eleanor with him to the houses, since women often had an instinct for these things. She might have known whether they should make the place a temporary haven, or whether it might be dangerous to them—perhaps a trap set by some unseen enemy.

While he pondered this, it seemed that the others had made up their minds. Godwin had taken off his tattered tunic, knotted it to the well rope and lowered it into the water. He brought it up and wrung it over the faces and into the thirsty mouths of his brother and Faber. The priest had gone in and out of every house, carrying his cross in front of him to bless it, and now, under his direction, the Monkey was carrying the wooden bench into the open space between the houses, so that Father

Nicholas could set up his altar. Simon turned, still undecided, to look back to the place where he had left the women under the care of Gyll and Magnus. They were already coming down, carrying the buckets and the blanket bags and all the party's belongings, and walking more quickly and with more determination than he had seen them walk for many days. He turned towards his brother with a slight shrug, and Geoffrey darted forward, freed by this, to join Eleanor and help her towards the houses.

The well became the center of their pleasure and attention. In the first half hour they used the water sparingly, drinking what they needed, sharing a bucketful between three of them, for the welcome washing of their faces and feet. But Godwin, peering down into the well, reported that there was plenty of water, and he took the next bucketful and poured it over Joice's head, making her shriek with surprise at its chill. Soon all the younger ones were playing like children, drenched and chilled but happy to have the dust washed from their hair and their clothes. "You'll be cold when the sun goes," Captain Faber warned them, but they knew that there'd be warmth for them that night. Normally they doused their fire at sunset, but tonight they would be able to take coals from it into the huts, and keep small fires burning there on the earthen floors.

When the young men had gone out to look for food the women, after washing what rags of clothes they could spare without being seen naked by Faber and the priest, stayed close to the well for the pleasure the water gave them. Clodagh leaned over it, trying to peer into its depths. Then she brought her gaze back to its surface, and saw her face. The afternoon sun made an elliptical patch of lightness on the water. It gave her a

poor reflection, but the best she'd had since she had lost
her polished mirror when the *Grace Dieu* went down.
Her face seemed darker and thinner, and her long dark
hair was as wild and rough as any gypsy's. She leaned
back, looking at the other faces to see what changes the
weeks had made in them. Godda's fat face had fallen
into hollowed pouches; Eleanor's white skin had
browned, and the dark circles under her eyes made
their sockets more noticeable than the eyes themselves;
the marks of hunger and fear seemed to have etched
themselves between Joice's brows and at the corners of
her mouth. She leaned in again over the wall, moving
her head from side to side for the pleasure of seeing her
reflection's reassuring movement in the little patch of
silver on the water. Nothing came up from the depths of
the water to distort it. The place was friendly. It was
her face. She didn't think it had changed very much.
Cucumber cream, honey-and-oatmeal paste would soon
soften the skin and restore its whiteness at the end of
their journey.

For the second night in succession the men came
back empty-handed. "Tomorrow is the promised day,"
the priest said. "The forty-first. We will celebrate the
mass fasting. Tomorrow we will eat."

Because they believed him, and because they were
comforted by being able to fill their bellies with water,
they bore the lack of food with resignation. Except
Godda, who suddenly, as the priest was preparing to
begin the mass, threw herself to the ground with a
chilling scream, and began to writhe there, biting at her
hands. Her sons rushed to lift her. Her trembling lips
were bleeding, and her eyes rolled wildly in her tear-
streaked face. "Stab it," she said. "Stab it . . . not a true
bread, not a true body, not true flesh."

"No," Eleanor said.

"Stab it," Godda said, turning to Edwin. "Take your knife and stab the priest's bread." He let go her arm to cross himself, and Godda lunged at his belt, trying to reach his knife. "I'll do it," she said, and burst into wilder sobs as Edwin took his knife and flung it aside, out of her reach.

"Be quiet," the priest said. He had not at first understood what she wanted, but now it was clear to him. "Be quiet. You are in the presence of God."

Godda tried to throw herself to the ground again, but Godwin still held her by one arm so that she crouched sideways, beating at the dirt with her free hand. "Stab it, stab it," she said. "If it's the Host it will bleed. If it's not the Host, it's a Black Mass, and God will punish us."

"Move her further from the altar," Father Nicholas said.

"No!" Godda screamed, and as they tried to lift her she broke away from them, and pitched forward so that she lay with her head over the buried relics and under the altar bench. The priest stepped forward and signed the air over her head, and at once she grew quieter, almost as though she had seen the cross he made. "God wants more sacrifice from us," she said. "He is greedy for more, more. The mass alone can't please Him, the mass isn't enough for Him. We should make a sacrifice of some of the food. We should take a lamb, and slit its throat under the altar . . ."

"My child, what are you saying?" the priest said.

"We'd have better things to do with a lamb, if we had one," Faber said.

"A blood offering," Godda said, "like it tells in the Bible stories."

"Be silent," the priest said firmly. "These are the larger ways to hell."

"Like it says," Godda said again, "in the Bible stories."

"Christ is that Lamb," Father Nicholas said, stooping to speak gently to her. "You are remembering the old stories, of the time before Christ was born. No more blood sacrifices. Christ was the last. He is our scapegoat, He took all our sins on Him, and carried them off into the desert places of the world, against infection. Lift her," he said to her sons. Godwin and Edwin lifted her and carried her away from the altar and put her down beside the well. Godwin held the leather bucket for her so that she could drink. She was quiet now, except that she was shaken occasionally by sobs. Father Nicholas began the mass. He told them the story of Azazel the scapegoat. He told them again, patiently and repetitiously, how Christ had become the scapegoat for the whole of Christendom, and would gladly take all their sins upon Him in return for a full and true confession of them. "God wants no sacrifice," he said, "except the sacrifice of your baser natures." He heard a general confession from his people. He prayed with doubled piety as Godda came to him, supported between her sons, to receive one of the last morsels of carob bread they had.

After the mass was finished, most of them drank again from the leather bucket, and then they prepared to sleep. Father Nicholas had promised them food on the morrow, and to most of them it seemed likely that the promise would be kept, and that to sleep early would bring the time of eating a little closer. On the march, Simon de Baude had not bothered with setting watches at night, depending on the young and active ones to wake instantly at any approach of danger. But here, where his party would be divided among a number of huts, he thought it wise to have two to watch while the others slept. "Edwin and Godwin take the first watch," he said and then, remembering Joice, he made a better arrangement of their time. "Edwin and *Gyll* will take the first watch," he said, "and Godwin and Magnus will watch for the second part of the night." After the others were settled he prowled for a little while between the huts. The division of his party worried him, and he thought it wise to know where everyone was. On the side where there were four huts Magnus and the Monkey had gone into the first, the priest was alone in the second, and Eleanor with Clodagh in the third. Faber and Geoffrey de Baude had gone into the fourth, and Simon would join them there when his patrolling was done. Opposite that one, Joice and Godda and Godwin were already settled, and he supposed Edwin would join them when he came off watch. Next to it was one of the huts that had been burned and was partly unroofed, and he hadn't expected that anyone would use it. But after a while he saw Clodagh come out of the house where Eleanor was, and go into the partly unroofed one, and he saw that Gyll, on watch at the windlass of the well, had seen where she had gone. Beyond Clodagh's place was the seventh hut, a little removed from the others.

In the late afternoon of the forty-first day it seemed that the priest's prophecy was to be fulfilled. Those who had stayed close to the houses had been occupying their time by digging where there were signs of earlier cultivation, and in searching among the branches of trees for any remnants of last summer's crops. Suddenly they heard crashing sounds and the unfamiliar sound of laughter in the bushes a little distant from the huts.

Gyll and Godwin and Magnus were bringing in a live goat—Gyll and Godwin holding it by the ears and shoulders, and Magnus pushing at its rump whenever it stopped. The others crowded around. It was a large and rangy female, its white coat splotched with wide patches of black, and its pendant udder half-distended with milk. Finding itself no longer being pushed forward, it stood quietly enough in the circle they had formed around it, turning its head and keeping up a soft neh-eh-eh-eh-eh in the direction from which they'd brought it. Joice had run to fetch the leather bucket from the well, and the others let her into the circle and watched as she bent to milk the goat. It sidled away from her until it was hard up against the legs of Gyll and Magnus, but then it stood quietly enough, as though it was used to being milked into a bucket. The sweet, thin, almost-forgotten smell of the milk was tantalizing to them as they watched.

"If there's one, there should be others," Simon de Baude said. "She must have gone wild, after the people went."

"She's got a kid," Godda said, turning to Godwin "Didn't you see a kid?"

"Probably eaten by a lion," Godwin said.

"Edwin and the Monkey are looking for it," Gyll said.

There was perhaps a pint of milk in the bottom of the bucket when Joice had finished. She looked at Simon, uncertain what should be done with it. "For the women," he said. "Give it first to the Lady Eleanor." Eleanor drank a mouthful of the milk, and put the bucket into Clodagh's hands. She bent her head over it, inhaling the aroma, but then she straightened and passed the bucket to Godda, saying, "Leave my share in the bucket, it's for the priest."

"My share too," Godda said, dipping one dirty fore-finger into the milk for the pleasure of tasting it, and then passing the bucket to Joice, who did the same. The priest was asleep, or at his prayers, in his own hut. He was, after all, the oldest and the weakest of the party, and he had predicted this goat. They owed him something for it.

While Clodagh carried the milk to the priest, the goat was quickly dispatched with a knife and skinned by Magnus while a fire was built in the open space by the well. Soon the air was full of the smell of roasting meat, while each of the watchers took a share of the entrails and grilled them, for immediate eating, on the ends of pointed sticks.

It had been Simon's plan that the goat should last them for two meals, but they'd been hungry for so long, and attacked it so ravenously before it was properly cooked, that he saw no point in issuing an order no one would listen to. He'd been concerned, too, at the long absence of Edwin and the Monkey, partly because of the rule that hunting parties always came back before dusk, and partly because he feared there might be no food left for them. They came running back with the last of the light and just as Godda pronounced the goat ready for eating. They hadn't, they said, found any trace of her kid.

After everyone had eaten they collected the picked bones of the goat; Godda would make a soup of them next day, after they'd been smashed with a stone to free their tasty marrow. Then the fire was put out after burning sticks had been taken to start a small blaze on the floor of each of the huts, the priest gave them his blessing for the night and they separated. Simon and his young brother, Geoffrey, were to take the first watch, and they would wake Magnus and Gyll for the second.

Clodagh had gone at once to her hut on hearing this, taking a burning stick. She had collected a pile of wood, choosing carefully only dry stuff that would burn without too much smoke. She was pleased that Gyll was to take the second watch. That would give them four or five hours of love and sleep in the flame-lit privacy of their hut before he had to leave her. She scraped out last night's ashes from the little bowl Gyll had dug for the fire in the center of the dirt floor, laid small twigs and leaves over her burning stick and bent to blow it into a little flame. She expected that Gyll would come to her almost at once.

But Gyll had gone to the other partly unroofed hut, and was deep in argument there with Godda and her sons and the other non-Norman members of the party. "If God is angry, then He's angry with her as well," Gyll said. "We waste everything if she isn't here."

"It's true," Joice said. She didn't care to have her own sin rated blacker than Clodagh's.

"She's a Norman," Godwin said, "which means proud and tricky and not to be trusted."

"She's not a true Norman . . ." Gyll began.

"And besides, she's Gyll's woman," Magnus said.

"Believe it when you see him take a stick to her," Edwin said. "Gyll's her man, which is a different thing."

"She has as much right to be here as anyone," Gyll said. "Ask the priest whether God divides people into Norman and English, or only into sinners and unsinners."

Magnus laughed. "Ask the priest nothing," he said. "God's a Norman himself. We'd best get this over with before Simon de Baude and his pup come looking and asking."

Edwin went to the door and looked out. "They won't come," he said. "They're full of good meat, and sitting at the far end, near the well."

"She has as much right as your woman," Gyll said, looking from Godwin to Edwin. "We need her to be here. It won't work, without."

"Let her come," Godda said, and Gyll knew that hers would be the final say, since hers had been the origin of the idea. "Let her come," Godda said again, "but don't let her try any of her high tricks."

The men had come on the goat grazing quietly with her twin kids in a clearing two or three miles from their camping place, and in a wild rush of chasing and wrestling they had captured all three of them within a few minutes. The sight of the twin kids had stirred first in Godwin and then in all of them a hope that they had in their hands the means of turning God's anger aside, of making their hunting fruitful again, their journey safe, their arrival certain. The priest's certainty that God was angry with them was worrying enough, but Godda's fear that their sacrament was a false one, and therefore unknowingly offered by the priest to Satan, was even more frightening. Now it seemed that God had sent them the young goats as a sign that he wanted another and better sacrifice.

"One goes to God and the other goes to the Devil," Magnus said, bowing his head twice, with equal reverence. Though he seemed to be a sort of unbeliever, he was a great source of knowledge about holy things, as he'd been a monastery orphan till the monks had shown him the gate for persistent pilfering.

"Fetch her, then," Godda said resentfully, and while

Gyll ran to bring Clodagh the twin brothers unwound the torn blanket that was usually used to carry what food the hunters found, and that now held the twin kids bundled together in it. Edwin, with the Monkey for company, had stayed away from the camp guarding the kids until darkness had almost fallen, and then he'd wrapped and knotted them into the blanket and hidden them in the furthest of the huts.

By the time Gyll came back pulling Clodagh with him, the little goats had been freed from the blanket and were tottering around on their uncertain legs, bleating with thin sounds.

"Better be quick or the others will hear them," Joice said.

"They'll never hear those little sounds," Godwin said, "and besides, I won't let anyone in that comes." He took a stand near the door.

The goats were a male and a female, the male black and white like the mother, the female pure white. Magnus explained quickly to Clodagh what was to be done. She'd been angry with Gyll for keeping her waiting so long and for then bringing her to this crowded hut. She was shocked now by what they meant to do. "You mustn't," she said. "You mustn't think of doing it. It may be witchcraft."

"It's not witchcraft," Magnus said. "It's in the Bible, and there's no witchcraft there. One goes to God, and one goes to Azazel."

"Who's he?" Godda asked.

"Who knows?" Magnus said. "Maybe he's one of Satan's brothers. But he's off there, in the wilderness, and one of them carries all our sins to him."

"Which one?" Godda said.

"The black and white one," Joice said, "because the

other's as white as the Holy Ghost, and ought to belong to God."

"We cast lots," Magnus said.

"We haven't any dice," Edwin said.

"Let *her* choose," Godda said, pointing at Clodagh. The mention of witchcraft had frightened her, and she wanted Clodagh deeply implicated.

"Bandage her eyes," Edwin said, and Gyll put his hand to her head and covered her eyes with that. Edwin and Godwin picked up the little goats and carried them, changing their position twice before they were satisfied. "Now put out your hand and touch one of them," Godwin said, "and the one you touch goes to old whatsisname."

Clodagh hesitated for a moment. She didn't want to do it, but if it was in the Bible . . . she hoped that her hand would fall on the black and white kid.

"Right," Godwin said, and she opened her eyes. Her hand was resting on the head of the little white female.

"This one's God's," Edwin said, and bundled the black and white kid back into the blanket and put it down against the wall.

"It's a very small goat to carry everyone's sins," Clodagh said in protest, looking at the white kid. "And it's so young it won't get very far before something swallows it whole for its supper."

"Then our sins'll give it a great burning pain in its belly," Magnus said. He began to sing softly, in parody of the *Vexilla Regis Prodeunt,* the Crusaders' hymn:

> *Oh goat, our only hope, all hail,*
> *Thou smelly lecherous young female,*
> *Get hither at the fastest pace*
> *And all the sinners' sins efface.*

"Get on with it," Godwin said. "We haven't got all night."

"Be still, goat, and take our sins upon you," Magnus said. "Now everyone take turns," he said. "Put your hand on the kid's head, and think of all your sins and they'll cross over." He took first turn himself, thoughtfully laying on the head of the little goat a tremendous load of treachery, blasphemy, lechery, perjury, infamy. "It's a very strong goat," he said with a grin when he'd finished. Then came Gyll, laying on the goat wrongs done to Robert Apelfourde, and to his own soul; next, Godwin and Edwin, offering up Joice, who seemed in everyone's view to be the ripest of their sins; Joice followed them, and took a long time, for she had to get rid not only of the sin of the twin brothers, but neglect of prayers for her dead husband if indeed he was dead, and old wars fought with her bitch of a mother-in-law, and ill-wishings on many people, and prides and angers. Godda followed her. She didn't think she had very much to offer, since she'd lived pure since she was widowed. But she acknowledged that she was too proud of her sons and too covetous for them, and that she'd once found a sheep dead and sold brazy mutton from it knowing she could lose her ears for the sale if she was caught, and she'd often thought that God was more for rich people than for poor, which was a small thing, but might have offended Him, so she laid that down, too.

Everyone had now laid their hands on the goat's head, except Clodagh and the Monkey. Magnus pulled him forward, and he put out his pink hand as he'd seen the others do, and grinned with pleasure and pulled at the lobe of his ear. Clodagh had hoped to escape it, but now they were all looking at her. She put out her hand and closed her eyes and said under her breath, "Run very fast, little goat, and escape all your enemies," and as she took her hand away she wondered whether that might be blasphemy, and she put her hand quickly back, as if to expunge it, and said silently, "Forgive me for doing this, if it's a wrong thing."

They were finished with the white kid then, but nobody wanted the job of taking it out, in darkness, and freeing it a mile or so from the hut. They decided that it should be left alone in the hut until first light when Gyll and Magnus would be watching, and Gyll could watch alone for a little while Magnus carried the goatlet out and set it free. "And be careful no one captures it again tomorrow," Magnus said. "I'd hate to eat all those sins for tomorrow's supper."

Edwin had taken the black and white goat from the blanket now, and it gave a quick bleat which was stifled by his knife at its throat. "Let some of the blood fall in this," Magnus said, and held out a hollowed length of bark to catch it. "Now you take it," he said, passing it to Gyll, "and mark a little cross with it on the door of every house."

Gyll looked at the blood held in the hollow of bark. "How can I do that?" he said. "They'll see me—Sir Simon and Geoffrey."

"Mark it on the back of the houses," Magnus said. "What does God care, whether it's the back or the front."

Gyll looked at him doubtfully for a little while, and then went out. Edwin was cutting up the small goat's body, searching deep under the rib cage for its heart and liver. "Everyone has to eat a little piece," he said.

"*Accipite et manducate ex hoc omnes,*" Magnus said, remembering from his altar-serving days. "Take and eat all of this."

"I won't," Clodagh said. "I won't do it." She had pulled back, getting as far from the small bloody body as she could.

"Lady, it's good meat," Magnus said kindly, giving her the title the others had omitted for so long. "Everyone should eat a bit, to complete the circle."

"No," Clodagh said. "No, I won't. I won't eat it."

"Make her," Godda said. "Hold her, and make her, or she undoes everything."

"*No,*" Clodagh said, her voice rising. "No, I won't. You've gone savage and mad." She turned and evaded Edwin's grasp, and ran out into the night.

Alone in her own hut, she crouched over the fire. She was shivering, not so much with cold as from nervousness and disgust. The men—Magnus and Edwin and Godwin—had frightened her with their half-mocking piety and their arms streaked with the blood of the goat. She rocked backwards and forwards moaning softly to herself, "Mother of God, Mother of God." She thought that she would bar the door against Gyll, that he was one of them, a barbarian. Remorse flooded her for the first time. It was not her sin that she regretted, but the bottomless folly that had pulled her towards these crude people who lived by spells and vileness and belief in the old gods. She would have liked to seek shelter from them in Eleanor's hut, but she couldn't do it without explanations, and what safety would there be, with a puny knight, a callow squire, a cowardly sea captain and a weak old priest? She went to the door, half determined to go out and join Eleanor, half concerned to find a way of barring it. As she looked out, four or five figures burst out of the doorway of the seventh hut, carrying burning sticks they had taken from their fire. She stood pressed against her dark doorpost, frightened of seeing what they were at, but frightened, too, of turning her back on them. They had made some noise as they came out, but quieted quickly when they saw Simon and Geoffrey de Baude start to their feet from their position at the far end, close to the well.

A male figure, one of the twins, she thought, was in the lead, and by the light of his fire stick she saw with shock that he was stark naked. The others lined up behind him. He led them off and, going very fast and in absolute silence, they circled the hut three times, going widdershins, with their fire sticks held aloft. The de Baude brothers stood stock still at the other end of the huts, watching them. The leader dropped his stick and made a back and the others went over him; and each in turn dropped their sticks and made a back for the others, and the sticks burning briefly on the ground showed bare buttocks, and bare thighs leapfrogging over them. It was finished as quickly and quietly as it had begun, and the figures followed their leader back into the hut, leaving the sticks smouldering on the ground.

Clodagh sank down in the doorway, afraid to leave it for fear they should come out again, and surprise her. She could hear raised voices from the hut, and excited laughter. She had been too frightened and they had moved too quickly for her to be sure how many dancing figures there had been. "Mother of God, Mother of God," she said under her breath, "don't let him have been one of them." She needed Gyll now. She had to have protection from these savages.

When Gyll came he was fully dressed, and he laughed at her terrors, pulling her away from the doorway and close to the fire again. "It's the dance they do, every midsummer, in the churchyard," he said.

"It's black foulness."

"It's only a bit of fun," he said, pulling her close to him. She was afraid of him, afraid of his flesh, afraid of his origins; and then, as he grappled with her, trying to subdue her, immensely glad of the hard evidence of his body that he had not taken part in the orgy she fancied must have followed the others' return to the seventh hut.

"Swear that you didn't eat," she said.

"Eat?"

"Any of the goat."

"I didn't eat it," he said.

"*Swear.*"

"I swear by my tool," he said, forcing her down onto the hard earth floor under him.

It seemed that Father Nicholas had been right about God's wish that they should spend forty hungry days in the wilderness. On the next day, the forty-first, the men had ranged a little further afield, and had come back with enough meat to supply a satisfactory evening meal. And, better than this, they had sighted a small number of wild pigs. Dogless, and on foot, they had had no luck with their first attempts at hunting them, but new lances, light enough to be thrown like spears, were being prepared by Magnus and by Faber with the hope that next day they could get close enough to bring one of the beasts down. They had found, also, in a little gully not far from the huts, a collection of cattle and sheep bones. These were not carcasses from which the flesh had rotted, but bones that had been expertly jointed before they were roasted or boiled, and the flesh was cut from them. It was obvious that people had once prospered in this place. The puzzle about why it had been abandoned remained, but it seemed likely that enough food could be found to feed de Baude's party, and even to fatten them. Clearly the priest had been right about the forty days— or else, clearly, God had been mollified by the death of the kid.

The scene in the end hut, the slaughter of the black and white kid and the banishment of its twin, and the dance that had followed it haunted Clodagh's sleep for several nights. The boundaries between black and white magic seemed so ill-defined that no one had ever been able to tell her quite where they lay. If she, with the others, had strayed onto the dark side of the boundary, then she, with the others, was guilty of a black sin. In her dreams she saw the little white female kid lying alone on stony ground, with its throat newly bleeding where some predator had torn it. As its body cooled, the sins they had laid upon it climbed up through its coat as fleas climbed out of the coat of a dead dog. Each had a black triangular body and the hideous face, in miniature, of a church gargoyle. Each paused for a moment at the end of one of the kid's white hairs and then each jumped to the ground and scuttled away, crabwise, into the dirt. In her dream it seemed plain that the sins would crouch there, concealed, until some warm-blooded creature came within springing distance, and that they might all walk unknowingly into a cloud of their own sins the next time they set out. Hideous to have her own sins coming back to her, but how much worse to have Joice's, or the twins'! The fear woke her and she reached for Gyll's body, for comfort. Four walls around them, and their little fire, nights of privacy outside the range of listening ears, had given them their first chance to make love slowly, variously and with words. "My unicorn, my white beauty, my one-horned wonder," she said, stroking to wake him so that he could comfort her into forgetting her dream. What he thought of privately as her Frenchie tricks startled and enraptured him. "Whore's games," he had said, guarding himself, the first time her hands went to his body and her tongue into his ear in the new privacy of their empty hut. "Mother of God, who taught you to do that?"

"Who but my husband," she said quietly.

"Now look what you've done," he said, flinging away from her. "I shrink to a shrivel when you mention him."

"He exists," she said. "And if I hadn't known him, I wouldn't have known these things." Robert Apelfourde's existence, somewhere there at the end of their journey, was often in her mind. Gyll, she thought, could put his existence totally out of mind, except when she reminded him of it. She moved a little closer to him, began again to stroke and knead his flank. From an equal, she would have found his words a rebuff too painful to be turned aside. But he was not her equal. And, despite his lies, he was younger. These two inequalities gave her a sweet sense of power and liability. "My unicorn," she said again. "My beauty, my white wonder."

"Only a virgin tames a unicorn," he said, still half-resentful.

She laughed. "You want to wager?" she said. "Lie down in my lap, little unicorn, and soon I'll trap you in my thicket."

The two inequalities worked on him, too. He was afraid of offending that leisurely possessiveness in her that said love was a twenty-four-hour matter, instead of a brief excitement after work and dark. And besides, her hands worked on him, and won arguments. He had known hands slapping, and hands pressed palms forward against his chest to ward him off before they were painfully locked in the small of his back to draw him closer. Hers had a power over him which he sometimes feared came close to being a form of bewitchment.

It was the opinion of the others, too, that he had been bewitched. They teased him about it. "She's a night rider," Godwin said. "She's turned poor Gyll into her broomstick." He took off the remnants of his right shoe and spat into it—a wise thing to do when witches were mentioned. There was no ill feeling in the way they teased him. Magnus envied him a little, Godwin and Edwin admired him, and all three of them saw ways in which he could be useful to their purposes.

The second day had brought them a half-grown pig, run down by Gyll and Magnus and stabbed in the bushes in a hullaballoo of blood and squeals and triumph. The third day had brought several large birds and a tough old sow and a tender young piglet, and they were satisfied that the next day would bring more food. They had no desire to leave the place.

To Simon de Baude, too, it seemed a good thing to spend several days there so that his people could eat well and perhaps store up a little stock of surplus food to take with them when they moved. Their rate of progress had got slower and slower as hunger weakened them, and the priest had become so frail that he needed ten minutes' rest to recover from every half hour's walking. For three days now he had eaten well and had moved only between his hut and a spot close to the well where he could sit propped to get the warmth of the sun. Already it seemed to the others that his cheeks had filled out a little, and his voice strengthened. Geoffrey de Baude made it his duty to bring wood each day to supply the priest's fire, and often at night he would leave the fire in the hut he shared with Faber and Sir Simon to go to replenish the priest's fire. Then he would lie down curled against the sleeping priest, to lend him a little of the warmth of his own body. Neither of the de Baudes had spoken to anyone else of the silent dance they had seen.

Despite their fires, the cold punished them cruelly at night now that they slept separated, instead of in the warm huddle of bodies around a common spot where the ground had been heated a little by a good blaze doused at sundown. They had been warmly dressed as protection against the cold of the *Grace Dieu*'s holds, the common soldiers in leather, the others in padded garments with a hood to them. But even these clothes, drenched and dried out, caked with the dirt of their journey, slashed by thorns, were not protection enough against the cold of the night. Twice already they had woken to find rime on the grass and a crackle of ice in their water buckets. Each had a blanket, also tattered now, with a head-hole cut in it so that it could be worn as as a cloak. There were four extra blankets that had come ashore when the *Grace Dieu* broke up, but these had had pieces cut from them to patch holes and bandage wounds. What was left of them was used in the daytime to make pack bundles for anything they had to carry with them, and whoever carried the bundle during the day claimed the right to the extra covering at night, and shared it with as many as could creep under its corners.

From the point of view of warmth and comfort at night, Simon de Baude thought the splitting of his party into separate groups in six of the seven huts was a mistake. But from every other point of view it made their condition easier. He had been irritated by the all-hours presence of the commons, with their stink and dirt and ignorant opinions, but had thought it might be both inhuman and rash, in their circumstances, to order any degree of separation.

It was Eleanor's view, too, that the separation by

choice might bring Clodagh back to a proper apprecia-
tion of her place in the party, her duties to it and her
own worth. "Leave her," she said when Simon spoke to
her of the scandal of Robert Apelfourde's wife being
seen by the others to share a patch of bare ground with
a peasant farmer. "She'll soon tire of his boorishness under those conditions. She's not used to a bedfellow who
scratches and farts and doesn't know enough to turn his
head away until he's chewed something to clear his foul
morning breath." Simon looked at her curiously. She
surprised him. He was often surprised by the knowledge
pure women had of things they couldn't have experienced.

Every roughness in Gyll's speech or manners had im-
printed itself darkly on Simon's awareness. He found it
difficult to look at the boy, and he had to guard himself
against the impulse to overload him with tiring duties
and to choose him for any hunting excursion that might
conceivably hold more than the normal amount of danger. But the place convinced him that they were on the
edge of territory taken by the Crusaders, that the houses
they were in had once been the houses of Moors driven
out by the Portuguese and their allies from the north.
Perhaps this was the most southerly point to which the
armies had penetrated, before pulling back a little to
consolidate their line. It seemed to him that within a
few days, within a week at the most, he and his people
would be back among their friends. It would then be for
Robert Apelfourde to deal with Gyll of Dittisham. No
need for de Baude to endanger his own soul by thinking
about a death that could be safely left in the hands of
someone else.

Down at the other end of the line of huts the fact that
their rightful owners had disappeared without trace

made the new occupiers feel by no means sure that the place was Iberia, and safety close to them. "These could be the last houses of the known world," Godda said. "Anyone who walks beyond them could be walking into the void. Why have we found pigs here, and goats, that don't commonly follow men about, but never a sign of any dogs, that do."

"They could as well have walked the other way, taking their dogs with them, and their horses," Magnus suggested.

"No," Godda said. "If they had, we would have passed them."

Magnus thought that this didn't make much sense, that the times were wrong and the houses seemed to have been long deserted, and that any party walking south with its household goods and its dogs and horses might have passed beyond the point of the *Grace Dieu's* wreck long before her luckiest passengers managed to get ashore. But he didn't argue it, because it was undeniable that in all their hard weeks of walking they had seen nothing to suggest that anyone else had ever walked that way.

"They could all have died," Joice said, and crossed herself at the thought of the foreign spirits that might now be sharing the air of the hut with them. "We've dug in the fields, but not in the trees and bushes. They might all be buried just a stone's throw away."

"And the last one dug his own grave and jumped in and pulled the earth over him," Godwin said.

"Don't joke about it," his mother said. "Stranger things have happened—best not to joke."

"I don't care if there are twenty buried underneath this floor," Edwin said. "This is a good place, where a man could stretch himself, yard up a pig or two, eat some fruit from the trees, plant some seeds . . ."

"There are no seeds," Magnus said. "The women have found nothing."

"There'll be seeds jumping into life when the spring comes," Gyll said. "Crops will always come up where crops have been."

"Like I said," Edwin said. "Some pigs, a crop or two, fruit from the trees, some rabbit hutches, birds and some birds' eggs, fish if there's a river anywhere near—a man could stretch himself here, and live comfortable." It was a thought that had occurred to several of them in the last few days.

At the other end of the row of houses, the people's thoughts were running differently. It seemed to them that Simon de Baude was right, and had been right since the beginning of the march. Clearly they were now on the outer margins of God's territories, and close to the southernmost point the Portugallers from England and Belgium had reached with their Portuguese allies. It seemed to them a good thing, and sensible, that they should rest for a few days, but they had no wish to remain in the place any longer than that. Ahead—perhaps only a few days' march ahead—lay a familiar world of leather tents and the possibility of news from home, bread and wine, hot water and servants to carry it, music, masses without makeshift, good soap made with ashes, fruit, physic, shoe leather and known rules for the conduct of each day's affairs. They had begun again to look into the future, to think of ships, and the Holy Sepulchre. The priest thought he would not see any of these things, that the Promised Land would not be granted to him because of the snares he had allowed his people to fall into on the way. But there was still a seed of optimism in him, and it had begun to flourish with the help of rest and food. A few more days of rest, a little more good and ample food, and God might give him the strength to wrestle with the sinners in his party, to baptize the Monkey as he had planned to do, and so to recoup his spiritual innocence. It did not seem entirely fair to him that God should plan to punish him for the sins of others, but even as that thought comforted him he remembered how God had punished Moses in circumstances that seemed to him remarkably similar. All he could do was resign himself to God's will, and pray assiduously in these blessed extra hours of leisure that he had. It was a pity that the sun made him drowsy. It was a pity, too, that hunger and tiredness seemed to have weakened his memory, so that now he could no longer recall what it was that had been said about a priest's responsibilities at his ordination all those long years ago. Certainly he knew that a mass was not worthless to the people just because it had been offered by an unworthy priest, so it seemed to him a possibility that the opposite would hold, that a priest might not be worthless in Christ's eyes, just because his people were themselves without any value.

Clodagh accepted the view that they were on the edge of Christian territory. It made a sort of biblical sense to her. They had been, quite literally, down into the depths, they had struggled against their own weakness and against great odds, they had been beset by unfair temptations and most had managed to triumph over them. Now it seemed that a few more days would see them free from danger, and that ahead of them lay feasting and rejoicing. Joice's troubles would be private ones, and a good and subtle confessor would soon deliver her from them. Her own case might be different. Of course there was the chance that Robert Apelfourde might already have made the supreme sacrifice and died in one of the battles on Portuguese ground. She didn't really wish him this ill, and she didn't have any confidence in its likelihood. If he was waiting there, then her safety would depend on the close mouths of Simon de Baude's party—and she didn't have any confidence in those, either. To try to win herself a place with them would have been to be drawn into their group. Instead she had tried to draw Gyll away from everyone else, to make a private third world between the two worlds of the travelling people.

But, against her will and before she knew what was happening, she had been drawn into the business of the goatlets, and the sin shedding. This troubled her conscience and disturbed her sleep far more than any fears of her eventual reunion with Robert Apelfourde. The more she rehearsed what had been done and said, the more heinous it seemed to her in memory. If it was witchcraft, then she had been touched by filthiness, and her soul might already be dying in her body. Would she know? Would it cause pain, shriek like a dying tooth? Or would it die soundlessly, like a child that stopped growing within the womb? She wished she had listened more attentively when her mother's chaplain spoke about the soul, but all she could remember was that if it died, a living body without a soul would quickly be invaded by some fiend. She was afraid for Gyll, too. She was afraid that he might have eaten some of the flesh of the sacrificed goat after she ran from the hut. Whenever she asked him, and she asked him often, he denied it. He said he had taken the meat to avoid argument, and then dropped it, unseen, to the floor of the hut. She didn't believe him. She believed he'd eaten it. She feared for him, and her fear was changing her fondness for him into a sort of love.

She would have liked to talk of all these things to the priest, but she could do that only by a full confession, and at the end of it she could hope for absolution only if she renounced the things confessed. She could renounce all stupidness and ignorance, since she had never wanted any part of them. But to renounce her adultery was another matter, since her life was ordered now in such a way that it offered very little else. On balance, then, it seemed more prudent to delay a full confession, and the church recommended prudence to women as a virtue. She thought there might be more help to be had from Eleanor, if she could find a way to open the subject without admitting her own part in it.

The Lady Eleanor was a strong-willed woman, and sometimes openly critical of church law. And she had, after all, taken the Cross in her own right, a thing unheard of except with women of very exalted rank and calculated, Clodagh thought, to bring her closer to God than anyone else in the company except the priest. She found her, in the late afternoon while the men were hunting, seated close to the well between the huts. She had a knife beside her, and one of the surplus blankets, and she was putting a patch cut from it over a large hole torn in Simon de Baude's plum-coloured cloak. "Watch this for me," she said to Clodagh as she put the needle down to tease out some more of the flaxlike plant fiber she was using as thread. "Don't let me lose it—it's the only one we have, and Godda will put the evil eye on me."

"Can she?" Clodagh said. "D'you believe she can?"

Eleanor laughed. "What other sort," she said, "out of that ugly face?"

"How can you tell what witchcraft is, and what people are witches?"

"Easily," Eleanor said. "Every time the thought enters your head that some woman is a witch, you are wrong."

"But there are witches," Clodagh said.

"How do you know? Tell me some way in which you can be sure?"

"How can you need to be told?" Clodagh said with exasperation. "Do you think there's no evil in the world? Haven't you seen it around you?"

"Of course there's evil in the world," Eleanor said. "For all I know there may be witches too. I only know I've never seen one. It's a blasphemy to think some fat old crone of a peasant can be a proper adversary for Christ."

There was silence for a moment, while Clodagh tried to wrestle with this thought. "Not adversaries, perhaps," she said doubtfully, "but minions—Satan's minions."

"He doesn't need them. Don't underrate Satan."

"It's a good thing you don't believe in witchcraft, or you wouldn't be happy using that needle," Clodagh said. "Godda says it's a charm needle, used for sewing the dead into their shrouds. If you prick yourself with it you're likely to run mad."

Eleanor got to her feet, holding the needle carefully. She looked, with her long gown belted over her barren hips and her hair cut off to shoulder length with Geoffrey's dagger, rather like the beardless Christs of the Saxon churches. Or perhaps she is actually a witch, Clodagh thought, and crossed herself as Eleanor turned away. Still carrying the needle with exaggerated care, Eleanor crossed to where Father Nicholas was sleeping in the sun, and knelt beside him. "Bless this needle for me," she said, shaking him gently to waken him. "It's done some queer work. Bless it for me."

The priest signed a cross over it, and took it from her. He fumbled for the wooden cross he wore in his belt, and rubbed the needle backwards and forwards across it as a woman rubs a needle to clean rust from it. "Be blessed in all the work you do," he said.

"Past, present and future," Eleanor said, prompting him.

"Past, present and future," the priest said obediently, and gave the needle back to her, and returned to his doze.

"I thought you didn't believe in that stuff," Clodagh said as Eleanor came back to her.

"I don't believe in taking risks," Eleanor said. "You'd better not tell Godda about that. She'll think her needle's ruined, with the spell off it."

"I don't know when you're serious and when you're joking," Clodagh said. "I thought you could help me."

"No one can help if you don't tell what help is needed. And even if you do . . ." Eleanor said, and left the sentence unfinished.

"And what about crops that are blighted?" Clodagh said, sheering away from the subject of the help she needed. "And great storms of rain and hail? And cattle that abort, and women?"

"Women and cattle—they go well in a bracket. You think I aborted because some witch put her mark against the Seigneur Joinville's women and his cattle?"

"You?" Clodagh said.

"Three times."

"I thought you were chaste," Clodagh said in some bewilderment.

"It's a matter of definition," Eleanor said. "And indeed, now you mention it, perhaps it was God's will for me, and His way of puttings things back the way He wanted them. Perhaps a little hard on my husband, though, who got no son, and only a short life."

"I am sorry," Clodagh said.

"For whom?"

"Will you marry again?"

"Why should I? I have my jointure back, and my two brothers are weak fools who can't find any way to force me to accept a marriage offer, or to live as a dependant in their houses."

"But the money," Clodagh said. "No widow controls her own jointure—not a young widow, not a widow without children. They can starve you into submission if they want to."

Eleanor laughed. "Only brave men would try it," she said, "and my brothers are neither brave nor sensible men."

"What can you do? Talk is all very well," Clodagh said, for the injustice of dependence and forced second marriages had often been talked about among her friends, "but you can't live on talk if your brothers close their purse strings."

"Talk, no. But the threat of it, yes," Eleanor said lightly. "A sister knows about her brothers things best not talked about when they have their way to make close to the throne."

Clodagh laughed uncertainly. "You shock me," she said. "It seems a great ungodliness that a sister should range herself against her brothers and threaten them."

"A great ungodliness that she should be owned by a brother, fed or not fed, sold in the marriage market like a cow. You are young, and perhaps stupid. But you've put yourself in a position where you must think, and quickly, whether you own your own soul or whether it, like your body, is a possession of your husband's."

"What choice have I?" Clodagh said, and it was a new thought to her that anyone might consider that she had a choice. "And besides, doesn't God say that we are to be ruled by men?"

"You listen too much to priests," Eleanor said.

"I don't *understand* you," Clodagh said irritably. "You've taken *that*"—pointing to the cross on Eleanor's cloak—"and yet you speak against priests, and you seem to speak against God."

"Not against God," Eleanor said. "I have given Him the whole of the rest of my life."

"Then why aren't you in a convent?" Clodagh said. "Widowed, childless and with no wish to marry, you should have taken vows."

"Alas, I have no talent for obedience," Eleanor said. "And since Christ is my brother, how can I be His bride?"

The obedience of women, and their proper submission to their men, was also being talked about in a sunny spot three miles away where Magnus and the twins and Gyll and the Monkey were resting in a clearing after pig hunting. Now that they had houses and fires, enough to eat and a set place to which to return at the end of their hunt, the territory in which they hunted seemed to them tamed, and safe. On the march it had seemed dangerous to linger anywhere when they were separated from the main party, and they had kept on the move until they had gathered enough food or else exhausted themselves in searching for it, and then gone quickly back to the camping place before they rested. But this country, reasonably supplied with animals, no longer seemed to be a hostile place, and they often rested companionably in the sun before they carried the day's supplies back to the others. They had a young boar, bleeding into the dust, and Magnus had propped himself against it, using it as a backrest. He had taken his knife and the bits of bones he carried in his waist pouch, and was at work upon the chess set commissioned by the priest. He had collected useful pieces of boiled bone from the heap of bones they had discovered near the huts, and already he had made a pair of dice from the knobs of bone at the head of two sheep shanks. The priest had promised him a rose noble for the chess set, when they got to some place where a rose noble would be of any use. It was Godwin's view that he was foolish to take any money for it. "Make it as a gift," he said. "Then it should be worth a day off purgatory for every hour you work at it."

"You should be able to do better than that," Gyll said. "Make a bargain with him. A day off purgatory for every hour's work, and half a day for every game of chess the priest plays."

"Better still," Magnus said without looking up from his work, "a thousand years off for my purity. I'd rather be making a different sort of set. I saw a beauty once. Indecent. Made from the shinbones of dead Leinstermen, they told me."

"Leinstermen?"

"Irish. Hundred years old, they said, carved up for some earl out of his enemies' bones after a battle."

"Go on!" Gyll said unbelievingly. "What earl would let you get your big hands on his dirty chess set?"

"No earl," Magnus said. "Not knowingly, that is. But I had a friend, see, and he had this girl, and she sneaked the pieces out for him to copy, one by one. I'll bet he got more than a rose noble for the set, if he ever finished it. A beauty! A king that fitted snugly over his queen, and a bishop with a crook that was part of his person in a way that ought to stop him getting through the pearly gates."

"Make one, when you've done the priest's set," Gyll said. "We can all live on the proceeds for a month when we get to Porto."

"If we get to Porto," Godwin said. "Who says we're going to Porto in the end?"

"About Porto I don't know, but if we go on walking we'll reach somewhere."

"Who says we'll go on walking?" Edwin said. "I don't say it. Godwin doesn't say it." The brothers moved a little closer, looking at Gyll and Magnus across the crouched body of the Monkey, who was at his usual game of tracing patterns in the dust with a stick.

"We can't stay here for the rest of our lives," Gyll said.

"It takes some hard thinking," Godwin said. "But where does easy thinking ever get you, except into doing what you're told? Suppose we walk on and on and on, and in the end we get somewhere, to the armies, or to some town. What happens to us then? We're back under orders. And what happens to us then? They put us back in holds, and ship us to the fighting in the Holy Land. What happens to us then? Either we die or we don't die. If we don't die we get back home after a dozen years, and all the rest of our lives, if we're lucky and get a bit of land, we'll work first for some stinking lord and second for ourselves, so that his corn comes in while ours stands rotting in the rain, and we'll cart his dung and gather his nuts and plough his fields and wash his sheep, and thatch his barns, and scour his ditches, and still he'll want a shilling a year rent and our women and children to work for him in the fields and the right to say aye or nay to their marriages." It was a long speech for Godwin, clearly the product of some hard thinking, and Edwin punctuated it with approving nods.

"What choice have we got?" Gyll said. His circum-

stances were very much the same. He owed Robert Apelfourde one day's work in every week, three days at every
harvest, three days to gather dung, every day to shear his
sheep while shearing lasted, hens and eggs for his table,
and his own horse and cart to carry for him when and
where he wanted things carried, within a radius of a
two-day journey.

"Only one choice," Edwin said. "Go with the others,
or stay here."

There was silence for a few moments, while Gyll and
Magnus thought about it. The idea of staying wasn't
unattractive, but Gyll thought perhaps they were assum-
ing too easily that the place was friendly, not inhabited
by hostile spirits, not perhaps visited from time to time
by some of the monstrous creatures of Faber's stories.

"They wouldn't let us stay," said Magnus, who had
spent all his life under soldiers' orders.

"Who'll stop us?" Godwin said. "That puny knight?
Faber with his soft belly? The priest forever pissing holy
water?"

"Who would stay," Gyll said, "if it came to a choice?
Suppose the four of us . . . who else?"

"Monkey," Edwin said, giving him a sharp kick.

"And Godda and Joice," Magnus said resentfully. He
didn't resent the idea that they might stay, but only that
they would be of little use to him.

"What about your woman?" Edwin asked of Gyll. It
was a question that had been in all their minds.

"I don't know," Gyll said. He thought a little longer.
"If she didn't choose to stay, I wouldn't stay either," he
said.

"Y'see? Bewitched," Magnus said to the others, with
a grin. He turned to Gyll. "Think it out," he said.
"You've had your fun. Now let her go on with the others

and when she gets back no questions asked and no harm done—not unless you've left a pup inside her."

It was true, Gyll thought, that for him to stay behind would remove most of Clodagh's problems in rejoining Apelfourde. But it would remove none of his. Was he going to spend the rest of his life, lonely in this place, with nothing better to do than hope that Joice would produce a daughter who would grow quickly? "If she doesn't stay, then I go with them," he said firmly.

"And if she stays what happens, how does she act?" Magnus said, not liking to make the point aloud that Clodagh, like Joice, would have to agree to being shared. "I don't spend the rest of my time here without a woman."

"We'll give you Godda," one of her sons said gallantly.

"Too old," Magnus said, taking the offer seriously.

"Or the Lady Eleanor," the other brother said. "She can be persuaded to stay. We'll give you old Nell."

"Too old," Magnus said with a grin. "And too dangerous. Women like her have teeth in funny places."

"Persuade the Lady Eleanor to stay and they'll all stay," Gyll said. "Simon de Baude won't go without her. Without her he wouldn't know when to chew and when to spit."

"And his lapdog brother . . ." Edwin said.

"But he's a good lad. A quick learner at low ways of taking game. We could use him. Food's not going to drop into our mouths while we lie back."

"That's true," Godwin said. "We'll have to work for it. But we're not going to work for it under any orders."

"And we'd have a priest," Gyll said. "Not a bad thing." The more he thought of it, the more he liked the idea. Land without rent, and no labour due to anyone, children growing up, no military service, good food, the sort of independence only the rich had. If they went on he would lose Clodagh first, and then probably his life to some stinking Turk. He began to be more and more in favour of the idea, but it seemed to him that clearly it all depended on Eleanor. If she went he thought Clodagh would go too, and the de Baudes. And he would go himself, for mixed reasons, and the chief among them would be the shortage of women. You had to look ahead, into the years. "It seems to me it's all or none," he said. "All stay, or all go on. Magnus? What d'you say?"

"Pigshit," Magnus said, laying down knife and bone. "If I didn't know you were as dry as I am, I'd say there was a bellyful of beer talking for all of you. A fine lot of freedom any of us've had so far. Fetch and carry and hunt and bring in the food, and Sir Simon says when we'll walk, when we'll sleep, when we'll eat. What makes you think they'd ever want to stay? And if they did, only because we're here, ready-made serfs."

"Like I said," Edwin said. "*We* stay—they go on. You and Godwin and me, Godda and Joice, Gyll and Gyll's woman, if he wants her. What d'you say, Magnus?"

"I say one thing to that," Magnus said. "I want a woman."

The question of when—not whether—they should move on had begun to bother Simon de Baude a good deal. He had agreed that rest and food were necessary to the party, but as the days slipped past he began to feel that command was slipping away from him. Nobody, not even Eleanor, spoke of the rest of the journey that lay ahead of them. The division of the party into little groups living in separate huts had weakened discipline. Those who went out to hunt went when they chose, and came back when they chose. The rest—Faber and the priest, de Baude himself often enough, and the women —waited for food to be brought in and didn't stray very far from the huts, except to look for edible nuts, and bees' nests. The priest had been too ill in the first days to celebrate mass or call the people together at night to pray; now that he was better he seemed to have forgotten the need for it. "The people are going to bed like heathens every night, and like heathens eating their meal without giving thanks," de Baude said to him.

"Yes," Father Nicholas said. "I am remiss."

"Will you celebrate mass this Sabbath?"

"Yes," the priest said. "When is it?"

"You have the tally stick," Simon said. He was sorry for the priest, but the discipline of his party couldn't be maintained without the proper observances.

Father Nicholas had taken the tally stick from his belt and was looking at it carefully. "The Sabbath," he said, "is . . . the Sabbath is two days hence . . . or perhaps tomorrow, or perhaps three days. How many days have we been here?"

"Five."

"It is possible I have forgotten to cut the notches."

"Does it matter very much?" Simon said. "The people will accept that it is the Sabbath when you say so. Does it matter much to God?"

"I think not," Father Nicholas said. "I think He will accept the intention to be right about the day."

"Then you will tell the people that the day after tomorrow is the Sabbath? And you will celebrate the mass? And the next day we will move on."

"Ah, yes," the priest said wearily. "I suppose we must."

Having made his decision, Simon went at once to have it agreed to by the Lady Eleanor. He found her washing her narrow feet in ice-cold water from the well. "Why do you go barefoot?" he asked her. "Are your shoes done for?"

"Almost," she said. "And if there's much walking ahead it seems wise to save them, and harden my feet."

"Will you be ready to move out from here in two days' time?"

Eleanor looked at him for a moment. "Yes," she said. "I suppose so. I shall be sorry to go."

"Sorry?"

Eleanor smiled. "I am a woman, Simon, and weaker than I thought," she said. "A few days of rest, and I'm no longer sure I have the strength for that long journey to the Celestial City."

"You're wrong!" Simon said. "You've done your part, and more. You are stronger and more tireless than most."

"I didn't mean weakness in that way."

"You have been my strength," Simon said. "Surely you know how much you've been my strength?"

"I'm glad," she said, "though it's very possible to borrow what isn't there. I've discovered things about myself that shock me."

"Perhaps we all have," Simon said, though in truth he couldn't think of any discoveries he had made. He hoped that she wouldn't tell him what those things were. Her strength and her probity and sweetness had inspired in him the sort of courtly love that every young knight longed for but found hard to come by in the workaday world of affairs, and he had no wish for her confidences, no wish to be drawn any closer. "Please tell me. Is there enough food stored? Are we ready to move?"

"Nearly," Eleanor said, and risked a sigh, knowing he would ignore it. He was, after all, what his rank and his

training made him—pious and good and empty of understanding. For a moment she almost envied Clodagh.
There was, she thought, probably rather more to that
rough young man than to this gentle and amiable one.
But on second thoughts, and more searching ones, perhaps it was Gyll she envied. "For the last two days Godda
has saved a little meat each night, and she is drying it,"
she said.

"From tonight we must ration the meat again, so that
there is more to be dried and carried with us."

Simon's announcement that food was to be rationed
to half a bellyful wasn't well received. There was argument about whether the hunters could be expected to
go on hunting on half rations, and for the first time
opinions were voiced openly about whether weak women
and inactive old men should share equally with those
who did the bulk of the work. Those who did the hunting weren't able to match the other men in argument,
but Godwin made his views clear by forcing open Joice's
clenched hand to take the last of her food, and eating it
while the others argued. The Monkey couldn't follow
the argument, but he understood this, and decamped
quickly to the outside of the group to finish his food in
safety.

When their small meal was finished and the saved
food put with the meat Godda had been drying, de
Baude announced that Father Nicholas would celebrate
mass on the next day but one, and that the party would
begin their walk again at dawn on the following morning. The announcement was greeted with a few minutes
of complete silence. It had taken the hunters by surprise;
they had not thought that the time was so close, and
though they had talked a lot about refusing to go on,

they were not ready yet to discuss their plan in front of the whole party.

The silence made de Baude uneasy. He had expected grumbling, perhaps even some argument. The time they had spent in the abandoned village had divided his people, and he saw no real way of reimposing proper discipline until they were on the move again, and exhausted by daily walking and foraging. He saw the looks they were exchanging, and Edwin's efforts to nudge Godwin into speech. To break the silence and prevent Godwin from speaking he said, "Plainly we are on the edge of occupied territory. A week, two weeks at most, will find us, with God's help, home and safe with our own people again."

"Good luck to you, Sir," Godwin said. "But some of us stay."

The silence closed in again. They stared at Simon de Baude. No one moved except the Monkey who, having finished his food, had come back into the circle and was staring from face to face in his efforts to get a hint about the meaning of the stillness.

"Who stays?" Eleanor said. But Simon de Baude spoke quickly before anyone could answer her. "Foolishness," he said. "Nobody stays. We go on, the morning after mass has been celebrated." He wanted to bustle them, to break up the group, to send them to their beds for the night before there could be open talk of mutiny and any sort of challenge to his command. He had no weapon against them except talk, no way of coercing them into obedience. He stood and Geoffrey, who had been sitting beside him, rolled forward onto his knees facing his brother, in the humble page and gentil knight position. "I command, under God," Simon said, "and with Our Blessed Lady's help I shall bring you all safe back."

"Who stays?" Eleanor said again, ignoring him.

"I stay," Edwin and Godwin said, together. "And Joice," Edwin added.

"And Godda," Godda said.

"And the Monkey, of course," Godwin said. "He stays. And Magnus?"

Everyone turned to look at Magnus. He had not yet made up his mind. In fact he hadn't taken it very seriously, or realized that the moment of choice might be so close. He still objected to the prospect of a womanless future. But agreement, he thought, wouldn't bind him in any way. "I stay," he said.

"That's six," Godwin said, with a grin that betrayed his surprise. "Who else? There's land, water, food and every man his own master." He stared around at the others. He didn't want them particularly, but he thought they must be given their chance, and they must understand the conditions. "Gyll?" he said, since Gyll was the only one of them who would be really welcome.

Gyll looked at once to Clodagh, but before the girl had time to speak Eleanor broke in. "I stay," she said. She had not, for an instant, considered staying, but she knew that without the commons they could not survive. Arguments must be found, and her seeming agreement might give her time to find them.

De Baude and Faber and the priest all began to speak at once, arguing with her, reasoning, pleading. She sat with eyes downcast, and a half smile on her lips. "Perhaps it is Our Lady's wish that we should make a bower here for her, with our prayers," she said.

"It is not God's will," Father Nicholas said, with a firmness they had not heard in his voice for many days. "Be governed. It is not God's will that any of us should stay."

"But perhaps His Mother's," Eleanor said, without looking up.

"Emulate her obedience," the priest said. "She did not urge her own course, or set herself up against Sir Joseph's wishes."

"No?" Eleanor was heard to say by those close to her.

"We stay," Clodagh said, putting a hand on Gyll's arm to indicate that she spoke for him as well. It was the first she had heard of any plan to stay, and before Eleanor spoke she had been about to reject it scornfully. Godwin's plan had suggested a hard peasant life, and she wanted none of that. But Eleanor's words suggested mistily to her some sort of Court of Love like the romances sang of, days filled with sun and music, undemanding love, avoidance of the reunion with Robert Apelfourde which she now dreaded. "We stay," she said again, smiling at Gyll.

Simon de Baude had now dropped to his knees beside Eleanor. He was bewildered. He had depended on her to strengthen him when he needed strengthening, and to reassure him by approving what he had done or said when he moved without consulting her. "My Lady," he said softly, "you are sick, you are tired. We will get safely back. Don't leave me now." Eleanor looked up for the first time, glancing directly at him for a second. "Shuttlewit," she said fiercely, and dropped her eyes again. Simon fell back onto his heels. Four of them—himself, his brother, the priest, Captain Faber. They couldn't go on alone. They would starve, suffer attack. And in any case his knightly oath enjoined on him so many things that could not be done if his party were to divide—protection of the church and reverence for the priesthood meant that he should go where Father Nicholas went; but if he went, how could he fend off injustice from the poor, since the poor people in his care were determined to stay? And he had sworn to do succour, upon pain of death, to all ladies, and to gentlewomen. He was bound, therefore, to the Lady Eleanor, and he was bound to Clodagh also. Christ knew she had demeaned herself, but it was Christ's job to judge her, not his. Sitting back on his heels, he began to weep quietly at the injustice of a fate that posed such problems for a knight without brother knights to support and steady him. "I stay," Geoffrey de Baude said loudly, in a cracked treble. He had been debating his duty silently all the time. As a squire he owed service and obedience to his brother, but he was in love with the company of women, and Eleanor's smile raised in him delicious dreams of a selfless death.

Faber respected Simon de Baude's tears. He didn't approve of the niminy ways of knighthood, but every trade had its tricks, and he would cover for Simon, little as he deserved it. "Are you all run wild?" he said on a roar. "Have you been eating birds' eggs with a haunt on them, so you're turned to asses? What do you suppose will happen to you, when you stay alone in this place?" He searched his memory, hunting for some appalling travellers' tale to impress the commons. "This is nasnas country," he said. They waited a little fearfully. Suddenly the captain burst into a roar of laughter. "So you don't know what the nasnas is," he said, "and yet you think of staying here, in the heart of his country."

"What is it, then?" Magnus said sullenly.

The captain crossed himself. "It is the most hideous creature in creation," he said, "for a sort of yellow blood drips all the time from its feathers. It has one eye and one hand, one leg and one ear, half a body, half a heart and half the head of a crocodile. And inside it, just before you die, you can see its brain curdling."

"Before you die?" Gyll said.

Captain Faber ignored him. "It is endowed with speech, and great profanities issue from it in a torrent of steam. It can hop so quickly on its one leg that it can easily overtake the fastest horse. And the worst thing is," he said, and paused significantly, "the worst thing is that when the sun strikes it, it throws the shadow of a man."

"*Nominedomini*," Godwin said, and laughed a little shakily.

"You may well say," Faber said, "for all know what that means. It must devour a man before it can get its own shadow back again, and until it has its shadow it can neither rest nor sleep nor eat nor drink nor copulate."

"It is true," Eleanor said. "I have seen one."

"Where?" half a dozen of them asked at once.

"At London," Eleanor said., "It was preserved in a great cask of honey, and brought back from Egypt."

"That one was resting sweetly enough," Magnus said.

"Are we in Egypt?" Joice asked nervously.

"Not far away," Eleanor said.

"Only a *hop* away," Faber said.

"There's one thing puzzles me," Magnus said. "If there are so many of these whatyoucallits about, why haven't we seen them?"

"Half a body, half a head, only one leg, one hand," Faber said. "They can only hunt down small parties, less than a dozen people, and parties with an unequal number in them."

"We'll be ten, with the Monkey," Edwin said.

"So we will," Eleanor said. "And if, as time passes, illness or accident should take one of us away, then we will

face the danger when it comes. Perhaps it may not happen till we are old."

"And by that time there'll be plenty of us," Godda
said. "Children born, and grown, and children's children."

Eleanor looked at her with sympathy. "Poor Godda,
you will have no grandchildren," she said. "It is not
the Virgin's wish that children should be born here."

"It's no virgin's wish, often enough," Godda said,
"but it happens, all the same."

"It won't happen here," Eleanor said. "Look around
you. The Lady Clodagh has been a wife for several years.
So has Joice. Each," she said delicately, "has had other
visitors in her husband's place. Neither has a child. You
are beyond it, Godda. I do not mean to attempt it."

Clodagh had turned angrily to Gyll, stung by the suggestion that she might be barren. "I don't know that I
want to stay," she said.

"Nor I," Magnus said. If there were to be children,
then in ten years, twelve years . . . but he had no mind
to stay with a lot of hopping half-men, if he was also to
stay womanless for the rest of his life.

"I think it is Milady's will that we should stay here,
living a life of prayer and hardship, and without sin,"
Eleanor said. "Indeed it is very necessary that we should
live without sin, for we'll have no priest, and each one
of us, when our time comes, will have to die unshriven."

"Gyll and I go on with you," Clodagh said, speaking
to Simon de Baude. He nodded at her, and turned to
look at Joice. "Why does she speak for him? Can't he
talk?" Joice said, and glanced from Edwin to Godwin,
seeking their decision.

"I'm going with them," Magnus said, and stood up.

"We are all going," the priest said, and no one con-

tradicted him. He stood up, and made an outsize cross
in the air above their heads. "Pray, sleep, wake and
pray," he said. He waited for them to kneel, and then he
prayed for a long time in Latin, with the idea that it
might be salutary for the unschooled among them. "Go
now, and sleep," he told them, when he had finished
praying. "Put all your trust in the great and famous
blood of God. Do not fear these beasts of which you have
heard. They are all God's creatures—it is a mistake to
think they mean us any harm."

When the others had gone Sir Simon knelt again beside the Lady Eleanor, thinking she might need comfort,
or persuasion. She looked at him with a wide smile on
her face. "Seem to go someone else's, if you want your
own way," she said. "We couldn't have got back safely
without them."

They began to walk again with a pretense of sullen-
ness, but with real relief. Magnus and the twins and
the others had frightened themselves a good deal with
the plan to stay. They had not expected so many of the
others to agree to it so readily, making what had been
only the beginnings of an idea into a firm plan and a
frightening possibility before they had had proper time
to argue it to a standstill among themselves. They were
not frightened so much by the named and nameless horrors with which Faber threatened them, or by the threat
of an unshriven death. What frightened them was the
threat of perpetual imprisonment, of a sort of death-in-
life unrelieved by friends, enemies, in-laws, children,
rulers, leaders, itinerants, landlords, tinkers, pardoners,
wives, witches, crones and the appeasable spirits of their
familiar places. So they were glad to be walking again,
and there was more talk than in the last days of walking

before they had come to the huts—more optimism, more talk of the food they would eat, the tankards they would empty and the foreign girls they would tumble when they reached the Crusading Armies in a few days' time.

They found no food on the first day, but this was not surprising, since they had walked very little further than the limits of the territory over which the hunters had been ranging for a week or more. Simon de Baude allowed them a small meal of the dried meat and a mouthful or two of the water they carried with them and they settled, fireless, in the loose circle they had previously made each night around the ashes of their doused fire. The long period of rest had divided them more firmly into two groups, so that now the gentles gravitated automatically to one side of the circle, the commons to the other. Clodagh and Gyll removed themselves a little from the circle, daring the dangers of the night for the extra privacy a removal of two yards could give them. "She was lying," Clodagh said fiercely into his ear. "If we'd stayed, there would have been children." She had discovered during the day that she was not yet with child. "There would have been many children," she said to the sleeping boy. "*Many.* Only God is not so unkind as to make me gravid while I have to walk." She spat ritually onto her crossed fingers as she said it, for fear God might be so unkind as to misunderstand her words and make her gravid too far ahead of the time of her reunion with her husband for her to explain it satisfactorily.

On the second day they found only enough food for a meager night meal, but they camped by water and drank gratefully, and Gyll was confident that he could trap enough fish in the withy basket if he began as soon as the sun was high.

The priest, like the others, was glad that they were

moving again, even though the daily walking took a toll
of his strength and he often needed the support of someone's arm during the last hour or two. He had been
glad of the long rest; in particular he had been glad of
the solitude the place gave him, and the chance to sleep
and pray out of the sound of straddlings and strugglings
which reminded him all the time of the sinfulness of the
people, and his failure to bring them back to righteousness. Now, though his strength seemed to have increased
only a little, his zeal had taken on a new growth. Time
was running out—his time—he thought. He did not expect to see Porto and the brave tents. He did not expect
to hear a sung mass again, to confess himself, to die the
quiet nun-attended death that had once seemed to him
the proper end of his road. He would die not at the end
of it but beside that road, he felt sure. God's last chance
to him would be the chance he would have, in the next
few days, to put right the neglects of the last weeks, to
strengthen the waverers, admonish the wicked and bring
his people to the edge of delivery in a fit condition for
their eventual salvation. The trouble was that though
he began each day in an evangelical fever, walking tired
him so much that when he stopped walking he dozed,
daydreaming about his early life and his boyhood, instead of concentrating his thoughts on the life to come
for him, and for these others.

Clodagh, walking with a supporting hand under his
elbow late on the third afternoon, found her thoughts
once again on the sin-shedding, a possible transgression
that frightened her more than the sin of her adultery,
which was, after all, so common a thing that, if the
priests were right about it, it must have turned heaven's
corridors into empty, echoing places. "I am confused,
Father," she said to him.

"We are all confused," the priest said. "It is natural. It is due to weakness and walking, hunger and lack of faith."

"I am confused between right and wrong."

"It is not possible to be confused between right and wrong," the priest said. "They are clearly defined."

"Not always. Not for me."

"They are defined," Father Nicholas said, stopping to face her, so that she was forced to stop walking too. "You are doing wrong. That is what troubles you, my child."

"I am doing *some* wrong. What troubles me is whether I have done more, and greater. Father," she said impulsively, "*is* there witchcraft?"

The priest sighed. "There is an evil belief in it, which amounts to the same thing," he said. He could see that she did not understand him. He gave her arm a small tug, and they began walking again. It would be a long business explaining it to her, and they would lose the others in the party if they lingered. "If you are going to tell me that you have sinned so hideously because some cunning-woman has worked a spell on you to make you powerless over the cravings of your body——"

"No," she said.

"——then you are talking nothing but foolishness. God has given you a choice. You can act in a way that pleases Him, or in a way that delights the Devil."

"I am not talking about that," Clodagh said. "Not about my . . ." She found it difficult to name it to him. "I am talking about sortilege, witchcraft. Is it possible to offer things to the *Devil?*"

The priest sighed again. At every step the bones in his left hip seemed to grind together with a burning pain, and the poor, stringy fare of the last few days lay cold and undigested in his bowels. "It is a great blasphemy to think that storms of thunder and lightning which may ruin a crop, or frosts that blight the buds or sudden falls of snow that kill the lambs, are raised by shrivelled, stupid old women. A great blasphemy, that God will not forgive. Storms and tempests, great winds, flood tides, lightning that strikes men's houses into fire, all these things are God's. They are His storms, His frosts, His flood, His scourges on His own unworthy people. It is a great sin to believe anything else."

"Then there are no witches?" Clodagh said, her spirits lightening.

"There is no *witchcraft*," Father Nicholas said. "That is a different matter. If all the witches in the world were drowned, do you think there'd be no storms? No crops and cattle blighted, no infants overlooked, no broken bones, no pox, no pestilence?"

"These are all from God?" she said uncertainly.

"From God."

"And no Devil?" she said hopefully.

The priest stopped again. "How can you believe that?" he said, searching her face. "You are a Christian. You have been baptized. You have been taught and told that the Devil is beside you, every moment of your life, tempting you with soft pleasures to betray Christ and leave Him hanging forever on His Cross."

"I know these things, I know them," she said hastily, seeing his distress. "But when you said . . . I am sorry, Father, I am confused," she said.

"Such things are beyond your understanding," he said kindly, beginning to walk again. "Turn your back on what you have been doing. Listen. Obey. Pray."

"And there *are* no witches," she said again happily, seeing the end of her fear of Godda and the business of the goatlets.

"There is no witchcraft," Father Nicholas said. "There are witches. They are poor sad old women, or sometimes young and foolish ones, who claim powers for themselves that no one but God has. And sometimes they do not even claim these powers, but have them fathered on them by the superstitious, who must find someone to blame for every ill chance that happens to them. Men will not acknowledge their sin," he said sternly. "They must forever turn and lay the blame on someone else. They will turn to the Devil for a scapegoat, when they should turn and confess themselves to God."

His words were a twofold comfort to Clodagh. They removed the nag of her guilt over the business of the goatlets, since clearly Father Nicholas, if he knew of it, would dismiss it as a piece of ignorant foolishness. And they explained to her, too, something about the nature of God that had always puzzled her. She had not liked to voice it to anyone, but the *weakness* of the Almighty God had always bothered her. If He was all-powerful as she had been taught, how was it that He could be defeated by such poor creatures as the little melancholy-eyed old woman she had once seen whipped at the cart tail through the town where she lived, and had afterwards smelled for half a day as she was slowly roasted on a bonfire in the marketplace? The priest had given God's power back to Him. She felt clean again, and confident. She had no sin of a monstrous or unnatural sort on her conscience. Adultery could be purged as soon as she was ready to abstain, and the time for that was not now, when she needed the nightly comfort of Gyll's body, but when abstinence was forced on them by Robert Apelfourde's presence.

But the others, as the days passed with no improvement in the food supply, and with a great increase of all their bodily ailments, felt more and more certain that they were being punished for some sin of omission or commission. The things that had bedevilled them before—night fevers, the ache of swollen limbs, coughs that cut at their chests like an assassin's knife and the pulpy swellings of their bleeding gums—had come back almost as soon as they began to walk and fast again. The country, instead of becoming kinder as de Baude had promised them, now seemed a waste of dry gullies into which they lowered themselves, to find dryness at the bottom and a treacherous climb through stones and powdery clay to the top again. They began to walk for fewer hours of the day, and to hunt for longer. Those who didn't hunt suspected the hunters of bringing in less than their full bag, and there were accusations and angry denials. And certainly Clodagh found that, when weariness and weakness prevented his doing anything else for her at night, Gyll often had for her a handful of berries he had hidden, or a couple of small eggs taken from a nest. She looked with some envy at Joice who, though she might be suffering a doubled deprivation, was probably being given a double ration of hunters' purloined pickings.

After the first week Godda, in her search for someone or something to blame for the hardships suffered by the party, began to worry about the immortal souls of her sons. "Fornication is an abomination," she said, quoting the priest. "You should marry."

"Which of us?" Edwin said.

"Either or both," Godda said. "You are twins. You've only got one soul between the two of you."

They decided against conveying this idea to the priest, since they thought it ran contrary to his beliefs. But if the marriage of one of them might lift some of the

load of ill luck off the party, then it was worth a try.
They sought out the priest. "We have been sinning long
enough," Godwin said. "One of us ought to be married
to Joice." A great happiness swelled in the priest's heart
at Godwin's words. If these two would forswear their
sin, if they would confess and receive absolution, and if
one of them would take poor sinning Joice in the sanctity and decency of marriage, then they would discharge
half of the great weight of responsibility Father Nicholas was carrying. "Which?" he said.

"It doesn't matter," Godwin said. "One of us. We'll
decide."

"Perhaps the woman should decide," the priest said.
He was silent for a moment, giving thanks to God for
this lessening of his burden. He looked from one to the
other of the brothers. "It is to be a true marriage," he
said sternly. "A marriage made and kept before God,
vows honoured, chastity preserved."

"A true marriage," Godwin said. The priest looked at
Edwin. "A true marriage," Edwin said, echoing his
brother.

"Will you swear it?" the priest said. "On pain of
cursing?"

"I don't think any marriage is possible," Eleanor said
from behind the priest. He turned to look at her, im-
patient at any interruption that might postpone half of
his heart's desire. "Father, you are forgetting," Eleanor
said. "Joice may be still a wife."

It shocked him for a moment. He had forgotten it.
"God have mercy on him, he can now be presumed
dead," he said.

"So can we all," Eleanor said with a smile. "I think
many people now hold that presumption about all of
us."

"A miracle is a sole act, a unique act," Father Nicholas said. "It is a miracle that we have survived the terrible dangers of the sea, and the terrors and hardships that have followed it. Isn't that so?"

"Yes," Eleanor said.

"And if a miracle is a unique act done by God for His special purposes, is it not foolish to think He would repeat the effect over and over again, saving this one and that one and the other one, so that the whole miraculous quality of His act is lost?"

"Perhaps," Eleanor said, seeing how much he wanted her to answer.

"Rest him, he is now presumed dead," Father Nicholas said. "I will perform the marriage, when all three of you have confessed yourselves and sworn a true and deadly oath about the marriage."

Joice's reaction to the news that she was to marry one of them came as a surprise. They told her of it the next day, while the party was resting midway on the day's walk. They had found water, and Magnus was carrying a hare and a leveret at his belt, so that they would have something to eat that night.

"Father Nicholas is going to marry you to one of us. You can choose which," Edwin said generously. Joice laughed.

"*Choose*," Godwin said threateningly. "If marrying one of us is going to take the curse off this bloody country, then you'll marry one of us, and quickly."

"Shit to that," Joice said, her voice rising angrily. Godwin leaned over and hit her with the edge of his hand, chopping down in the angle between her shoulder and her neck. She toppled over, clutching at her shoulder.

"Don't knock her out," Edwin said reasonably. "She has to choose."

Godwin pulled her upright and held her chin in a painful grip, jerking her head from side to side as he spoke. "Choose," he said. "Choose. Him or me. Hurry up. Choose. It's got to be one or the other."

Joice jumped back, pulling herself free. She spat on the ground at Godwin's feet. "What choice?" she said. "Two coarse braggarts. Two bigmouths. Two poxy cutthroats with half a prick between them. I've made my choice," she said, and spat again. "Neither."

Godwin reached for her again but she jumped back to evade him. "You had your chance," he said. "Now the dice'll decide it. Magnus," he called to where the others were resting. "Come over here. Lend us the hazards for a minute."

Joice was beside herself with anger now. She dashed at Magnus, knocking the dice from his hand into the dust. Then she turned again to face the brothers. "So that's it," she said. "So that's my value, worth so little that two ugly farts can play for me with two little dice, two bitching bits of bone. All right. I have to marry. I have to choose. All right. I choose him," she said, flinging a dramatic arm to point at the Monkey.

Her raised voice had caught the others' attention now, and all except the sleeping priest had sat up to watch the scene. The Monkey, pointed at, stared at Joice apprehensively. The twins laughed.

"Well, laugh," Joice said. "He's a whole man, and clean and young and strong. Any girl'd fancy him, any girl."

Her words infuriated Godwin, who came at her in a rush with his hands raised ready to catch her throat. The girl saw his intention, and raced for the other group, throwing herself at the surprised Monkey. They went over together into the dust, and Godwin hurled

himself on top of them, kneeing at them and punching
indiscriminately with both fists. His violence had surprised the others, and it was a moment or two before de
Baude and Faber and Gyll could pull him off and hold
him with an arm twisted behind his back.

"I'll kill him," Godwin said. "I'll cut off his stones
and make him swallow them." Joice had scrambled
away, her torn clothes torn again, and her face streaked
with dust and with blood from her punched nose. Magnus reached a hand down and helped the Monkey to his
feet. "Bugger you ver' much," he said politely, and
moved himself to the outer edge of the group.

"Let him go, let him go, you're hurting him," Godda
said, plucking at Faber's arm.

"Yes, let him go," Joice said from a safe distance, and
spat again. The three men relaxed their grips slowly,
watching him, ready to grab again if he made a move to
go after the Monkey or the girl.

"Has she made her choice?" the priest said, having
woken too late to understand anything that had been
going on.

"*I've* made a choice," Godwin said. "I'm for living
single." He turned away from the group and went off to
rejoin his brother. Simon de Baude kept an eye on him
for the next hour, but it seemed that his anger had
burned itself out in his brief bout of punching.

Joice kept away from the twin brothers during the
rest of the day, and when the group settled for the night
she took herself to the gentles' side of the fire, and edged
into a place between young Geoffrey de Baude and Eleanor. One of her eyes was blackened, and her lip was cut
and swollen where Godwin's fist had jammed it hard
against her front teeth. She seemed subdued, but she de-
fended herself when Eleanor threatened her with penal-

ties if she made herself the cause of any further fighting in the group.

"It wasn't my fault," she said. "Anyway, I was sick of them. Two men are too much, when you walk all day and live on sparrows' food."

"Then the answer's easy," Eleanor said. "Keep away from them. Spend your time with the women, and pay some attention to the state of your soul."

"Besides, it wasn't a proper thing," Joice said, as though she hadn't heard Eleanor's words. "I shouldn't have been asked to make a choice, not like that, not as though it didn't make a farthing's difference to them which I chose. I'd choose easy enough *now*, if they asked."

"You leave the Monkey alone," Eleanor said. "He can't protect himself, and he can't understand——"

"*Him!*" Joice said. "D'you think I'm an animal? I'll take Godwin, if he asks again."

"You like a bloodied nose and a black eye?"

"I like a proper man that knows how to fight for what he wants," Joice said.

"Sleep, slut," Eleanor said. "Don't keep me awake any longer with your whining."

By nightfall on the next day Joice seemed to have forgotten her difference with the brothers, and was back between them on the ground when the party settled for the night. Godda spoke no more of the necessity of putting the party right with God by arranging marriages, but she hunted ceaselessly for explanations of their miserable misfortune, and for magical ways of turning it aside. Sir Simon's hastiness in deciding to move the party on, Clodagh's haughtiness and the Monkey's heathenness might all, she thought, be partly responsible for their trials. "There *must* be villages," she said. "The earth is full of people. Perhaps the villages have been made invisible to us."

"And us to them, let's hope," Edwin said, "for they'd be as hungry as we are, and as likely as not to eat us."

"It's the bad minds and the proud hearts," Godda said, staring at Clodagh. "It's the ones that are too proud to put their sins away that put them onto other people's backs."

Clodagh stared back at her. It was the first time she remembered looking directly at Godda since the night of the small goats. Godda, she thought, had changed in appearance more than anyone else. When they'd set out she'd been a round, tight, bouncy woman with a straggle of greying hair over a high-coloured face. Now she seemed many sizes smaller, with hollowed temples and a longer face. Her shelving breasts spilled down over the gap left by the disappearance of the high stomach that used to hold them up. All that had kept its former fullness and firmness was her double chin, which looked plump and edible, like the crop of a well-fed bird, under the lean lower jaw. What sort of characteristics would be transferred with it, Clodagh wondered, and half smiled at the thought that they'd be righteousness and an inability to stop the chin wagging in endless talk. "Grin your fool grin," Godda said, "but there's ways of taking a haunt off honest people."

Clodagh didn't answer her. The habit of not answering was growing on all of them. There was much less talk now than there had been in the early days of their march. Weariness kept them silent while they walked, and when they were resting their silences were punctuated more by random remarks than by any interchange. She looked at the others, noticing how blue the priest's lips looked against the grey tones of his skin. Faber, on the other hand, now had a permanently high colour, as though he was fevered, or as though his blood boiled at the injustice of his lot. The younger men looked a little better. The long hours of walking and hunting had stripped the flesh off them and tanned their faces, making them look haggard and dangerous. The Monkey had fared better than the others. His pale hair was now matted and grey with dirt, but the pink skin with which he had started out had taken on an even olive tone instead of the leathery look of ingrained streakiness that the other men had. His skin still looked reasonably healthy, and he had only a few of the spots and pustules that disfigured all the other faces.

She looked at the other two women. Eleanor had started thin and had got even thinner, so that the bones of her wrists and ankles looked brittle and not to be depended on. She had cut her hair at the beginning of the march with one of the hunting knives, and it fitted close to her head, like a dirty yellow cap. Joice had suffered or contrived a slit in her fustian skirt which exposed, to the knees, legs scabby with sores and marked by deep scratches. One side of her face was pushed out by the painful swelling of her gums, and there were small pieces of leaf and twig matted into her coarse red hair. Clodagh pulled a strand of her own hair over her shoulder to look at it. At home it had been her great pride, brushed through for many minutes every morning and evening with an oil made from bitter almonds, rose petals and gillyflowers, and washed two or three times each year, so that it shone like the wing of a plump blackbird. Now she had nothing but her fingers with which to comb it, and she wore it bunched at the back and tied with a piece of grass in place of a ribbon. "It's changed," she said to Gyll, shocked. "I think it's gone bad."

"It's only filthy dirty," he said. He took the strand of hair and pulled it across his upper lip, making himself a dark moustache to cover his own fair one. "And it smells vilely," he said, returning it to her. "Don't worry. It'll wash clean—if we ever come to running water."

Godda had been watching them. "Say a babble over it before you drink," she said to Gyll. "There's some have hair that can turn drops of water into drops of poison." Since the night of the sin-shedding, resentment of Clodagh had burned steadily in her. She had become afraid of the girl—afraid that she might tell the priest what she knew, afraid that she might have destroyed the efficacy of their sacrifice by refusing to join in—and her fear showed itself in sudden, sneering attacks which she hoped would weaken Gyll's attachment to the girl. Since Clodagh had rarely addressed herself to Godda except when it was absolutely necessary, and since the business of the goats and the naked dance had so disgusted her that she now had as little to do as possible with those who had taken part in it, she didn't take any outward notice of these remarks. They confirmed for her her mother's wisdom and her own foolishness. Her mother had warned her against familiarity with inferiors, though in fact Blanchefleur had been thinking of the foreign servants of her new household. Circumstances and Eleanor's insistence that they were all equal under the priest and Simon had forced them into association too close for comfort, and the creature had now begun to pretend a moral superiority. It gave Clodagh pleasure to think how different their circumstances would be, once again, when they reached Porto.

The harsh nature of the country, and its emptiness,

had revived in some of them the fear that they had taken the wrong direction, had walked out from under God's cover and gone beyond the margins of the inhabited world. The captain, who had opposed de Baude's decision to strike inland in the beginning, and had many times recommended a return to the coastal areas, began to argue for it again when they had had almost no food at all for two full days. To de Baude it seemed that Faber argued this way only to weaken his authority. He didn't answer the captain's arguments, but while he sat silently, appearing not to hear them, he seemed to see in his mind's eye the shallows of an estuary where gorged birds floated above shoals of fish. Perhaps he should have listened earlier, perhaps he should have allowed Faber to command. But the code had been against it—the code had only foul scorn for carpet knights who stayed at home and left others their responsibilities. But there had been no question of his staying at home—hunger was muddling him. He had led his party inland because he had a memory of a map which said that the coast curved east before it curved west again, and that they would cut corners by going inland. He hoped that his memory and the map maker had been right. Faber, after all, was only a sailor, and sailors knew nothing beyond the beaches and the brothels. He cursed his left-handedness, and all that followed from it. He prayed for a long while before he lay down between Eleanor and the priest to sleep. And when he slept he saw his mother, ashy with sorrow, wringing her pale hands over the body of her youngest son, Geoffrey.

On the next afternoon, weak from walking without food or water under a sun that seemed fierce to them in their defenseless state, they came to a wide riverbed.

Simon de Baude decided they would halt there. He thought they had walked perhaps four miles, five at most, but the priest had fallen several times, and it was becoming difficult to get him up without someone else being pulled over onto the ground. There was no water in the river, but Gyll turned a stone or two and found dampness underneath, and it seemed that digging should produce enough for them to drink. The priest, propped on the high bank until water could be brought to strengthen him for the climb down to the riverbed, looked at it waveringly through painfully swollen lids, and was reminded of something he had never seen. "I think we are come to the end waters of the river that flows out of Paradise," he said.

"It's dry and stony and full of sand, Father," Geoffrey de Baude said.

"Is it?" the priest said eagerly, leaning forward. "Is it truly? Ah, then it is indeed that paradisiacal river. Tell Sir Simon that. Tell him we are only three days distant from Paradise."

"I'll tell him," Geoffrey said, and crossed himself hastily, out of the priest's sight.

"There is a spring which changes its flavour every hour," the priest said musingly, "so that it tastes of strong waters and of weak, of sweet waters and of sharp, and any man who drinks from it will never again feel any sort of fatigue, but will as long as he lives be a man of thirty."

The thought of the spring—raspberry water, ginger water, apple juice—reminded the boy once again of the painful dryness of his mouth. "I think we're a long way yet from that spring, Father," he said glumly.

"Only three miles," the priest said, closing his eyes.

"There's no water here," Geoffrey said querulously.

"Look for yourself. It's nothing but sand and stones."

"That is the nature of the river of Paradise," the priest said. "A stony, waterless river rolls down from the mountains, into a sea of tumbling billows of sand never at rest. As soon as the stream reaches the sandy sea its stones disappear in it, and are never seen again. And though the sea lacks water altogether, fish are tossed up, of various kinds, and very, very tasty," the priest said, seeing them from behind his closed lids. "And there are women there, called salamanders, which live in fire and build cocoons like silkworms," he said to the boy, not knowing that Geoffrey had deserted him and gone to join the others in the bed of the river. "And when the cocoons are unwound and spun into cloth, the garments made from it must be cast into fire and flames to clean them. Very strange," the priest said, without opening his eyes. "Perhaps we are salamander cloth. Perhaps we have just been sent here to be cleaned."

Geoffrey had joined his brother in the bed of the river. "He's wandering in his mind and seeing things," he said.

"What things?"

"Fish," Geoffrey said hungrily.

De Baude looked sharply towards the priest. He, too, had thought he saw fish while he had listened to Faber and had seen in his mind a kind sky over a calm estuary. He thought of going to the priest and questioning him. Wasn't the fish used as a symbol for Christ himself? He thought there must be some meaning to this dream or image that they both had, but the bank was steep, and the first need was to dig down far enough for water. He turned back to the others, who were scooping with their hands. Let the priest sleep now. There would be time to ask him later.

A little water had begun to seep into the hole Simon was making when a shout from Gyll and Magnus sent everybody crowding to their sides. They had unearthed, from the moist sand deep below a stone, the torpid bodies of half a dozen crayfishlike creatures. They were no more than three or four inches long, and about the thickness of Gyll's little finger, but they moved their claws lethargically when they were handled. Clearly they were alive, and fit to eat. The others began digging in the same area, and within an hour they had half a blanketful of the creatures, and enough water left over to boil them in after they had all drunk. The cooked fish proved to be very sweet and tender. Even those who could scarcely chew because of the swelling of their gums managed to make a meal of them, breaking them from their shells and then sucking the empty cases to get the last drop of goodness from them. It was the first full meal they had had since de Baude had reimposed rationing two days before they set out from the huts on the second part of their journey. Twice they had sighted small herds of wild pigs, but their low diet seemed to have slowed the hunters, and they'd exhausted themselves without being able to corner and kill a pig. Magnus and Gyll had got one among bushes growing against a wall of rock, but just as Gyll had raised his lance to pin it, the beast had broken away, gashing the muscles of Magnus's lower leg and leaving him with a wound that made walking difficult for him, and hunting impossible.

The discovery of the little shellfish seemed like a miracle, and a miracle that would recur again and again, for they had dug in only a small area of a river that, for all they knew, might go on forever. They settled happily to sleep, confident of a bright tomorrow.

But the crayfish, or the water they had drunk so greedily, had disagreed with them, and the night was full of windy moaning and the painful loosening of their tortured bowels.

They didn't move the next day except, from time to time, to change their position in order to avoid the sun. They dug again at midday and in the evening for water, and ate a few of the green things Eleanor chose for them, but they vomited up the green stuff and the water. They spent most of the day lying quietly, watching the moving orange patterns the stone-reflected sun made, even in shadow, on the inside of their closed and swollen lids. There was very little talk, except for the repeated suggestion that the only proper course for them was to return to the place of the abandoned huts. Simon de Baude listened to the arguments, but took no part in them. The more he thought of it the more uncertain he felt about the possibility of finding the place again.

On the next morning there was no talk of going back. They dug again for water to take with them, and drank sparingly and refilled the leather buckets before they set out, still going towards the north. Simon de Baude called the first halt when they had covered little more than three miles. Already the priest was stumbling and had two or three times fallen to his knees. And Magnus, with the festering wound in the calf of his leg, was moving nearly as slowly as the priest. An angry argument broke out over the question of water. They were used to drinking a little at each halt, but since they could not be sure of finding more water before night, de Baude ruled that no one should drink so early in the day.

"We need water and we've got water," Magnus said.

"We can't walk in this sun without," Joice said.

"The women need it, and the priest needs it."

"And we've got it," Godwin said, raising the bucket.

De Baude thought it was true that the priest needed water, and he would have liked to offer Eleanor the comfort of a half-cup. But unless they were lucky, their need would be far greater by the afternoon. "Each one can dip a forefinger twice into the bucket, and suck the water off it to moisten their mouth," he said.

"You suck your fucking finger," Godwin said. "I'm going to drink," and he raised the bucket and took two good mouthfuls. The others watched in silence, aware that if they tried to stop him the rest of the water might be spilt. He wiped the back of his hand across his mouth, and grinned guiltily. Simon stepped forward and took the bucket from him. "Everyone may dip a finger twice," he said.

"Where's the fairness in that, when he's had two swallows?" Edwin said resentfully.

"Dip your finger only once then, to make up," Simon said, holding the bucket firmly. He would have to carry it himself, or give it to Faber. He would have to remember to watch it throughout the day.

He found a stick with a fork in it at waist height, reshaped it carefully with a knife during their rest period and bound the fork with a strip torn from one of the blankets. The others watched him listlessly while he worked, thinking he was making it for himself, but when he ordered the party to start walking again, and took the stick and gave it to Magnus, the soldier's smile of gratitude and surprise warmed his heart. They are good enough people, he thought. God had put them in his care, and with God's help he would bring them home.

The plain seemed to stretch before them, straw-coloured and streamless, to the end of the world. They saw no birds overhead. Once, in midafternoon, a rabbit broke from underneath their feet to streak away. Magnus, who was closest, flung his crutch after it and cursed it, but it was gone before the others could give useful chase. An hour later de Baude halted the lagging party. They protested against the shadelessness of the spot, but he insisted that the main party must stay there. Ahead he had seen a fold in the plain too small to be called a hill, but the top of it was wigged with a thatch of brushwood and small trees. While the others rested he went forward with Gyll and the twins and Geoffrey and the Monkey, carrying their weapons and the nets and snares they had made from reeds and grass. If there was any game in those poor brushes, they would have a better chance to snare it without Faber and the priest and the women crashing about.

While they waited Eleanor moistened the priest's cracked lips with a little water, and gave a mouthful of the precious stuff to Magnus, who was burning now with a high fever. Suddenly a hoopoe alighted on the ground a few feet away from them, raising and lowering his brilliant crest as he watched them. Stealthily hands moved out for stones, but as Clodagh let fly with the first of them the bird rose, squawking, and climbed and sideslipped harmlessly away. "I could have eaten his feathers, and enjoyed them," Clodagh said sadly.

"Anything. Anything in the world my teeth would cut. The liver of a Turk," Godda said.

It was almost night before the men came back. What they brought was pretty poor fare—four small birds, a dozen fat sluglike creatures they had found in the lower leaves of a fern, two handfuls of the new fronds of the fern—but comforting to stomachs that had been so painfully emptied out. They cut all this into small pieces and stewed it for a little while, till it was well warmed through. It didn't fill them, but it made sleep possible.

They drank a little water before they set out in the morning. The priest seemed stronger and prayed aloud for them all—a thing he had neglected to do recently. Magnus was no better. He burned with fever and every movement of his leg made him grimace with pain. He lashed out with his stick at the Monkey when the boy came too close, jostling him; and the Monkey, who normally spent his days close to Magnus, removed himself to safety on the other side of the party, close to Gyll and the twins.

Again Simon de Baude stopped the walk early, and sent the hunting party forward into areas that had not been disturbed. Again they came back with the last of the light, and this time with only enough food for two good mouthfuls each. Godda prepared it and divided it under Eleanor's supervision, and when she had put each person's share of the solid part of the food out onto a ring of stones she suddenly let out a shriek and began to cross herself repeatedly with a flying hand.

"What have you seen?" Eleanor said sharply.

"The number, the number," Godda said. "The number. One is doomed. One has to die."

"Why?" Clodagh said, bending to peer at the food, expecting some augury to present itself in the birds' innards.

"The Creature himself sat down to dinner with twelve, and the next day they had Him on the Cross," Godda said. She was still crossing herself with an agitated hand. The others looked about them, counted, looked at the portions of food, crossed themselves. It was the first time most of them had made the count that ended at the unlucky number thirteen.

"We have been thirteen since the day of the wreck," Eleanor said. "There's no point in making a song about it now."

"One's doomed, one's doomed," Godda said, looking around. Her gaze fixed first on the worn priest, then on the fevered soldier. Sir Nicholas and Magnus were the most likely, she thought. One of them would go. "When one is dead, the rest of us will be safe," she said. "When Jesus was dead, the rest from the supper were safe."

"Except for Master Judas," Joice said. "Didn't he go raving out and stretch his neck in a rope?"

"Two have to die," Godda said, speaking more calmly. "When two have died, the rest of us will be safe."

"You do wrong to talk like that," the priest said, speaking with his old authority. "It was ordained from the beginning of the world that Christ should die as our saviour, taking all our sins away. Do you think it would have made any difference if twenty-six had sat down with Him to eat, or even fifty-two, or a hundred people?"

"It would make a sad difference if there were twenty-six or a hundred here," de Baude said, and reached forward to take one of the portions of food. The others crossed themselves hastily and reached forward to take their share. Nobody wanted to be left with the last serving.

Those days became the pattern of the days that followed. They walked more and more slowly, rested more often, were harder to get started when de Baude, against all his own inclinations, decreed that walking was to begin again. There were times when it seemed to him that he walked for an hour at a time without being conscious, only to jerk fully awake to check their direction against the moving sun. The food they were getting, he thought, was barely enough to keep them alive, and if a day should come when they got nothing, half the party might well be unable to move on the next morning. Godda had become an extra problem, walking along in a muttering grumble all the time and, if she was not watched, sometimes stumbling off at an angle to the party, so that somebody had to be sent after her to bring her back.

At night the party no longer split into two groups, nor did Clodagh and Gyll separate themselves a little from the others. To choose company and move around the circle to get close to it seemed too heavy a demand on their strength, and except for Eleanor, who stationed herself always where she could be of use to the priest if he needed her, everyone else ate what there was to eat where they found themselves, and slept in the same place. The first night that Clodagh found Gyll wasn't beside her she felt bereft, and thought of moving, but slept before she could make up her mind to the effort. When she woke she found that Gyll had sought her out, and was sleeping with his head on the calf of her leg. But the next night they found themselves separated again, and both were too exhausted to remedy it, so that though they walked side by side during the day, they now often spent their nights apart. The twins still guarded Joice jealously between them, though neither now had any craving for their possession. The Monkey, always the last to settle, slept alongside Edwin or Godwin now, since Magnus's new temper frightened him.

The weakness of the party now became Simon de Baude's chief concern. He found himself, against his own heart and conscience, remembering Godda's words "two must die" and thinking how much even the death of two would improve the rations of those who remained. He began for the first time to consider seriously that those who hunted should have more of the food than those who were hunted for. There seemed to him to be good logic behind this—unless a little more food could be found for those who brought food he thought that the time must be close, perhaps no more than two or three days away, when weakness made it impossible for them to hunt any more. Godda's two sons, who had been the strongest and the most tireless of the party, were now so weakened by hunger that it was sometimes difficult for him to persuade them to go out. And Gyll and Geoffrey and he himself—the only others of the party who were hunters—were now incapable of running more than a few yards without rest, and even after rest walked slowly, stumbling as they went. He was troubled by visions while he hunted. The visions were pleasant enough, but it was hard to look beyond them, watching the grass for any small movement that might betray the presence of some edible thing. His visions were always concerned with chivalry, with his brother knights, brave banners, galloping horses. It was hard to come back from them to the contemplation of his ragged people, and the thought of which of them should be allowed to die in order to feed the others.

Visions came often to Clodagh, too, as she walked, narrowing her sore eyes to shield them from the glare of the sun and the monotony of the plain. She would see the bright plaits of hair of a roomful of girls bent over their spinning, great mounds of cheese cool under muslin in her mother's dairies, her little cat, Blanchette, who would mother anything from an orphan pup to a clutch of yellow ducklings. "I had a cat, once, that mothered a fox cub," she said to whoever was walking beside her, and opened her eyes fully to see Joice regarding her strangely. On another day Robert Apelfourde walked beside her over the plain throughout a long afternoon, and though he didn't speak he looked at her with deep affection, and she knew that he was promising her water at the end of the day.

On the fifth day after they had left the stone river— or maybe it was the sixth or seventh day, nobody could be sure that the priest had marked the tally stick correctly—they came under sparse grey trees again, found a small stream of water and saw signs that wild pigs had been there recently. There was mast—a little of it—lying on the ground, hardened pig droppings and the little excavations they had made with their snouts, searching for truffles. "A hog or two would put new life into us," Simon de Baude said, and his bones ached with the thought of the effort necessary to catch and kill a pig. Obviously the hogs had now left the place, and they would have to find them again before they could hunt. In the meantime they dug under the trees in places that the pigs had left undisturbed, and found a few handfuls of the distasteful white truffles they had been eating.

They moved only a short distance the next day, pushing painfully over the dry ground to where the threadbare trees grew a little more thickly. By noon they had come to a water seepage where some rocks held back a slide of earth from a small slope, and again they found signs that pigs had been digging underneath the trees. Simon decided that the party should walk no further that day, giving the hunters a full six hours of light when the pigs might be torpid with afternoon sun. He and Gyll and Geoffrey went off to the northeast of their camping place, while the twins and the Monkey took a northwest line. Whichever party first sighted the pigs was to send a runner to summon the others. In their weakened state, they would need all hands to corner and kill successfully. The others rested, dug for truffles, rested again. There was little vegetable food to be found. The only plants growing under the trees were spiny things even Eleanor couldn't recommend to their sad stomachs.

The afternoon light faded. They had collected enough water from the seepage for their needs that night and in the morning; they had found enough of the truffles to give each of the party a handful for their night meal. They hoped for meat to go with them, but they had heard no sounds from the hunters, no comforting crashing through bushes nor shouted warnings. Suddenly they heard a screaming sound, distant at first, but coming steadily closer. "Hide," Eleanor said, recognizing the sound of wheels, and afraid of the people who might accompany them. She looked quickly around, but there was no close hiding place, and Magnus and the priest could not be moved quickly. Godda and Joice had bolted, without concern for the others, to concealment on the far side of the clearing. There they clutched each other, expecting a panther to break into their sight, or a manticore with its human victim screaming from between its triple row of teeth.

The bushes parted thirty yards away. The twin brothers, Edwin and Godwin, came into sight. The fearful sound went on advancing behind them. The bushes opened again, and a cart came hurtling through, pushed by the Monkey. He speeded up as he came to open ground, broke into a jog trot and pushed the contrivance to where Clodagh and Eleanor and Faber stood. It was a square box made of thick timber, mounted on a wooden axle and solid wooden wheels, with shafts wide enough to take an ox between them. Joice and Godda came cautiously back and the four women crowded around the twins and the cart asking questions about where they had found it, what other signs of human beings they had seen, what horses, what fields, what wells or stores of food?

They had found the cart, Godwin said, standing alone and abandoned under a tree. There were no markings on the ground close to it—no sign of human feet, nor hooves nor claws.

"It didn't build itself, or pull itself," Joice said, and they all agreed that its discovery proved they were close to human habitation—until Faber pointed out that the grain of the wood was weathered and opened up, like wood that had stood uncovered through long hot summers and long winter rains. The disappointment made Godda turn angrily on her sons. "We can't eat that, you fools," she said. "What else did you find?" They pointed to two rabbits bleeding from clubbed heads on the floor of the cart. Godda picked up the corpses and made off, to begin skinning them. Eleanor took the shafts from the Monkey, who was still holding them, and pushed the cart backwards and forwards a couple of times. It screamed again, as soon as it was moved. "It's not too heavy," she said. "We can push Magnus in it, and Father Nicholas, by turns."

"And we can load the weapons on it, and the water buckets, if there's someone in the cart to steady them," Clodagh said. "But it will frighten all the game away for seven miles."

"And the evil spirits," Eleanor said with a smile, "for they're said to hate the sound of cartwheels almost as much as they hate the sound of church bells."

Their meal was even smaller that night than on the previous night, for de Baude and Geoffrey and Gyll had brought nothing back except some honeycomb. But the signs, they thought, were cheering, since the finding of both cart and honeycomb suggested that people had been close, and were perhaps still not very far off. They had had no honey since they left the hut place. Bees were known to be born out of the bodies of dead cows, so clearly people had been here with livestock not long ago. They put Father Nicholas and Magnus under the cart for the night, though the priest would have preferred to be under the stars and further away from the stink of the soldier's wound. The rest of them clustered close to the cart—it gave them a center, almost like having a roof again.

By morning Simon de Baude had decided to split the party during the days as well. The cart could be made to work for them. Pushed steadily forward at a slow pace, it would tend to drive any game away to the sides where, with luck, it would fall to the two hunting parties. He sent Godwin and Edwin and the Monkey off to the left of the cart's path again, and himself led Gyll and Geoffrey half a mile off to the right. In this way the hunters would have all the hours of light in which to hunt, and there would be no fear of their losing the way back, since the cart made a beacon of sound by which they could steer.

But the plan didn't work as well as he hoped. The hunters were so weakened now by hunger and sickness that their eyes wouldn't focus quickly enough on small movements. The spiky bushes and the starved trees seemed empty of life, and the food they found during the day would have made a fair meal for one hungry man. The women, too, had found the day hard almost beyond their endurance. The cart, light enough in itself, became almost too much for their weakened muscles with Magnus's fevered body aboard, and with such dry and stony ground to be covered. They took short turns at it, in pairs, Eleanor and Clodagh pulling it while Godda and Joice walked free, then lending a hand to the stumbling priest while Godda and Joice took their turn at the shafts. They had decided against carrying the water in the cart because it was too precious to be risked in an accidental overturning. Faber carried the two partly filled leather buckets, walking carefully behind the party on the safe track the cart had already tried.

But on the next morning there was no real possibility of abandoning the plan or the cart. Magnus was sleeping heavily there, or had lost consciousness, and unless they deserted him along with the cart they had no option but to push it ahead of them. It was later than usual in the morning before they started out. They were now so weak that their will to move was gone, and although Simon de Baude could muster enough determination to issue orders, he couldn't hold to it for very long at a time, and his bullying would peter out against their apathy. "If we don't get food today, I don't think we can go on tomorrow," Eleanor said. It was the first time she had taken a hopeless tone.

"We will get food. Today we will get food," Simon de Baude said. He managed to persuade Gyll and his brother, Geoffrey, to their feet and led them forward and to the left of the line he had pointed out to the cart-pullers. He looked back just as his little group were about to disappear into the bushes. Godwin and Edwin had gathered their weapons, and seemed about to set out. The Monkey was a pace or two ahead of them, and looking back, waiting for them. He had lost flesh and the spring from his walk in the last week, but he seemed to have better reserves of strength than the others.

The day was a hard one for Faber and the priest and the women with the cart. It became a long agony of walking and of pushing. They forgot the hunters, stopped listening for them, forgot to wonder whether they were having any success. Magnus lay motionless in the cart, with a flushed face. His breathing scarcely seemed to move his chest wall. Once or twice they looked at him hopefully, thinking he might be dead, but clearly he lived on in some painful place of his own. Several times they had to stop at a shout from Faber, because the priest or Godda had wandered off at an angle into the bushes; and once, when Eleanor had gone off to bring the priest back, Clodagh had to go after her to stop them both because Eleanor had fallen in behind the priest and was following him into the distance. When the shadows began to lengthen, Godda and Joice put down their shafts and sat on the ground. Everyone stopped, as though they had reached agreement without speaking. Faber took a small horn cup from his belt and dipped it and drank and then passed it in turn to all the others. Normally they didn't drink until all the people were there. Now it no longer seemed to them to matter. Half an hour passed, and an hour, while they sat slumped about the cartwheels. Then a sound disturbed them, and they looked up. Edwin and Godwin were standing close to them, with a heavy carrying blanket slung between them. "Meat," Edwin said. "We killed. We killed a pig." The twins dropped the blanket and opened it. There were two roughly butchered haunches there that would feed the party admirably that night. Godda reached a hungry hand towards them, and then remembered. "Fire," she said. They had started no fire, had gathered no wood to make one.

Gyll and de Baude and Geoffrey came back to the

smell of meat cooking, and to the sound of voices. Their camp had been a silent place during the last days, but now they were gripped by hope and a quick excitement that made it natural for them to talk again while they waited. Eleanor had taken a little of the meat and crushed it with a stone and set it over the fire to make a broth for Magnus. The smell of it, hėld beneath his nose, roused him as their words had been unable to rouse him throughout the long day. He opened his eyes and looked about him, and took a few drops at a time when it was held to his mouth.

It seemed to the others that it took an interminable time for Godda to prepare the meat for them. De Baude had decreed that only one of the haunches should be used, and had taken the other and put it, for safety, beside Magnus in the cart. "There's more meat," the brothers argued. "We couldn't carry it all. We can go back for it."

"Then go back for it tomorrow," Simon said. "We eat one piece tonight. Any more would be lost, because it would make us sick."

While the meat cooked, Clodagh had been walking restlessly on the outskirts of the group—walking a few paces, stopping, turning to stare off into the bushes, walking again. As the meat was lifted from the fire she rushed back into the group. *"No,"* she said in a high voice. "Don't touch it. Don't touch it." They stared at her with dull eyes. "Rest," Eleanor said, reaching up to pull at her arm. "You'll feel better soon, when you've eaten."

"The Monkey," she said, staring at the twins, and her voice rose in a howl of mingled hunger and terror. "What have you done with the Monkey?"

Edwin and Godwin looked at each other. They looked

at the others. "Where is the Monkey?" Godwin said. In the excitement of finding that there was food at last, none of the others had noticed that he was absent.

"Well?" de Baude said, watching the brothers.

"We thought he was with you," Edwin said.

"Not with us," de Baude said. "He went with your party."

"But we sent him," Godwin said. "Like arranged. When we sighted the pigs."

There was a long silence. "He didn't find us," de Baude said. "And you didn't wait."

"No," Godwin said. "Because this . . . this one . . . we didn't wait because this one got separated. He came at us, asking to be killed."

De Baude left the group and went into the bushes, and in a moment they heard him begin to call "Mon-key, Mon-key, Mon-key." Edwin and Gyll got up too, and followed de Baude, and soon their three voices were calling in unison. After a time Faber and Eleanor each took a shaft of the cart where Magnus slept and began to push it backwards and forwards, and in the failing light the place was eerie with the men's calls and the scream of the wooden wheels.

They kept it up for ten minutes or more, and then de Baude led the others back to the fire where the meat had been set to cool on a flat stone. "He'll be coming now," de Baude said. "He will have heard us," and the others nodded agreement.

Clodagh stood over them, shaken with sobs, an accusing finger pointing at the meat. "It's not pig. It doesn't look like pig," she said. "It looks like—" and found it impossible to say what it looked like to her. "It looks like—it looks like—if it was pig meat, there'd be fat on it."

"Not in this country," Faber said. "Not any more than there's any fat on us." He coughed uneasily, finding his words had made his own gorge rise.

"It wasn't a pig, exactly," Godwin said. The others stared at him apprehensively, waiting for him to go on.

"Well?" de Baude said, when he didn't speak. Godwin looked for help to his brother, but none was forthcoming. "One of those foreign creatures, as the captain has seen and sworn to, many a time." The people looked at the cooked meat, and crossed themselves. They looked back at Godwin, wanting and dreading further information. "It had a light-coloured hide."

"Silvery," Edwin said.

"And one great horn, and arms that grew from its shoulders, though it had the proper number of legs."

"What sort of a beast was that?" Edwin said, questioning Faber, the expert.

The captain cleared his throat. "I don't know," he said. "It could have been any of many things."

"And it could have been something quite ordinary," Eleanor said. "I myself have seen many odd things in the last week while I was walking and fasting. The eyes of these two may have played them tricks."

"All things live by eating each other," the priest said. "It is the law of God. All flesh is grass, and all creatures are subject to man."

"Do you swear that what you have said to us is the truth?" said Simon de Baude, questioning Godwin and Edwin.

"Swear," they both said together.

De Baude took his knife and reached forward, and began to divide the meat. Clodagh found herself gagging with fright. "Don't," she said. "Don't begin to eat till the Monkey comes." De Baude went on with the equal distribution.

"Don't touch it, don't touch it, I beg and pray you not to touch it," she said, clawing at Gyll and clutching at his arms. He pushed her aside and put out a hand to take his share of the food. She ran off then, away from the fire and into the gloomy bushes, and for a long while she stood there, out of their sight, repeatedly calling "Monkey, Monkey" into the waning light. After a time Eleanor joined her, bringing her a double handful of the white truffles that nobody wanted now. "It's all right, it's all right," Eleanor said, encircling the girl's shoulders and rocking her against her own body. "Pray, pray. It will be all right tomorrow. It's not only you. We are all a little unhinged by what we have suffered."

Clodagh didn't answer her, and she wouldn't go back with her to the fire when Eleanor urged it. She ate the truffles, and she stayed for a long time by herself in the bushes, but she didn't call for the Monkey any more. When there was no longer any sound from the group and no light showed from the fire, she went back and stood looking down on them in the dim light of the stars. They were sleeping now. She found Gyll in the circle, and settled on the ground close beside him. But she was careful that she didn't touch his body.

In the morning everyone's waking thought was of the Monkey. He had not come back during the night. Simon de Baude changed his mind several times about whether the party should move. His first feeling was that they should go on. Food would have strengthened them a little and made it possible to hunt more effectively and the Monkey, if he was still walking, must be walking somewhere ahead of them on the route they would take. In any case they had meat for the next night, and if there was more meatless country ahead of them, it seemed wise to press on while they had strength to do so. Magnus's fever seemed to have died a little. His breathing had improved, and though the jolting of the cart caused him great pain whenever it was moved, his colour had improved and he seemed further from death than he had on the previous day. But just as de Baude was about to announce his decision, the Lady Eleanor began to argue for a day of rest where they were. "People who are lost," she said, "commonly walk in circles. It may be almost night before the boy finds his way back to us. We have food. We need rest. Father Nicholas is not yet strong enough to go on." In the end de Baude allowed Eleanor to make the decision. The party would rest during the morning. In the afternoon he and Gyll and Geoffrey would hunt again, while the twin brothers returned where they made their kill to bring back any of the meat that was left. They expected to find it. The twins said they had covered it with boughs and bushes against birds, and in all the weeks of walking they had seen no sign of wolves, or of any other meat-eating creatures. Three of them moved Magnus from the cart, lifting him carefully into a patch of shade where he could sleep more comfortably and where it was possible for someone to lie beside him, keeping the flies from his wound. Eleanor had made a concoction of crushed leaves steeped in water, and a little of this, poured into the wound, seemed to give him relief. "When you find it, bring back one of its tusks," she told the brothers repeatedly. "It could be the same beast and to smear its tusk with this stuff might still heal Magnus, as balm smeared on a dagger will heal the wound it has made."

The fact that they had eaten well the night before and that they weren't exhausting themselves by walking made their pangs of hunger far greater than they were used to suffering in the middle of the day. In the end de Baude agreed that the second haunch of meat should be cooked and a small piece eaten by each member of the party before the hunters set out. The rest was to be kept for the night meal, in case their hunting should be unsuccessful. The smell of the roasting meat reawakened Clodagh's black terrors, and she ran away again, going deep into the bushes where she was hidden from the sight of the camping place. She lay on the ground there, underneath a bush, and as distance and silence calmed her fears a little it seemed to her a good plan not to rejoin the party when it moved on. Somehow she would have to keep walking by herself, find water and a handful or two of some sort of food each day. She didn't mean to separate herself entirely from the party. She would follow them, using the sound of the shrieking cart to keep her in touch with them, watching them from a distance to see where they found damp spots and water seepages. She opened her eyes at the sound of movement in the bushes some distance away from her and saw that, on the thick bark at the base of the bush she was sheltering under, there were three little blobs of pinkish spongy pulp. She broke a piece off and sniffed at it, and it smelled deliciously of the earth, and of mushrooms. She nibbled at it delicately with her eye-teeth, and the good earthy taste of it matched its smell. Gyll had come into sight now, and he was calling her, but she had no wish to answer him or to speak to him, unless he found her by his own efforts. She ate the rest of the piece of fungus she had picked and, since she would now have no food except what she found for herself, she moved her body to shield the stem of the bush and the other two pieces of fungus from his sight. She lay with her eyes closed, hoping he would go away. Her mouth now felt as dry as the inside of a manger, but a great and delectable heat spread through her body, raying itself out to the very extremities of her hands and feet. She was aware that Gyll had found her, and that he had dropped to his knees beside the bush where she lay. She knew that he was speaking to her, but though she could feel the grasp of his hand on her leg, she couldn't distinguish his words. "Promise and swear to me that you won't eat any of that meat," she said without opening her eyes.

She made a particular effort to listen to his answer, and she thought she heard him say "I promise and swear."

"Because it's the poor Monkey they're eating," she said, and burst into soft laughter.

It seemed to Gyll that she was ill, that she was perhaps dying, and that he should fetch Eleanor at once, and the priest. But when he moved she clutched him quickly, as though she had seen his movement without opening her eyes. "Take this," she said, without giving him anything. "It makes God available. Give it to Magnus, to heal him."

"Give him *what?*" Gyll said, standing over her, seizing her shoulders. She laughed again. "I can see right through your skin and into your heart," she said. "It's green, palest green, like a starling's egg." She put a hand beside her, felt blindly for the stem of the bush, broke off a second small piece of the spongy fungus. "For Magnus," she said, giving it to Gyll. "So he can see to the inside of his bones."

When Gyll came back to her, bringing Eleanor with

him, she was sleeping deeply, and smiling and murmuring in her sleep. They took the last piece of fungus from the bark behind her, and they searched carefully among the bushes for many yards around, finding about twenty more little pieces of the pinkish stuff which Eleanor gathered carefully in her belt satchel. "Will you give it to Magnus?" Gyll asked. Eleanor watched Clodagh for a little while before she answered. "If she wakes, and is well," she said. "I'll watch her while you're hunting." He told Eleanor what the girl had said about the meat and the Monkey. "She is a little mad," Eleanor said, "but she'll recover, if she's fed. Any food that you find this afternoon is to go first to her."

It was midafternoon before Clodagh woke. Godda was crouched over her, holding her chin with one hand, trying to force something into her mouth with the other. Clodagh struggled violently, guessing what it was, knocking the piece of meat out of Godda's hand.

"Everyone has to eat," Godda said, searching for it. "Everyone. It's not right that one should stand back, and not eat." She found the meat again, tried again to pry open Clodagh's jaws and force it into her mouth. "Eat. Eat. Everyone has to eat," she said doggedly.

Clodagh sprang away from her, knocking her to the ground. Her mouth was still dry, but the colours and the beautiful warmth had gone, and her head ached in the clear light of the afternoon sun. "Slut, mother of monsters," she said. "Leave me alone. Keep away from me. Don't come within four paces, or I'll strike you dead where you stand." She left Godda grovelling on the ground and went off further into the bushes. But she stopped after she'd gone a few yards and remained motionless, waiting for the woman to go. She didn't want to go too far, didn't want to lose the way back to the others. And besides, she wanted to go back to her bush and pick the last piece of fungus which she clearly remembered having seen there before she slept. When Godda had gone she went back to the bush, and she also searched a wide area around it on every side, but the comforting stuff seemed to have disappeared.

Simon de Baude's party had done better than on previous days, bringing back half a dozen birds and two thick-fleshed lizards they'd found sleeping in the sun. Godwin and Edwin had brought nothing. The other party had seen a bird of prey hovering on ragged sails over the trees in the direction in which the twins had gone, and had thought that it must mark the place of their kill. But they came back empty-handed. At first they had been unable to find the place, Godwin explained. Then they had found it at last, but *something* had been there before them. The rest of the carcass had gone, and the dust where it had been lying hidden under bushes had been swept bare and smooth. "Lions commonly do that," Faber said, "using their tails." It was noticed by some of them that Godwin had a new habit. He was pulling at the lobe of his left ear with his fingers.

No one questioned the fact that Gyll had reserved one whole bird of their catch to be given to Clodagh. "On a clean fire," she said when he had plucked it and was preparing to cook it. He took a coal from the common fire and bent to blow it into a blaze over some twigs, and when the bird was cooked she ate all of it, and her headache receded a little. For the rest of the party there were the five other birds, the lizards and the meat that had been left from the previous night. This was eaten with the other stuff without attention by the priest and Faber, sparingly by de Baude and not at all by Eleanor and Gyll, at least while Clodagh watched them.

There had been very little talk about the Monkey except for the report, from each party, that they had seen no trace of him while they were out. It was agreed that they should move on again, the next morning. After they had eaten, the priest prayed for a long time for the Monkey, calling him Jonae Insciens—Unknowing Jonah—and begging God's merciful protection of him until he could be restored to them, or to his own people. Those who had no Latin thought that he prayed for the Monkey's soul, and made what pious funeral responses they could think of.

From behind them, as the priest finished his prayers, came a loud "Amen" from Magnus. It was the first time he had spoken strongly for several days. Then, in a gay voice, he said, "I can see the way out. It's clear. Through pied meadows." Joice and Geoffrey de Baude started up to go to him, but Eleanor waved them back. "Leave him," she said. "I have given him something that will stop his pain."

"What?" Faber asked, since his own waking hours seemed to hold nothing else.

"A plant," Eleanor said. She looked at Clodagh. "It is harmless, seemingly," she said.

"Give it back to me," Clodagh said. "I found it."

"It should be kept for those who need it."

"How much is there? Show me," Clodagh said. Eleanor took half a dozen pieces of the fungus from her wallet, and laid them on a flat stone in front of her. Clodagh broke half a piece, and then broke the piece again and put one fragment in her mouth, chewing it slowly while she watched the fire. The dryness in her mouth and the sweet feeling of warmth began almost as soon as she swallowed it. She got up and went around to her place beside Gyll again. She sat down on the ground and pulled him suddenly, so that he fell across her, with his head in her lap. The others watched them, more than a little shocked. They were in no doubt about what Clodagh and Gyll did together under cover of darkness, but so open a show embarrassed them. Clodagh put the second piece of fungus into her mouth, pressed her mouth over Gyll's in a long kiss, and forced the morsel with her tongue on to his. "Eat," she said. "Join me in Avalon."

"And peacocks," Magnus's voice said from behind them. "Spit-roasted peacocks."

Clodagh closed her eyes. She could no longer see the others, but Gyll's face came to her clearly through her closed lids, calm and quiet and with all the hungry strain washed out of it. She began to sing to him, choosing the Breton song about Loiza that had been the rage in her mother's house for a month or more before she left for the *Grace Dieu.* "I change myself into a black bitch, or a raven, when I wish it, or into a will o' the wisp, or a dragon," she sang. "I know a song which splits the skies asunder, and makes the great sea tremble, and the earth quake." Gyll didn't know the words of it, but very soon he began to hum it, following a little behind her, with a dreamlike drag. Absently, as she listened, Eleanor broke off a small piece of the fungus and passed it to the priest, who looked at it for an instant without interest and passed it on to Simon de Baude. Sir Simon held it in his hand until he had seen Eleanor break off a second small piece and swallow it. He chewed and swallowed his own piece and let himself down to lie, spreadeagled, like a man surrendering to the *coup de grace.* Very soon the stone in front of Eleanor was empty. Everyone had taken a morsel of the fungus. Everyone except the priest, who was praying. No one spoke or moved. They lay still, warmed, and absorbed by the sound of Clodagh singing over and over again the lines about Loiza's illicit love for her clerk.

They set out on their walk soon after dawn the next morning. Most of them had headaches, and the noise of the cart was nearly intolerable to them. Magnus seemed better. The wound in his leg had putrefied horribly, but the pain seemed to have lessened, and he was conscious and quiet. "Is there any more of the mushroom?" Clodagh said, contrite at having eaten it when clearly it could help Magnus so much.

"I've a little piece left, if it's needed again," Eleanor said, tapping her wallet. She didn't intend to tell anyone how much of it she had, because she thought the time might come when they all needed it.

Again, in the evening, the hunting parties returned to the squealing cart almost empty-handed, but the women and Faber and the priest had been luckier. They had come on a patch of carob beans again, and had gathered enough to supply the party for a couple of days. Ground between stones, mixed to a paste with water and baked in the ashes of the campfire, it made a grey bread, saltless and savourless, but the hard crust and the soggy crumbs were a delicacy for the few who could still chew comfortably. The rest soaked the bread in their water rations. They prayed again for the Monkey before they slept, and for themselves. It seemed that something had turned God's glance on them once again. Perhaps it was the fact that now there were twelve.

Gradually, in the next few days, the country began

to soften and improve. Now it no longer stretched endlessly before and behind them in a flat circle that went
as far as the sky. Now they were climbing gently through
wooded slopes, and going down again into moderate
little valleys which, though they were dry, sometimes
had an inch or two of still water left in isolated pools in
their dried-up streams. On the second day they found
carob beans again. They collected a store of them and
put them in the cart with Magnus for future need. On
the third day the twins and Geoffrey snared four rabbits
just at dusk, and Gyll managed to tickle a trout from
a shallow pool. Its flesh, shredded and pounded into
water, proved to be something that Magnus's stomach
could tolerate. He was growing weaker. The foot of his
injured leg was now monstrously swollen, and the toes
discoloured. Each night Eleanor gave him a piece of the
mushroom so that he could sleep, and in the daytime,
when the constant shaking of the cart became more than
he could bear any longer in silence, she would put a few
shreds of it between his lips to ease him. The weight of
the cart with Magnus lying in it was now too much for
the weakened women to pull throughout the day's
march. Once, on an incline, when Eleanor had fallen,
it had run backwards down the slope, pulling Clodagh
with it, until it was stopped by a jolting crash into a
tree. Now that they had a reserve ration of St. John's
Bread stored in the cart, Simon no longer sent the hunters forward during the day's march. They hunted during the late hours of the afternoon, and pulled the cart,
in pairs, while the party walked. Even the younger men
were now so much weakened that the two at the shafts
needed help whenever they were on rising ground. But
with the cart's movement shared by a greater number,
they were walking a good deal further every day, and

their distance was limited only by the priest's weakness. He had become strangely silent, walking doggedly in whichever direction he faced as though he walked in some other place and in other company. They had tried, with the extra hands available for pulling the cart, to lengthen their day's march a little by putting the priest into the cart with Magnus, but his weight made the work almost too heavy for their strength, and somebody was needed to walk beside all the time to restrain the priest, who stubbornly tried to climb out as the cart moved, and was in danger of falling.

But despite their weakness, there had been a lifting of the spirits of most of them. They believed now that they would reach somewhere in the end, that they would be saved, that some of the evil that had been hanging over them had removed itself in search of other occupation. They had taken to more assiduous prayer at nightfall, and again before they moved off into each new day, and it seemed that the sum of good things granted to them during that day—an extra rabbit, a couple of birds, a handful or two of green stuff that was not unpalatable and that didn't scour their insides—was directly related to the length and fervency of their morning prayers. "If we clear ourselves of *every* sin," Godda said, "Milady will argue God into taking us back." She had become a zealous guardian of their righteousness, reproving all weakness, blasphemy and despair.

The fact that Clodagh and Gyll spent all their waking hours side by side, except for the times when Gyll was absent to hunt, nagged constantly at Godda. In turn she nagged constantly at Gyll to separate himself from the girl. Godda's twin sons took no notice of Joice during daylight hours. Their forbearance satisfied their mother's new orthodoxy, since even God, she thought, couldn't be absolutely certain what happened after dark. But the open flaunting of Gyll's and Clodagh's fondness seemed to Godda to endanger all the rest of the party. She appealed to the priest to stop it. "They are filthy," she said. "God will punish them."

"If that is certain, why should I interfere?" Father Nicholas said, and went back to his own thoughts.

"The Father says you are damned, and God will punish you," Godda reported to Gyll. Gyll thought it very possible, but the remission of punishment he would gain by giving up now something that would be taken from him in a few days' time seemed scarcely to balance the pain he would have to inflict on Clodagh. She depended on him now. She wasn't able to bring herself to speak, except for a monosyllabic answer when it was really necessary, to any of the other members of the party. She could have talked to the priest and would have liked to, but he had no strength left for any problems but his own. She was no longer certain whether what she feared had happened, or whether her mind had been disordered even before she found the fungus. Perhaps the Monkey was not dead at all. She had a constant daydream in which the party toiled to the top of a hill and found there, spread out before them, a fair town of houses and churches and orchards and water meadows studded with calves and lambs, and the first person who ran out to welcome them was the Monkey, grinning and pulling at his ear, and resplendent in new clothes and a new understanding of the English tongue. But, on the other hand, if the Monkey was dead, what was the penalty for all these people? Death for those who took life; the lopping off of hands and ears for those who knowingly ate human flesh; but what earthly penalty for those who ate unknowingly? And what heavenly one?

And if the Monkey was indeed dead at the brothers' hands, which of the party could say that they had eaten unknowingly? The priest for certain, for there were few things now he knew except things from the past; Gyll perhaps, for he swore, to her repeated questionings, that he had eaten none of the suspect meat. But if he had eaten first, and now swore, didn't that suggest . . . she put the question away from her—it had become too hard a problem in philosophy. If there was blood guiltiness, then it belonged to the twin brothers, and to their evil old mother, perhaps, and perhaps to Captain Faber. Not to the others. Not to the priest, who was too uncertain, nor to Eleanor, who was too pure, nor to Sir Simon or his brother, Geoffrey, nor to Magnus, who was half in the next world. And not to Gyll, not to Gyll, not to Gyll. As the days passed, she put the whole worry of it further from her mind. She had been weak, near death from lack of food, and her mind had been disordered for a time. The whole evil dream had been put into her mind by some malign spirit, angry that she had found consoling pleasure in the midst of their hard times. It had been a phantasmagoria, hateful and frightening, but powerless against rest and food and good sense. The Monkey would be found again. She preferred Gyll's company to that of the others, until he was.

On the next day, late in the afternoon when they were about to stop walking, they came on a wheel track. It was faint and had been disused for a long time, dusted over with windblown sand and litter dropped from the surrounding trees. But where wheels had been, men had been as well. Without consultation they decided to keep walking, climbing the slow slope towards the crest of the hill. When they reached it the light was already fading, and there was nothing in the vista before them except more slopes, more trees, more distance into which the faint track quickly disappeared. They retreated a little from the crest, so that they would be sheltered from the night wind. Simon decreed that they should make their meal of little loaves made from carob flour and then sleep at once, so that they could start early and use the whole day's light for following the track as far as it led. While Gyll and Sir Simon, with Eleanor's help, lifted the partly conscious Magnus from his place in the cart, the other men quickly began gathering wood to make a fire. Suddenly there was a summoning shout from Geoffrey. Those who were still on their feet hurried back to the crest of the hill. The boy was a little way down the further slope, on his knees in front of a shallow niche cut, long years ago, into a rock face. He had found a calvary, a little wooden Christ no more than a foot high with a rough blank face and a crack in his side that a spider had patched neatly with a plaster of web. They went back for the priest, and brought him to it. He knelt in front of it, for a long time, weeping. He had grown desperate with the fear that he was the last of God's lieutenants on the earth, that he was condemned forever and forever to the sole responsibility for these people. The calvary reassured him, freed him. There were others at hand, they would come before long to the promised place, and he would be free to sink onto the hard ground, to give up, to surrender himself, to die. The others had expected that Father Nicholas would make some prayer there for the whole company, but he seemed absorbed in his own devotions. Gradually they drifted back to the campsite, and the empty cart. They felt happier than they had in many weeks. Not only were there people ahead of them, but they were Christian people. They began, for the first time, to see the end of their journey.

They followed the track throughout the next day. It became a little clearer and a little easier to follow as the day passed, but though they watched very carefully, they saw no other shrines, no signs that the track was used, or that people had been there recently. Mirages bothered some of them. They saw beckoning figures that dissolved as they approached, and little lakes with boating parties on them. They had been very short of water through the day, and again at night they had nothing to eat but carob bread, because it had seemed more important to them to press on along the track than to stop and hunt. Magnus needed none of the mushroom to make him sleep that night, because they hadn't been able to rouse him when they stopped. He swallowed the drops of water Eleanor put on his tongue, but he didn't open his eyes, or speak to her. It was hard now for anyone to stay beside him for long, because the stench of his wound had become overpowering. They left him in the cart for the night because it seemed almost beyond their strength to lift him. But they moved the cart a little way from their sleeping place, in case the vapours of his wound might prove to be poisonous.

At noon the next day, after a morning that seemed to have doubled its hours in order to let them be defeated by exhaustion, they came suddenly on the first people they had seen since the ship sank—two men and a woman who had stopped their work of stripping the bark from trees at the sound of the squealing approach of the wooden cart, and were now openmouthed at the sad and skeletal look of the people who surrounded it.

"We are English," Simon de Baude said. "Shipwrecked English." They stared at him without comprehension. The priest, shaken to life again by the nearness of delivery, repeated the words, speaking this time in

Latin. They touched their foreheads in respect for the tatters of his priest's gown, but clearly they understood him no better than they had understood Sir Simon. The woman fetched a wicker basket from under a tree and opened it and displayed bread and olive oil and a pound or so of cheese—a good-sized midday meal for three working people. The woman pushed it towards them, urging them on with encouraging gestures. They hung back at first, obeying their established rule of taking nothing until the food was fairly divided and the division carefully looked at by all. Eleanor took the loaf of bread and divided it carefully into eleven small portions. They watched anxiously as the woman took one up and dipped it into the wide-mouthed jar of oil. Then she passed it to Godda, urging her to eat. One by one the others dipped their bread too. The oil was headily flavoured with crushed garlic, and the oiled bread tasted to them like manna. While they ate the delicious bread, mumbling it slowly in their festered mouths, Eleanor divided the cheese into little portions, setting aside a few crumbs of it for Magnus. She mashed the crumbs into a thin paste with some of the olive oil, and when she went to give it to Magnus the three people followed her, craning to look at him, and exclaiming at his wound. Eleanor smeared the cheese gently over his dry and swollen lips, but he didn't open his mouth, and he seemed to have lost all consciousness.

The woman pulled at her arm, pointing continually along the track in the opposite direction from the one in which the party had come. The men pointed too. Clearly they were urging the party to get moving again. "We can't move yet," Simon de Baude said. "Not yet. Some are too weak. They must have an hour's rest before we move." But the men kept gesturing, and the woman put the empty basket in beside Magnus and lifted the shafts of the cart and Sir Simon shrugged—plainly there was no good way of making them understand.

The men took up their own tools, and gathered up the party's weapons, to carry them. All surrendered them willingly enough except Godwin, who stepped quickly back, keeping a firm hold on his sharpened lance. The woman moved quickly forward between the cart's shafts and soon, with a strength that shamed them, had disappeared from their sight down the winding track. They followed, making as good a speed as the weakest of the party could manage. After half an hour's walking at a better pace than they had managed for a week or more, the priest suddenly stopped, wavered for a moment, fell to his knees and toppled sideways to the ground. One of the men passed what he was carrying to the other, and with a quick movement bent and slung the priest onto his shoulders. "I wish I'd thought of that first," Godda said sadly.

They walked for another hour before they reached the place where these people lived. It was a small settlement in a clearing, not unlike the place where the party had rested halfway through their journey. But here there was life—hens bustling around the doors of the four little one-roomed houses, two empty stalls made for housing oxen, a haystack, a well, children playing, tethered goats, women coming out from the doorways to welcome them. Their cart was there, standing empty beside the well, but there was no sign of the unconscious Magnus. "Aveiro, Aveiro," the people kept saying when Eleanor and Clodagh pressed into each house in turn, looking for him. "They are a good people, Christian people," the priest said. "They have taken Magnus where he can be helped."

The people cleared babies and grandmothers out of one of the huts, and brought a blanket for the priest, and another for Eleanor. They could not supply blankets for so big a party, but they swept the earth floor, and stacked extra wood so that the fire could be mended during the night. Then they brought a plentiful supply of bread, honey, an egg each and a flagon of thin white wine that went to the newcomers' unaccustomed heads and, since conversation was impossible, withdrew to the other huts and left them to sleep. The wine and the fire warmed them, and they slept easily. To many of them it was very like home again—a fire, a crowded sleeping place, a picture of the Virgin on the wall and a cat with newborn kittens bedded in straw underneath a bench.

In the morning there were two oxcarts standing near the well—the one that belonged to the people of the settlement and another that had been brought back from wherever it was they had taken Magnus. The people of the settlement stood around, watching the loading of the carts and lending a hand to anyone who found the climb difficult. The four women and the priest and Simon de Baude and his brother made up one cartload. The rest of the men climbed thankfully into the other. They had been offered no more food, perhaps because the provision of their night meal had left the people short of ready supplies; but they had lost the habit of expecting morning food. It worried Simon de Baude that they had nothing to give these people—no means of paying them for their help and their food. But the only things of value the party had were the relics that had been buried under each of their temporary altars, and these belonged to Geoffrey and Faber and the Lady Eleanor, and were in any case far too precious to be given away. Father Nicholas stood at the tail of the oxcart to bless the peo-

ple, and they accepted his blessing with their heads
bowed. Then the oxcarts moved off, the one carrying the
men leading the way, and the people made themselves
as comfortable as they could, not knowing where the
journey was to end, or how long it would take.

The country they covered was very like the country
they had been walking through—dry, sparsely treed and
often very stony underfoot. They passed no other houses
and no signs of cultivation, though occasionally there
were patches of trees where the bark had been stripped
and stacked neatly, ready to be moved. As the day wore
on the country became more open, and the soil sandier,
and in the late afternoon they came onto the banks of a
lagoon. Here their track was more sharply defined. The
wheel ruts had cut deeply down into tussocky grass.
There were birds feeding on the water, and it seemed to
Sir Simon that this might lead them to the place of his
dream. The feeding birds meant that there must be fish
and he thought that they should stop now, make camp
for the night and try to get some fish before darkness fell.
But when he pulled at the oxcart's driver's arm and tried
to indicate all this with words and gestures, the man
shook his head, repeated the word "Aveiro" many times
and kept pointing off towards the west. They went on
for another hour. The lagoon had broadened so that
they could no longer see to its far side, and the fresh
salt smell of the sea came to them on the wind. In the
very last of the light they saw, still some distance off to
the west of them, a cluster of houses and barns. "Aveiro,"
the driver said, smiling and pointing with his whip.

Darkness had fallen by the time they reached the little town, and flares were held aloft to light the carts
through wooden gates into a stone-walled courtyard. In
the light of the torches a group of nuns came forward to

help the people down from the high carts. The men were led away to the guest quarters near the gate, the women housed, two to a cell, in the nuns' own quarters. Clodagh found herself sharing with Eleanor. There was still nobody to whom they could speak, either in French or English, but there was a little novice in smiling attendance on them, beds with thick palliasses, metal bowls of water and a brazier at which they could warm themselves while they ate a thick stew of barley and chicken and beans. They tried to question the novice about Magnus by pointing at the calves of their legs, limping, miming his sickness. When at last she understood them the smile disappeared from her face, and she clasped her hands together and looked downwards, as in prayer. They didn't know what to understand by this, whether he was alive or dead, whether she prayed for him or for his soul. "We will have to wait until tomorrow," Eleanor said. "There must be a priest within reach of a convent of this size. He can give us news, if only to Father Nicholas, in Latin."

Clodagh woke to the sound of a bell. She thought it was the bell calling the nuns to prime, but when she got up and went to the little barred window of the cell, she could see that the sun was high. The bell that had woken her must be for tierce or sext. Eleanor had gone from the cell, leaving yesterday's rags in a pile on the stone floor. Clodagh added hers to the pile, took off the woollen bedgown that the novice had brought her and dressed herself slowly in a shift and a habit that she found folded on a stool beside her bed. It shocked her to see how thin her body was, as though her sore and spotted skin had been thrown loosely over naked bones. She covered her lank hair with the oblate's veil they had left her, and went out. She had no wish to obey the bell's summons to the chapel—it was enough to know that it was there, and that prayers would rise in it seven times in the day.

There was nobody about in the courtyard, and the wooden gates stood wide to the dusty road. She went out, followed a footpath down between two houses and found herself on the grassy edge of the lagoon. The water stretched away, flat and unruffled and bluish under the sun. There were seabirds overhead and small sandy islands, lifting themselves only a few inches above the water. Grey cranes walked there on their stick-thin legs. Far off along the curve of the bank there was a barge beached, and two men were loading lagoon weed from it into the panniers strapped to a donkey's back. The air was rich with the smell of salt and weed, and she was overcome with the longing to ease her tiredness and heal her sores by sinking slowly into the still shallows. She turned back and went as quickly as her weakness would let her to the cell. She took off the habit, and dressed herself once again in the woollen bedgown. At home, in the height of summer, she was used to going naked into the backwaters of the millstream with a bunch of laughing girls whose screams would drive off any trespassing men. Here the bedgown would have to protect her against the stares of anyone who might be passing along the bank.

The journey back and forth to the cell and the effort of undressing again had tired her, and at first she only sat at the edge of the water, letting it wash across her scarred feet and soak the dragging hem of the woollen gown. But the coolness of the water tempted and revived her, and gradually she pushed herself forward with her hands, feeling the delicious coolness of the water on the back of her knees, her thighs, around her waist. The sand shelved very slowly, and she had pushed herself a long way from the grassy bank of the lagoon before she was in a foot of water, and could float. She lay back then, letting the water wash through her matted hair and fill the cavities of her ears so that it shut the world out. She moved her arms gently to keep herself afloat, putting a cautious heel down at short intervals to be sure that she hadn't floated into deeper water. A seabird came over her at a height, turned and glided down to get a closer look. The water had stung the sores on her legs and her back hotly for a moment or two, but now she felt nothing from them, as though they had been instantly healed. She raised her hand to her mouth and tasted it. It was neither salt nor fresh, she thought, but something midway between. She sat up, still in the shallows, and bent herself forward and scrubbed at her scalp and her hair. Then she filled her lungs and pushed herself forward, floating face downwards and feeling the exquisite coldness at her temples. She lifted her head sharply when her breath was done. In a great splashing of water, Gyll was hurrying towards her. He stopped when she sat up, and a grin of relief spread over his face. "I thought you were dead," he said. "*Jesus.*" She smiled at him and sank backwards again to float in the water. He came on, till he was standing over her. "Nobody could find you," he said. "They sent me to look. You'd better come."

"When I've finished my bath," she said.

"Better come now," he said. "They're waiting. They've got news from a priest of what's going on in the world."

"An English priest?" she said, sitting quickly up.

"Not English," Gyll said, "for I listened without understanding one word."

The rest of the party were gathered in the sunlight close to the wall of the guesthouse in the courtyard. Father Nicholas had been provided with a priest's gown. The rest, including Sir Simon and his brother, were in rough peasants' tunics that were belted with rope at the waist, and left their knees bare. They stared at her wet gown and her streaming hair. "Go and cover yourself," Godda said loudly.

Clodagh looked down at her body and said, "I am covered," before she remembered that Godda should be ignored now that they were back among people. She looked towards Father Nicholas, longing for his news. "What has happened to Magnus?" she asked.

"He is there," the priest said, pointing over the roofs at the far end of the convent buildings. "In the infirmary. He is being cared for." Father Nicholas was sitting with his back against the wall of the guesthouse. Alongside him, but standing, was a priest in a black robe, with an elaborately carved wooden cross in his rope girdle. "Father Duarte has no English," he said. "He's a Cistercian, of the Portuguese order." He sighed and looked down, trying to order his thoughts so that he could tell them what had to be told, without going through the weariness of recounting the whole of his conversation with the priest. "A man will be sent," he said. "It will take two days or more—Porto is fifty miles off to the north. I asked that a man be sent. This is not a big town, or a rich one, and men to guide and carry our party cannot be spared. A man will be sent, to tell the English in Porto."

"But are there English in Porto, or have they left?" Simon de Baude asked.

"They have come back," the priest said. "Father Duarte was there himself, fourteen nights ago. They have fought a great way down the peninsula, retaking Santarem from the Moors, and the town of Lisbon. Now they have come back, some say to embark themselves for the Holy Land, since God has prospered this venture and so may prosper that."

"And Robert Apelfourde?" Clodagh said, and waited anxiously while Father Nicholas asked the question and was answered by the Portuguese priest. "Not by name," Father Nicholas said, "but the English have come back in great strength, and with few losses. It will be four days, five days, six before we can hope for them to send for us. We are welcome here, Father Duarte says. Rest, eat, pray, go to mass, make you confessions to him."

"How?" Edwin said in an undertone to his brother. "My sins would sound bloody strange, in his parrot tongue."

"They would sound strange in any tongue," Clodagh said. She had meant nothing in particular by it, but she found Godda watching her with hostility.

In the six days that passed before their messenger came back to them from Porto, the party split into groups, never coming together in its entirety during the day. They saw little of the Lady Eleanor, who took her meals with the nuns and spent all her waking hours in the convent's chapel. They saw little of Faber, who had recovered sufficiently after two days of rest to be able to walk to the anchorage at the lagoon's mouth. He spent his time there waiting for a place on any fishing vessel that was going north. On the fifth day he came and took swift leave of Sir Simon, and didn't bother himself with any of the rest. He was going north among the nets and the fish pots on a small boat. He would be in Porto be-

fore them, and away from it, probably, before they
reached the place. He would take the first ship that
would carry him to Dartmouth, find somebody who
would trust a new bottom to him to replace the *Grace
Dieu*, fill it with any cargo that was offering and head
again for Alexandria and the rich spoils of the war. The
others didn't envy him his journey. They had had
enough of ships. All they wanted was to be in Porto, to
be among their own people, to rest and recover themselves before they embarked again, either for England or
the Holy Land. "Now there are only ten of us," Godda
said superstitiously when she heard of Walter Faber's
departure. "How many more, before we're purged of it?"

She couldn't stop her twin sons from wandering about
on the banks of the lagoon, or following Portuguese
girls with their high head bundles of produce along the
roads to the marketplace; but she kept Joice close to her
through the day and she watchdogged through the night,
waking at any sound to make sure that the girl was not
leaving their cell to cross the courtyard to the place
where the brothers slept. The strictest chastity now, she
thought, would go far to undo unchasteness that had
not been chosen, but forced on Joice and her sons by
malign powers too strong for them. The girl believed her.
The return to a peopled place had thrown her into a
nervous passion of guilt and fear and penitence. In spite
of the good food, it seemed that she was becoming thinner and more owl-eyed, and a dozen times a day she
would seek out Father Duarte to confess herself and
then kneel, wordless and weeping, until he sent her
away. Simon de Baude, too, seemed more and more har-
rowed by nervous suffering as the food and rest lessened
his physical pains. He spoke very little, even to his
brother Geoffrey, and spent almost all of his time alone

in his place in the guesthouse. He could have talked to Eleanor if she'd been available, but she was content in the nuns' company, and with her prayers, and had washed from her mind all concern for the others of the party.

For Clodagh and Gyll, the days were not without happiness. They were warm and safe and fed, and the time they spent together had the extra sharp sweetness of something with a definite term to it. They would be sent for. They would be parted. It was unlikely that they would see each other again; if they did, it would have to be without particular recognition.

For Gyll the parting would be more painful than for Clodagh, for the faults he saw in her—her feeling that she was superior to him and her unwillingness to defer to his wishes and opinions—were faults that would spoil her as a wife, but added a romantic value to her as a lover. For Clodagh there would be a sort of relief in their eventual parting, because she had grown to need him almost to the point of love. Its unworthiness troubled her. The coming loss of it troubled her as well. Even the memory of it would have to be put away because it would accord so ill with the sort of life to which she would be restored. Father Duarte's news of the war had cheered her. She no longer believed that Robert Apelfourde might be dead. She longed to see him. She looked with satisfaction on the breaking-up of the party, Eleanor's absorption in her prayers, Faber's departure, the priest's retreat into uncertain old age. There would be nobody who felt duty bound to tell Robert Apelfourde that she had been impure. Godda's open hostility to her would carry no menace, because hardship had turned Godda into a viciously whispering, half-demented crone.

Eleanor seldom came to their shared cell now at night, and when she did she slept with utter exhaustion after her hours of prayer. When the last bell of the night had rung for compline Clodagh would creep out, going barefooted and silent over the stones of the courtyard, to the end room of the guesthouse where Gyll had his bed. She would stay with him there until the false dawn, going back to her cell to sleep a little longer just before prime.

In the daytime she and Gyll went out from the convent, usually taking the boy Geoffrey with them. He had nothing to do, now that Eleanor had withdrawn herself and there were no duties for him to perform for his brother. Together the three of them would wander through the houses to lie on the edge of the lagoon, watching the birds and letting the sun heal them. Once or twice, to the great scandal of Godda, they went into the water, the two boys naked, and Clodagh wrapped in the trailing bedgown the nuns had given her. The people of the town, passing with loaded donkeys or with goats being brought in from their pasture place, stared at their peculiar foreignness; but Godda, thinking it a further sin that would have to be purged, hurried Joice away from the sight of it.

The man who had gone to Porto, carrying Father Nicholas's messages, came back on the sixth day, bringing with him three men, a string of little donkeys, an English priest, a surgeon and Robert Apelfourde's lieutenant, Thomas Daubeni. Daubeni didn't recognize Clodagh at first when she ran to him in the courtyard, wearing her nun's habit and her oblate's veil. "Is he well, is he safe?" she said.

"He is well, he is safe," Daubeni said, "and he sends me to bring you back." He called to one of the men to

undo the packsaddle of the donkey whose rein was tied
to the saddle of his own horse, and when it was undone
he brought her a bundle tied up in linen. "My master
sent these," he said, "the best he could find at short notice, for you and the Lady Eleanor."

"No letter?" she said. "No message?"

"Only his thanks to God that you are safe," Daubeni
said.

While the others crowded around for news from
Porto, Clodagh took the linen-wrapped bundle into the
cell she shared with Eleanor. There were two gowns in
it, of good soft stuff that gave her pleasure when she held
it to her cheek. The better of the two, a gown in the
pure deep blue of the Virgin's pictures, she put aside
on the bed for Eleanor. The other was the green of
English woods in summer, with a yellow girdle of finely
plaited wool. She put the gown on, letting it hang free
from her shoulders, and bound the girdle around her
brows, looping the ends loosely two or three times
around the swing of her long dark hair, to make a head-
dress. It made her feel taller and stronger, and she
wished there was some way that she could see herself,
but the convent had nothing that would mirror her face.
She went out again to the courtyard where the others
were still standing, and saw it mirrored in their surprise
and deference.

Thomas Daubeni had brought money with him.
Those who had fed them could be paid for their food,
and a large meal was prepared that night for the party
and the newcomers in the refectory of the guesthouse.

Eleanor joined them, wearing her nun's robes. She
had admired the blue gown, stroked its fabric, shaken
her head and moved the gown from her bed back to Clo-

dagh's. "I have taken the Cross, remember," she said. "I want no vanities."

Father Gilbert, the new priest, had spent a long time with Father Nicholas, while he unburdened himself of all his doubts and his insufficiencies. The old man would not come to supper that night. He was asleep now, happy in the knowledge that he had passed responsibility for the party to a priest who was strong and zealous and without any hampering doubts about the true wishes of God. "I will hear each person's privy confession tomorrow," Father Gilbert told them. "In the afternoon I will say mass. And the next morning we will begin our journey back."

The Lady Eleanor was the first to go to confession. She was there a long time, and when she came out, there was no rush to be the next to go in. They left the decision about who should go to Sir Simon, and he put his hand under Clodagh's arm, and led her to the door. She had not gone to Gyll's bed the night before, fearing that one of the newcomers might be sharing his room, and she was glad of it now. She came slowly to the point of her adultery, confessed it flatly, had to be drawn with prompting questions about reasons and occasions and future intentions and repentances. Father Gilbert was at a loss. Adultery was heinous enough in itself, but lasciviousness with someone of low station clearly deserved the punishment of public confession at the door of the church. But she was Robert Apelfourde's wife. He had brought his soldiers back from Lisbon victorious, and few English in Porto now stood higher than he did. "Spend the day on your knees," he said. "I will send for you again, before the mass."

Since it was to be only a part of her penance, with more to be imposed on her later, she didn't go at once to the chapel, but stood for a little while with the others in the courtyard, listening to their talk. She was careful not to glance in Gyll's direction—all that she had abjured a few minutes ago. Suddenly, from beyond the complex of convent buildings, a terrible screaming rose in the air and seemed to hover over them. Everyone turned, huddling together at the sound, and Sir Simon fell to his knees, crossing himself. The scream rose and fell and rose again to an agonizing pitch, prolonging itself for longer than it seemed possible that human lungs could hold any breath. Then it stopped suddenly, leaving the air aching. "Another one gone," Godda said superstitiously, not remembering that she had already counted Magnus.

Clodagh went to the nuns' chapel, leaving the others in the courtyard. The uneasy waiting and the unwilling entries stretched on and on through the morning, deep into the afternoon. Each confession seemed to take longer than the last, and as each came out they turned away from the others, preferring to be alone with their consciences. When the last of them—Edwin—had been confessed, Father Gilbert stayed a long time closeted with Father Nicholas. Next he spoke briefly with Thomas Daubeni and Sir Simon, out of the hearing of the others. Then he and Daubeni called for their horses and, in the late afternoon, left the place without a word to anyone else.

Clearly no mass was to be celebrated. Father Nicholas was at his prayers, and they couldn't question him. Sir Simon could tell them nothing except that the party was to set out, as arranged, on the next morning; and, which seemed to have no bearing on their case, that Father Gilbert had told him that the temper of Porto was incorruptible, since Bernard of Clairvaux had said, and the

campaign against Lisbon had confirmed, that only the
stainless and inviolable would be blessed with any success in God's holy war.

It was a quiet party of people who set out the next
morning, sitting sideways on the little donkeys that had
been provided for them. At intervals the men would
slide heavily to the ground and walk for a time, but
none of them was yet recovered enough to keep up for
long with the donkeys' steady jog. The surgeon had
stayed behind, making his horse available to Sir Simon,
but in fact the knight surrendered it to the Lady Eleanor, and either walked, or joggled on a donkey.

In the early afternoon they came to a monastery—a
long, low wooden building surrounded by gardens and
inhabited by half a dozen monks. The man in charge of
the donkeys indicated to de Baude that they were expected here, and when they dismounted they found that
there was food ready. It was a rough place, and poor-
looking, but the monks had provided a good fire for
them, and straw pallets on the floor. Again, there was no
possibility of talk. Father Nicholas was the only one of
the party that the monks might have understood; but he
was nodding with weakness when they lifted him down
from the donkey, and was soon asleep. There was no way
in which Sir Simon could find out from them how much
further they had to go, but he thought the journey
would probably take them two more days, at their present pace.

The monks provided them with bread and a thin ale
in the morning, and soon after sunrise they began their
journey again. It was necessary now for a man to walk
beside Father Nicholas, supporting him on the saddle
pad, but the rest of them were strong enough to bear,

unwillingly, another long dreary day of journeying. On this day, they passed a few people working under the trees, saw a hovel or two from the surrounding soil of which a bare living was being scratched. But everywhere the dryness of the soil worried them, and they thought with longing of the green grass and the dampness underfoot of places which, until a few days ago, they had given up hope of ever seeing again. At midday, while the donkeys were being watered at a slow river broken up by sandbanks, they heard horses cantering through the trees, and looked up to find Daubeni and another man, with a lead horse between them, coming down to the ford.

"The Lady Clodagh is sent for," Daubeni said, drawing rein alongside the tree where Simon de Baude was resting.

"Only the Lady Clodagh?"

"Only she," Daubeni said. "Make haste, Lady," he called, looking towards her. "We are expected back in Porto tonight."

"I am ready," she said. She had nothing to do, except to walk from beside her donkey to the horse Daubeni had provided. She was too tired to be pleased at the thought of the long ride, but it comforted her that her husband had sent for her. She turned to look at the others when she was mounted, wanting a last sight of them before she left. They were resting, drinking, paying no heed to the horsemen, or to her departure. Only Eleanor was watching her, and Gyll. Eleanor smiled at her, and raised a hand in farewell, without speaking. Gyll made no sign, but she knew that he would watch for a long time, till she was out of sight. She would have liked to say some parting word to him, but the risk would have been too great. She had been reclaimed now. She was Robert Apelfourde's woman.

It was almost dawn of the next day when they reached Porto, and she was dizzy and weak again, with hunger and weariness. Their horses slithered down the steep track to the riverside, and she thought that they must be going to cross in one of the boats that were tied there. Across the river, in the dim light, she could see what appeared to be a large town. Streets climbed the bank at steep angles, so that the thatched roofs of the houses rose above one another like stacked nests. It seemed they were not to cross. Daubeni led the way along a narrow footpath at the edge of the water, till they came to a dark stone building, standing alone. He pushed at the door and led her into a stone-flagged kitchen. The other man had not followed, but had stayed outside, holding the three horses. There was a rushlight burning on the table, and a cloth-covered plate of bread and a jug of milk. Daubeni gestured towards them, inviting her to eat, but she shook her head wearily. She wanted to see her husband, and then to sleep. He took her arm, and led her along a narrow corridor. There was a wooden door at the end and, outside it, a sleeping monk crouched on a three-legged stool. Daubeni kicked the stool to waken him, and then opened the door for Clodagh and followed her in. She expected to find her husband waiting, but the room was empty. She saw a doorway beyond it, and went to look. It contained nothing but a bed with a fine fur rug thrown over the foot of it.

"Where is he?" she said, turning to Daubeni.

"Later," he said, "sleep now," and he left her. She stood for a moment after he had gone, and then she opened the door again, and looked out. The old monk was awake, and he shook his head at her solemnly. She closed the door again and went back into the room and through the connecting doorway to the bed. She stretched out on it, and pulled the fur comfortingly to her chin. She would sleep now. It would be better to see her husband when she was rested, when she had washed, when the long hair he loved had been combed and dressed.

Five days were to pass before Thomas Daubeni came back. Her two rooms were comfortable, and the old monk kept her fire burning brightly. For the first two days she slept, waking only to eat her meals by the fire, and then being drawn back to the comfort of a soft bed and her fur coverlet. The food, brought to her on a tray, was the food that she had dreamed of during the long hungry weeks—heavily spiced meat cooked in butter, dishes made with eggs and cream and honey, milk and wine and walnuts and pickled cherries.

It was very clear to her that she was a prisoner. The old monk seemed to do guard duty outside her door for eighteen hours out of every day, and when he was not there his place was taken by a tall young monk who wore the same dusty brown habit, and looked at her with a cold scorn that spoiled her appetite for any meal he brought.

At first she had scarcely thought of it as imprisonment. But when two days of sleep had restored her strength she found herself angry, and a little afraid. Her anger was against Robert Apelfourde. He well knew her fears of thick walls and closed doors, and he knew the reasons for them. Because of her mother's vow and her mother's ever-changing attitude to it, she had never felt herself safe until her marriage. On one day Blanchefleur would weep because soon the vow must be honoured and she must be parted eternally from her only child; on the next she would weep again and sweep Clodagh into her arms and vow that her soul's damnation was a tiny price to pay to keep her beloved child always beside her. So, as a child, Clodagh had thought of her perpetually threatened parting from her mother as her death. As she grew she had seen many other girls go gladly in, welcoming a safe future of undemanding duties cushioned by companionship. Their happiness didn't alter her view. For her, life was sunlight, laughter, impulse, movement, Blanchefleur; walled places, days divided by bells, the absence of change and uncertainty and bustle and stir seemed a long death from which marriage to Apelfourde had delivered her. For that she would be forever in his debt, even if her marriage should now be close to ending.

From her window she could watch the river traffic, and see a little of the activity on the further bank. There was an armourer's shop there and, during daylight hours, the place was loud with the sound of hammered metal, and the comings and goings of fighting men, bringing armour and arms for mending. The near bank of the river, under her window, was a playing place for children. By pressing her head against the bars of her window she could just look down on them, getting some entertainment from their play. They played exclusively at war games, laying siege to a mound of heaped-up dirt and rubble or, with two riding pickaback on two others, fighting mounted battles with sticks and shields.

She watched the children and the river and the armourer's for hours at a time, because she was so short of employment in her rooms. She was provided with brushes and combs and a mirror; a manuscript Book of Hours, of which much of the Latin, written in a crabbed

Portuguese hand, defeated her; and a little ball, tied to a cupped stick, with which she amused herself for a few minutes each day.

The sound of church bells came to her sweetly across the water at all the prescribed hours, reminding her that though she had confessed she had not yet been given Absolution. She spent a long time each day on her knees, praying that Gyll of Dittisham should be spared from torture. Her adultery could be the only reason for her imprisonment, and although she meant to deny it if she was accused she was tormented with the fear that Gyll's denial of it would bring him only to the rack and the tongs. This fear, and the images it brought her of his body under torture, made her pace from wall to wall of her prison, desperate for some employment that would take her mind from it. When the old monk, who often smiled gently at her when he brought her food, came one evening at dusk bringing her a rushlight, she pantomimed her need for cloth and needle and thread to give her something to do. He nodded as though he understood her, but when he came back after an interval he had brought draughts and a board—something even more welcome because it gave her an hour or two of human company. It was plain that he preferred guarding her from the other side of the board rather than from his stool on the other side of the door. They played for several hours every day, the old monk concentrating fiercely on victory, and celebrating it with wide smiles that bared his toothless gums. The board and the game reminded her of Magnus, and the chess set he had been making for the priest. She wondered if it was finished— or if he was dead. She wondered if the others had yet reached Porto; if Eleanor had elected to stay with the nuns; if Joice had separated herself completely from her greasy stud rams; if Gyll's smooth skin had been broken, and his supple joints twisted out of shape.

Thomas Daubeni came back on the fifth night, being let into the room by the young monk, who stood watching her with disdain while Daubeni spoke.

He had brought her a cloth-wrapped bundle which she hoped came from her husband, but when she unwrapped it, it contained the blue gown Eleanor had chosen not to wear at the convent. As she shook it to free the cloth of fold marks something tinkled on the stone floor. She stopped to pick it up and found it was the little vial of crystal-stone holding the Virgin's tears, miraculously unbroken by its fall. The vial frightened her. Her danger must be great, if Eleanor thought so valuable a gift was needed.

"My husband?" she said, looking up at Daubeni. He shook his head. She got to her feet, wishing to stand on a level with him while she questioned him. She did not care for Daubeni, had never cared for him in the days when he was constantly employed about her husband's house and lands. She could not, now, expect any sympathy or comfort from him. "You will tell my husband that I wish to see him, urgently and at once," she said, speaking with cold formality.

"He will not see you," Daubeni said.

She was taken aback. "You will tell him, nevertheless," she said, less forcefully. Daubeni inclined his head. "How long must I stay here?" she asked.

"Two days, three days," Daubeni said carelessly, as though it was of very little importance. "They are collecting evidence."

"Evidence?" she said, her voice rising with shock. "What evidence?"

A small, sour smile appeared for a moment on Daubeni's face. "That will be made known," he said.

"I have a right to know it now," Clodagh said.

"But I no right to tell you," Daubeni said, "for all charges must be made suddenly and at the same time, lest a charged person should use the time to invent arguments, and conceal the truth."

When he had gone, telling her nothing else except that she would appear before the archidiaconal court, she flung herself down in a passion of angry weeping. The Virgin's tears were still clutched in her hand, but they brought her no comfort. The news was no surprise to her, it was what she had expected, but the certain knowledge that she would be tried as an adulteress brought home to her the humiliation of it, and the unfairness, and the pain. Was adultery, after all, so rare a thing, that she should be publicly charged and shamed and left without any future to her life? Would her mother take her back when it was done? And would she want to go, to live on without purpose or authority in her mother's house? Perhaps only the convent, with its large charity, would be left for her—the convent that she had only finally escaped by her marriage to Robert Apelfourde. Suddenly she had a great longing for her mother, with her managing ways, her easy laughter and her skill in finding means of handling priests and men. It was Blanchefleur she needed now even more than the Virgin's tears, for Blanchefleur had weathered church censure at the irregularity of her own marriage. She wondered whether her mother could be brought, whether she could demand the right to make the ecclesiastical court wait while her mother was sent for.

She got up from her bed and went to the outer door. The old monk smiled at her, proffering the draught pieces and the board. She shook her head at him and closed the door again. There was nothing she could do until some English-speaking person came. Then she would demand the right to see Father Nicholas. She no longer wanted Robert Apelfourde. The whole of her anger now was turned on him. He had asked no questions, waited for no proofs—and indeed no proofs were possible unless she was carrying a child, and she thought she was not. Who then could swear positively to her adultery, if she swore against it? Except Gyll, who would not swear. And if he swore under torture, surely even the church must know what slender evidence that was. Her hatred of Apelfourde grew from hour to hour. Who would he marry next, what woman was already carrying the child he so wanted? Adultery charged and found against her here would give his suit a swift passage in Rome. With luck he would celebrate his new marriage on the same day as his child's first anniversary.

Thomas Daubeni, with two other men in Robert Apelfourde's livery, came for her on the seventh day of her imprisonment. She dressed carefully for her appearance in the ecclesiastical court, putting on the blue gown of the Virgin's colour, keeping Daubeni waiting while she dressed her hair carefully in a dark shining braid, said her prayers, put the Virgin's tears carefully into the pocket at her belt. She thought a knowledge of ecclesiastical law might serve her better than Eleanor's relic, but since she had none of the first, she would have to depend on the second. Waiting had fed her anger against Apelfourde. But she was calmer now, and determined to defend herself.

Daubeni stood in the stern of the boat as they were ferried across the river, then led her at a fast pace up the steep hill on the opposite bank. She had little time to look about her, but she could see that the whole town was like a camp. Loads of stores were being brought in, armourers and swordsmiths and tentmakers were working at their stalls, knights' horses were being walked in pairs by their grooms, the streets stank of arrowmakers' glue, and everywhere respectable women were trying to chivvy their girls in from the streets and away from the lecherous blandishments of Flemings, Germans and the English goddams. The stench and the busyness of the streets were a delight after her long confinement, and if Daubeni had not been in front of her, with his lieutenants watchfully behind, she might have darted into the crowd in the hope of finding a strolling pardoner who would sell her an absolution for a shilling.

At the top of the long street, when she was breathless with climbing, Daubeni turned into the courtyard of a monastery. Beyond its walls, Clodagh could see the squat bell tower of a church. Daubeni led the way in through a doorway, up a half flight of stone steps and into a large square chamber where a court had been improvised. Her three judges sat at a long table at one end of the room. Below them, with writing materials in front of them, were two young religious who would act as scribes. On the left of them a separate table had been placed for the priest who was to be Promoter. A square stool had been placed for Clodagh six feet away from the table where her judges sat. The stone room was very cold, despite a number of charcoal braziers that had been placed about it. The judges were not pleased by the long wait they had had for their prisoner, but Daubeni surprised her by excusing it as being due to the difficulty of finding a wherryman to bring them over the river. While this was being discussed Clodagh looked quickly around, expecting to find her husband there to bring the charge against

her. There were two young knights, armoured and wearing helmets with nosepieces, standing watchfully at the
back of the room, with Apelfourde's badges at their
shoulders. He had not yet come himself. She drew a
deep breath of relief. She would at least have time to recover from the climb, since her husband's charge that
she had dishonoured him could scarcely be brought
against her in his absence. The President of the judges
began to speak.

"I am Canon Morkere, chaplain of the Lord Gilbert,
Bishop of Porto," he said. Clodagh inclined her head to
him, deeply grateful to find that his speech was English.
He moved a heavily ringed hand to indicate the priest
who sat to his left. "Monseigneur Guilliame of the Bene-
dictines." Clodagh hoped nothing from him, because of
his name. The President's hand moved to indicate the
priest who sat to his right. "Father Leofric, of the Chap-
ter at Sarum," he said. "We are your judges. Father
Wulstan of Ely acts as Promoter and accuser. Kneel
down."

Clodagh knelt on the board floor, feeling the cold
draft from the doorway on her knees. The Promoter
came forward and placed a silver cross in her hands.
"Kiss it," he said, "and swear by the rood that you will
tell the utter truth of what you know, what you are
asked, what you have done."

Clodagh hesitated, looking up at him. "Swear," he
said again.

"I cannot swear," she said. "I have not been accused."

"Swear," the Promoter said, giving the cross a push
so that it banged against her mouth.

She closed her eyes, fighting the nervous shaking that
made it difficult for her to speak, and then kissed the
cross lingeringly and put it back into his hands. "I can-

not swear when I do not know what I am accused of," she said, getting to her feet. "You may ask me things of which I have no knowledge."

The Promoter looked towards the judges for guidance. They conferred for a moment, and then Canon Morkere spoke to the Promoter. "Accuse her," he said.

The Promoter turned towards her again, raising the cross high between them. "You are charged that you are heretic, blasphemous, idolatrous," he said. "In short you are charged to be an arrant witch."

"What?" she said stupidly, looking up at him open-mouthed in her utter surprise. Neither the Promoter nor her judges moved or spoke. She felt the beginnings of a smile on her lips and did her best to suppress it because, though it was a smile of deep relief, she was afraid it might be misinterpreted. "No, by my faith," she said firmly, "you have made some error here. I am Clodagh, wife to Robert Apelfourde, an English knight." She looked quickly behind her to where Daubeni stood, expecting a protest from him that the wrong charge had been made.

"And so you stand charged," the Promoter said. "And so you must answer, on pain of burning."

She looked wildly around her at the impassive faces. She had no friend in the place, no one who would speak up for her against the nightmare foolishness of such a charge. "Messire," she said, addressing herself to her chief judge, "by the virtue of every mass that ever was said I swear someone is in error." He stared unblinkingly back at her. "Tell me what I have done," she said. "Who accuses me? Who have I bewitched?" Canon Morkere still watched her closely, leaving it to the Promoter to answer her.

"There are half a hundred charges against you," he

said. "Of incantation and exhortation, sorcery, conjury and devilry, the making of spells and enchantments, the most impious and detestable blasphemies, that you did heinously endamage the souls of others with abominable wickedness, and that you are, by the instinct of the devil, a foul strumpet and a succubus."

She put a hand behind her, needing the support of the stool. "None of it is true," she said weakly. "None of it, none of it."

"You must answer, whether you are sworn or not," the Canon said. "Will you swear now?"

"I'll swear," she said. "Give me the cross." The cross was put into her hands again and she dropped to her knees, pressing her lips to it. "I swear by the blood of Christ I have done none of these things," she said. "I swear that I will answer truly, whatever you may ask." She knelt on for a few moments, trying to pray, but her great terror made it impossible.

"I interest myself that she can weep," Monseigneur Guilliame said in his slow and heavily accented English.

"Three tears from the right eye," Father Leofric said. "It is the common ability of witches."

"I would like to see her face lifted into the light," the Benedictine said. The Promoter reached forward and lifted her face by its chin. On both of her cheeks there was a wet shine of tears.

"I interest myself that she weeps," Guilliame said again. "I should like to hear her say a Paternoster."

"Monseigneur, we waste time," Leofric said. "The examination should follow fast upon the accusations, that she is not given space to invent dissimulations."

"Might not we save time?" Guilliame said. "For if she did bite through her tongue while attempting a Paternoster, would she not have condemned herself by her own mouth?"

"There will be opportunity for such trials," Morkere said peaceably. "It will be best to follow the established lines. Was your mother a witch?" he said, turning back to Clodagh.

"No," she said, half startled into laughter by the absurd question.

"Or any of your godmothers?"

She shook her head vehemently.

"Have you any marks on your body, such things as warts or moles in your armpits, under your hair or on your buttocks?"

"No," Clodagh said.

"It will be wise to check the answer," Leofric said. "How many nipples are there on your body?"

"Two."

"Is there anything concealed in the cavities of your body, under your skin or at the roots of your hair which would cause and empower you to withstand pain, if you were put to the torture?"

"No," she said faintly.

"Have you about you any charm, spell, unholy trinket or written incantation?"

"No," said Clodagh. "I have only this." She took Eleanor's precious vial from her pocket, and held it up so that the light displayed it.

"What does it hold?" Morkere asked.

"The Blessed Virgin's tears. *Three* of her tears," she said, glancing at Father Leofric.

"Do you resign to your Holy Mother the Church all decisions as to your disposition for the rest of your mortal life?"

She was silent for a moment, not understanding what

the question implied. "I am a true believer, and faithful," she said.

"That is what we will determine," Leofric said. He nodded to the Promoter. "Begin the examination," he said.

The Promoter unrolled a parchment on the desk in front of him, and rehearsed a number of questions dealing with her birth, her parentage, her marriage, her childlessness, her voyage, her miraculous survival in the wild seas on the night the *Grace Dieu* sank. "Was some unearthly help given to you?" he asked.

She answered all the questions with a simple "yes" except the last, to which she answered, "Only God's."

"And yet many were lost, and did not reach the shore?"

"Rest them," she said, "but I was not alone. Others were saved."

"It is they who accuse you," the Promoter said.

The long series of harmless questions had reassured her a little, and given her time to see how unfriended she was and how much her safety would depend on her own firmness and lack of fear. "You have told me no clear thing of which they accuse me," she said. "You have told me only generalities."

"*Item*," he said, with a small sour smile. "You have a familiar that gave birth to a fox cub, against all nature, since it was a cat. *Item*, you were heard to boast of demoniacal powers of transubstantiation, to wit, the power of appearing as a dog, a dragon or a raven; likewise that you could raise storms, carry water in a sieve and pull down great hills to the level of the plains. *Item*, when you were crossed, you threatened death to those who disobeyed your will."

Clodagh spoke quickly, animated by her relief at finding how foolish all these accusations were. "I had a little pet once, a white cat," she said, remembering Blanchette. "One of my mother's tenants brought in a fox cub from the fields, and the cat mothered it, having lost her kittens. I do not remember speaking of this to anyone, but we talked of many things while we walked. As for the other things, *I* made no such claims," she said, and the absurdity of the charge made her smile. "Claims of power to split the skies and make potions and change into will o' the wisps and dragons are from the song about Loiza, and indeed I do remember that it was sung while we walked."

"By you," Father Leofric said. "A lewd song, with which no good woman would profane her tongue."

"Perhaps," Clodagh said. "And yet it is much sung by good people in my part of England. As for the rest, I never threatened death to any person, nor ever would."

The Promoter ran his finger down the parchment, looking for the place. "The woman Godda swore and deposed you to say 'Come one step nearer, and I'll strike you dead.' "

"It means nothing," Clodagh said. "It is a thing people say when they are angry." She turned to face the Judge President, Canon Morkere. "Messire," she said, "I have noticed that the scribes write down all of the questions, but only a little part of what I answer."

"Perhaps only a little part is true," Father Leofric said from beside the Canon.

Morkere frowned. He did not care to have remarks addressed to him answered by another. "Keep your heart and your mind on the truth," he said. "The scribes are not your judges, but only us, under God. Proceed," he said to the Promoter, but she interrupted, speaking to Morkere again.

"I have confessed all the sins and omissions of the journey," she said, "but I have not yet been given Absolution. When can I be brought to confession again?"

He stared at her, trying to measure the sincerity of her plea. "There will be a time for it," he said. "But to confess now, openly, would be a thing most pleasing to God and persuasive of his mercy."

"Private confession is forbidden," Leofric said. "For a witch may cozen her confessor, and so dishonour God greatly."

"Are you chaste?" Morkere said, again ignoring Leofric.

"Yes," Clodagh said. The lie appalled her. She did not think he meant had she lived chastely since her last confession, because he must know she had. But with so many untrue things charged against her, surely Almighty God Himself would not expect her to add to those accusations?

"Proceed," Morkere said to the Promoter.

He moved now from accusations to questions. "What is the name of your incubus?" he said.

She stared at him, colour draining from her face at the new direction of his questions. He pressed on with them, not waiting, nor, she thought, wanting any answer to them. "How is he summoned? At what hagging place in England did you first have carnal copulation with him? Why has God withheld children from you? By what means did you so bewitch the privities of some of the party that they could no longer serve, and their testicles were withered up like raisins? By what abominable incantations did you make the dumb boy appear? By what change him into a dumb beast?"

In her panic she could do nothing but stare into Morkere's face. The Promoter was silent now. They were all waiting. She tried to moisten her dry lips with her tongue. "If you were asked," she said, addressing Morkere, "if you were asked how you had caused the Saracens to capture Jerusalem, what would you answer, except to say that you hadn't? How can I answer? I have done none of these things."

"Nevertheless, they must be answered," Morkere said, not without sympathy.

"I can't remember them," she said, closing her eyes.

"We will take the accusations one by one," he said, "giving you a full time to refute any you can. All the first questions related to Satanic bondage, and the fearful rites by which it is imposed. First you should answer us——"

"I am perjured," she said, interrupting him. She fell forward from her stool, so that she was on her knees before him. "I beg forgiveness for the lie. I was confused, I was afraid . . ." Tears streamed from her closed eyes, and she covered her face with her shaking hands.

Monseigneur Guilliame broke his long silence. "It is interesting, that she weeps again," he said.

Morkere leaned forward, seeing a quick end to the proceedings. "You admit all these things that have been charged against you?"

She let her hands fall from her face. "No," she said, her voice rising. "No. Not any of them. Not one." She tried to get up again, but found that she had caught her foot in the folds of her gown.

Morkere sighed and sat back. "Help her," he said.

The Promoter stepped forward and helped her, with a hand under her elbow. She shook his hand off as soon as she was up, and moved forward from the stool, so that she stood facing her judges.

"What was the nature of the perjury to which you have confessed?" Morkere said.

She found it a hard and heavy thing to keep her head up, to face her judges while she answered. "I have sworn to tell the truth," she said. "I have told the truth in all but one thing. During the bad time, when we were lost and starving, I lived unchaste."

"With how many?" Father Leofric asked.

"With *one*," she said angrily. She made an effort to subdue her tone. "I have confessed it, at Aveiro, and abjured it and done penance for it."

"But have not been absolved," Leofric said. "You were refused Absolution, I believe."

"Can that stand as evidence against me," she said gently, "when I am tried by the power that refused me?"

"Are you questioning the authority of the Church?" Morkere said.

"No, Messire, *no*," she said passionately. "I am only trying to understand it. Help me. Please help me. Accusations are brought against me, but no accusers. How can I answer things that I have not heard said, but only heard read from a parchment that I have not seen? Cannot those who accuse me be brought to accuse me here, where I can see them?"

"It is against law and sense," Leofric said, "to bring her accusers into the presence of a witch, lest she suborn them with the glance of her eyes."

Clodagh threw out her hands in a gesture of helplessness. "Bandage my eyes," she said. Her judges leaned together, and for a moment she thought they were considering doing as she asked.

"Proceed," Morkere said, as the others drew back to their places.

It seemed to her now that she would get nothing except by fighting for it. Appeals to their pity would not help her. She was allowed no one to speak for her. She would have to speak for herself. "I will answer nothing," she said, "until I am told who has spoken against me, and for what reason and with what claims. Do not tell me what was said, unless you tell me also who said it, for I will not answer." She turned and went to the stool again, and sat down, putting her clenched hands between her knees to conceal their shaking. She looked down, afraid to look at Morkere and the others, for fear her tone might have turned them implacably against her. But a strong tone seemed to her the only alternative to hysterical weeping, and *that* she knew would be taken as a sign of fearfulness and guilt.

"The man Gyll of Dittisham deposes that she was his succubus, that he was bewitched into venery with potions and incantations, and that when he tried to withstand her she detached his privy member and threw it into a tree, later rejoining it to him on his promise of obedience."

"You lie," she said.

"The woman Joice deposes that she made game appear or disappear at will, caused streams to dry up and robbed men of their virile powers. The man Magnus deposes—"

"Is he alive?" she said.

"—that she wounded his leg or caused it to be wounded so that it putrefied and had to be cut off in the thigh, and further that she caused poisonous visions in the people, by persuading them to eat a noxious weed. The woman Godda deposes that she mocked the Host and forced them by spells to partake a Black Mass, to the everlasting danger of their souls. The man Godwin and his brother, Edwin, depose that she brought a creature among them that none of them had seen before, and that later she caused this creature to disappear, or to be transmogrified into the body of a beast."

A black horror seized her, so that the room and her judges wavered before her eyes. She closed them, holding to the edge of her stool to stop herself from falling. She had believed the almost unbelievable; she had believed that the twins, desperate for food, had killed the Monkey and that all of them—Gyll, Eleanor, Simon, Father Nicholas—had eaten his terrible and forbidden flesh. She had believed it strongly enough to separate herself, to shudder a night away, preyed on by inexpressible fears. But then she had found and eaten the mushroom, and a small and comforting doubt had crept into her mind. Now no doubt was possible any longer. Someone had confessed something to the English priest at Aveiro, something so insupportable that it could only be explained away by witchcraft. Somebody had admitted eating the Monkey's flesh, and had excused the abomination by charging her with having magicked him into the shape of some animal. She opened her eyes and found her three judges watching her. "We are waiting," Canon Morkere said.

"Have you seen these people?" she asked faintly. Nobody answered her. "I do not think I can be accused by a strumpet and a cunning-woman, a common soldier and two murderers," she said. "If they have sworn these things, they have perjured themselves. I cannot be accused by perjurers."

"It is laid down," Leofric said heavily, "that such people, and only such people, can accuse a witch, for none that are honest can detect one. The testimony of infamous and perjured persons is good, and allowable."

"Six have spoken against me," Clodagh said. "Seven,

he says"—indicating the Promoter—"but of one at least I know he speaks no truth. I ask that two be allowed to speak for me. I demand it," she said in a shaking voice, that made no real demand.

"Which two?" Morkere asked.

"I have *said*," Leofric said before she could answer, "the testimony of honest people is not to be heard in a matter of witchcraft."

"I am not asking for that," Clodagh said. "There is no matter of witchcraft. Surely their testimony is good in matters of fact?" She searched her memory of the accusations to find one that could be so considered. "I am accused that I conjured up a sailor, out of thin air. Will you refuse the testimony of honest people as to where he came from?"

Canon Morkere looked from one of his brother judges to the other. Guilliame nodded his agreement, Leofric shook his head.

"Which people do you ask for?" Morkere said.

"The priest," Clodagh said. "The Lady Eleanor of Canterbury."

"On one condition," Morkere said. "They will be sent for, if in the meantime you will answer every question put to you, without dissimulation or lie."

"I will answer," Clodagh said.

"Did you use spells or incantations or any monstrous or illicit things to persuade others into venery?"

"No."

"She is already perjured," Leofric said. "There is no credence left in any of her answers."

Clodagh started up from her stool. "You are damnable," she said. "How is that fair? How is that just? You will take against me the lying words of murderers and sots, but you will hold against me one small lie which I admitted and retracted myself."

"No lie is small, sworn on the rood," Guilliame said.

Clodagh fought for control. She could ill afford to antagonize Father Guilliame, since he was the only one who had yet appeared to have doubts about her guilt. "You are right, Monseigneur," she said humbly. "The lie was great. My plea is that I allowed it to stand only a short while."

Father Guilliame smiled and nodded at her, pleased that this point had been made. He did not care very much for his brother judges. He thought that a Porto court should have a preponderance of Porto priests, just as he thought that Porto should have a native bishop, instead of the Englishman who had been given the See. Besides, these two spoke their damnable English much too quickly for his understanding.

"Have you profaned the mass?" Morkere asked.

"Never."

"Or taken part in any Satanic mass?"

Clodagh hesitated. "Answer me," Morkere said.

"I do not *think* so," she said.

"I do not see that there can be room for doubt," Leofric said.

"Tell us your doubts. We will resolve them," Morkere said.

"They caught two little goats . . ."

"They?"

"The commons who accuse me," Clodagh said. "They did with them, in my sight, things I thought blasphemous."

"What things?" Morkere and Leofric said together.

"They called it a sin-shedding," Clodagh said. "They believed that God was punishing the people for their sins. One of the goats they killed. The other they released again, in the bushes."

"The priest allowed it?" Morkere asked.

"He didn't know," Clodagh said. "They ate the dead goat. And then they danced."

"And you neither ate, nor danced?"

"No," Clodagh said, "I swear it."

"We know the value of what she swears," Leofric said. She kept her eyes down, determined not to be trapped again into anger.

"You must answer now the graver charges about the dumb boy," Morkere said.

"He was not dumb," Clodagh said. "He had no English, that is all."

"How did he come to be aboard the ship?"

"I do not know."

"He was not aboard the ship," Leofric said. "This the people have sworn. He was not seen until the next morning. He came with this woman from the further end of the beach."

"They weren't on the beach," Clodagh said. "How could they swear to that?"

"The soldier Magnus was there," Leofric said.

"I had forgotten."

"He swore to it."

"But the boy was a sailor," Clodagh said. "Captain Faber can tell you that."

"He didn't tell us," Canon Morkere said, "and now he has gone from Porto. What happened to the boy?"

"Mother of God, do I have to speak of that?"

"If you hope to live," Morkere said.

Clodagh looked at her hands, opening and closing them convulsively, afraid of death and fire, eternal damnation and the very present danger that she might be going to be sick. "I think they ate him," she said speaking very slowly. "I think so. I . . . think . . . so." Their faces swam in front of her. Someone took her arm and pressed her down onto the stool. Someone else held a cup to her mouth, and she felt the coolness of water on her lips, but she couldn't swallow it. The judges had their heads together again, and this time she fancied that they were conferring in Latin. They talked for a long time, and several times a young priest went between them and the courtyard through which she had come earlier.

When at last they had reached some conclusion in their argument, the Promoter took her by the arm, raised her and led her to a curtained alcove at the back of the room. "Go in," he said. "You may listen, but you must neither speak, nor show yourself."

She raised the heavy curtain to go in, and was astonished to find Robert Apelfourde there, leaning forward in a listening position. *"You!"* she said.

"Let me past," he said quickly, moving to go out under the fall of the curtain.

"No," she said. "Wait. Why are you doing this?" It was what she had meant to ask, when she had thought he was bringing charges of adultery against her.

"I am doing nothing," he said. "The matter is between you and the Church."

"You could save me," she said, pleading. "I am your wife."

"But you are no good to me," he said coldly. "I couldn't get you with child. No more, it seems, could that young stallion you've been galloping with. He'll gallop no more, after he's gelded."

"It was not his fault," she said, keeping her voice low and level. "I am going to die. I shall use the last breath of my life to pray to the Virgin that if you harm him you will never have a child by any woman."

Apelfourde crossed himself. "Die easy," he said. "I swear I won't touch him."

"Nor have him touched," she said.

"Nor have him touched," he said, and crossed himself again and went out. She burst into tears as the curtain swung back behind him. His coldness and his anger were understandable; his fear of her and his ready promise not to revenge himself on Gyll could only mean that he believed she was a witch.

For a few minutes she forgot that she was there to listen, and gave way to weeping that would have gladdened Father Guilliame's heart and gone a long way to persuading him of her innocence. After a time she became aware of the sound of Father Nicholas's voice. She went to the curtain and took up the listening position in which she had discovered Robert Apelfourde.

". . . only of the flesh," he was saying, "as many have done, even as many priests have done, forgetting God's altar and their holy orders. The Lady Clodagh is very young, sinful and weak. I think she is guilty of no incurable sin."

"Nevertheless, bestial things are charged against her," Morkere said, "and they must be answered." He spoke gently. The old man was a fool, he thought. Or perhaps his wits had been starved away during the journey. In any case, since he was a priest, he must be listened to with courtesy; and then, Morkere thought, it would be as well to expunge his testimony from the scribes' record, since he seemed bent on blaming himself for every sin of commission or omission. "A priest can only do what he can do," he said. "He cannot turn his people away from error, if their hearts are closed."

"It was so long since God had smiled on them," Father Nicholas said wearily, "that I think they could no longer remember His face. Nevertheless," he said more strongly, remembering why he was there, "the Lady Clodagh committed no incurable sin. Her sin was of the flesh, not of the fiend."

"It is said she blasphemed—in treading on crosses, in spitting at the Elevation, in breaking fast on fast days and in fasting on Sundays."

"We all fasted on Sundays. We were hungry," the priest said. "As for the rest . . ."

". . . and that she used charms and potions, and did instigate a form of the Black Mass."

Father Nicholas sighed. The weight of his age and his failure robbed him of arguments in the face of these confident priests who had forgotten, if they had ever known, how peasants went back to old practices if God did not answer their prayers with alacrity. "The commons do these things," he said. "They dance in the churchyard, they burn torches against spirits, they mix potions to drive away dragons from their fields. The Lady Clodagh was not one of them. She was demeaned, but she was not one of them. They blamed her for this, not for the demeaning. What they did frightened them. They are looking for ways to alter the history of what happened, so that they can live with themselves, and perhaps deceive God."

"You have a kind heart, Father," Father Leofric said. It did not sound like a commendation. "It is also charged against her that she turned the foreign boy into a pig, and so deceived the others into unspeakable sin. *Veneficam non retinebitis in vita,* the Scriptures say. Thou shalt not suffer a witch to live."

"Translated out of Latin into English," Father Nicholas said, "the word sounds in every man's ear rather 'poisoner' than 'witch' or worker of miracles."

"What do you say, then, to the charge that the boy was killed, and his body ęaten?" Morkere asked.

The priest smiled. "It is an absurdity," he said. "The heathen wandered away and, I doubt not, was devoured by wild animals, as only the mercy and love of God prevented the devouring of us all. Who charges this absurdity against her?"

"Godda's sons," the Promoter said. "The twin brothers, Edwin and Godwin."

The priest shrugged. "The charge is benothinged," he said, "by the fact that both are rogues, and headed for purgatory."

The judges conferred again for a few minutes, keeping their voices low. Then they thanked Father Nicholas, and dismissed him. Clodagh put a finger between the curtain and the alcove opening to make a peephole, confident that no one in the room could see into so small an opening. Father Nicholas was walking slowly from the room, with his shoulders slumped. At the doorway he turned and, as though dissatisfied with the force of what he had said, spoke again in a firm voice. "She should be absolved of her sins of unchastity," he said, "after whatever strong penances the Church may lay on her. As for the rest, it is foolishness. If the powers punish people, as we were punished, the people look into their hearts, and find a reason for it. Everyone has a feeling of unworthiness. *Unworthiness*," he said again, remembering his own. "Those without proper faith cannot support their unworthiness. They try to put it on to the shoulders of someone else. That is all." Canon Morkere nodded at him in firm dismissal, and he turned and moved out of Clodagh's sight.

His place was taken by the Lady Eleanor, whose upright bearing and clear voice made it plain that she was

not easily to be overawed. Her cropped hair was clean
and shining now, and she wore a brown robe of plain
rich material, with a new cross of scarlet silk over her
heart. She was asked to tell what she knew of the Hyperborean boy.

"Very little," she said. "He had no name, he spoke no
language any of us could understand. He was found,
sodden with good English ale, in a laneway close to the
docks at Dartmouth, and brought unconscious aboard
the *Grace Dieu*, to make up a deficiency in the crew."

"Do you know this absolutely?" Morkere said.

"I swear to it, and I know it absolutely," Eleanor said.
"Captain Faber stole him from one of the far-north
ships. As for what became of him, who knows? He went
away from us of his own accord."

"The woman Clodagh says that he was killed, and his
flesh eaten."

"The Lady Clodagh is wrong," Eleanor said, hoping
to reprove Morkere's failure to accord her proper respect. "This is chop-cherry logic. You do not believe her
when she denies things that no sound person would find
believable, but you believe her when she voices a sick
fancy that attacked her when she was much weakened
and distressed by hunger and illness."

"Do you believe in the Devil?" Father Guilliame said
earnestly, leaning forward.

"Yes, absolutely," Eleanor said.

"And witches?" Guilliame said. "You believe in
witches?"

"I believe in Christ," Eleanor said. "If He had known
them, He would have mentioned them in His Book."

"Yet there are amounts of old women, many
amounts," Guilliame said, "that say they have powers
to do strong harms."

"A mewing cat is never a mouser, Monseigneur," Eleanor said.

Guilliame sat back again, to ponder the meaning of this.

"You are not here to air your views on such matters," Morkere said, "but only to tell what you know of the foreign boy and what became of him."

"I hope I am too good a Christian," Eleanor said, ignoring this, "to believe that some baggage old woman, or some greensick young one, has the power to do miraculous works that are rightly in the domain of the most high God."

"You will not deny that there are spells made, and incantations recited," Morkere said, forgetting his ruling that she should speak only of the boy.

"To make a spell is one thing. To make it work is another. If the pagan gods still walk in the furrows, Messire, then the Church must take itself to task that it does nothing to cure the blind ignorance of the man with the hoe. His childishness is not binding on better people."

"You are wrong, daughter," Morkere said earnestly. "Unpunished, these beliefs can bring the whole world down in destruction. And you are arrogant. All Christian people are equal in God's sight."

Eleanor smiled. "Who can tell what God sees?" she said. "All people are not equal, though, in places like this." She swept her arm out, indicating the room and the row of judges. "I do not feel myself equal, in matters of argument or of faith, with coarse peasants who cannot think beyond their next meal. I do not feel the Lady Clodagh equal with them."

"But you feel her to be equal to you?"

"No," Eleanor said, considering it. "I do not. She is

young and foolish, with a mind that is set only on worldly things. She is sinful, but she is not corrupt. As for the things said against her, surely it is a blasphemous assertion and not to be taken seriously, that a man made in the very image of God could be turned by this poor girl into a beast? As for her other sins, they are common enough, God knows, and should be excused because of the imbecility and frailty of her sex."

"For which good reason, also, Lady," Leofric said, "little store should be set by your opinions."

"So I would think," Eleanor said with a smile, "had not the Canon just reproved my rashness in thinking all were not absolutely equal in God's eyes. The charges against her are impious and malicious, made up by fools who have uneasy consciences. 'Be strong in the Lord,'" she said, quoting St. Paul to them. "'Put on the whole armour of God that ye may stand steadfast against the crafty assaults of the Devil, for we wrestle not against the flesh and blood: but against Rulers, against Powers, and against the worldly Governors, the princes of the darkness of this world, which are in high places.'" She turned on her heel without waiting to be dismissed, and walked out of the room.

Clodagh, watching her go from her peephole at the edge of the curtain, was full of love for her, but no gratitude. She had not understood the import of what Eleanor had just said, but she could see from the judges' faces that they were not pleased by it.

Again her judges conferred for a long time. It was impossible for Clodagh, in the alcove at the far end of the room, to hear anything of what they said. Father Leofric had left his seat and come around to the front of the table, leaning in across it to speak closely into the faces of the others. After a time she tired of watching

Leofric's back, and went to sit on a narrow stool against the wall of the alcove. She sat there a long time while they talked. She kept trying to bring her thoughts back to the accusations, to ways of refuting them, to means of discovering a single passionate plea that would melt their hearts and make them see her innocence. But she was too much frightened, too shocked by Robert Apelfourde's rejection of her, to keep her thoughts usefully on what she must do next. Instead her mind was crowded with old stories of enchantment and the awful penalties with which it had been punished. Suddenly she was startled by a great clanking and clattering in the court, as though an armload of staves and mattocks had been dropped to the stone floor. She went forward to look again through the curtain, but as she reached it, it was lifted by the Promoter. He reached in and took her by the arm, and led her back to her stool in front of the judges. She looked fearfully down. Beside her on the floor were tongs and straps and unidentifiable things which she thought were all instruments of torture. She tried to swallow, but her throat had tightened too painfully to allow it. She tried to speak, to say "Don't, don't, I will say *anything* rather than suffer such pain," but fear had made her tongue immovable.

"We charge you," Morkere said, "that you accept this last and merciful chance we give you, to acknowledge your wickedness, recant your heresy and throw yourself on God's indulgence and pity."

Slowly she dragged her glance away from the things at her feet, and raised her head to look into Morkere's face. Twice she swallowed painfully, but still she was unable to speak.

"Admit your errors," Morkere said. "God and His Church are merciful. If you refuse to answer, you must be put to the test."

She swallowed again, and found the remnants of her voice. "I am not brave," she said faintly.

"Then you must answer now."

She could think of no answer that would move them, no answer that she had not given already. "If I were possessed of powers, perhaps I would not fear these things," she said, glancing briefly at the things on the floor beside her. "I am no witch. I have no powers. And I am very much afraid."

The others looked in surprise as Father Guilliame rose from his place and came forward to stand in front of her. "Feet," he said, gesturing for her to stand. Then he took the cross from his belt and held it in front of her at the level of her eyes. "I conjure you," he said, "by Christ's amourous tears shed on the Cross for the saving of the world: by the hot tears of His Mother the glorious Virgin Mary that fell on His wounds that late night: and by all the tears of every saint poured in this world: that if you are true you pour down many tears: that if you are guilty, you pour down none. *In nomine patris et filius et spiritus sancti*, Amen."

She stared at him. She was beyond tears, beyond satisfying him in this way. He waited a little while. Then he lowered the cross and, looking surprised, went back to his seat behind the judges' table.

"Proceed," Morkere said, speaking this time to the two men who had brought the torture instruments into the room. One of them took her by the shoulders and forced her down on the stool. The other stood close, holding a small bowl of white powder and a horn spoon.

"Open your mouth," the first man said, putting a heavy finger on her chin to force her lower jaw down. She jerked her head away, and covered her mouth by cupping both her hands.

"Poison," she said, speaking through her fingers. She looked at Morkere. "Poison?"

"No poison," Morkere said, "but good wholesome flour. If you are guilty, fear will dry your mouth and you will choke. If you are innocent, you will swallow the flour and live."

The first man took hold of her again, forcing her chin down so that the other could spoon the choking flour into her mouth. She tried to mound her tongue into a hump, but he pushed it down with the bowl of the spoon, turning it on her tongue to empty it a second time, so that her mouth seemed crammed with the dry flour. Then they stood back to watch her. Everyone in the room was still, watching.

She was afraid to breathe, for fear that she would smother herself and die. Her eyes bulged with the effort of holding her breath, and with terror. She moved her tongue gently inside her mouth, and a little of the flour was forced out of her lips and spilled down on to her chin.

"If the flour is spat out, it is a presumption of guilt," Morkere said.

She closed her eyes, asking the saints for help, and one of the kindly ones put into her mind the image of a lemon. Behind her closed lids she held to the image, imagining the fruit cut and sucked, its sour juice stinging the inside of her lips. She felt a little of the smothering flour begin to cake with her spittle, but she was still afraid that she might die from lack of breath before she was able to swallow. She put a hand to her mouth to stop her lips from opening, and drew a cautious thread of breath through her distended nostrils. She added green gooseberries to her thoughts, and the caking of the flour increased, allowing her to breathe a little more.

Everyone in the room was still, watching her. She didn't open her eyes. Slowly the flour was becoming manageable in her mouth, but she didn't yet dare to try to swallow it, for fear it would not pass down her tightened throat. She began to work her tongue and her cheeks, shaping and moistening the mass that had now shrunk in size. Now she could breathe more easily, now it was safe at last to half fill her lungs. She chewed at the stuff for a few seconds more, and then she swallowed it, and opened her eyes. They were still staring at her. She held out her hands to show that they were empty and then, like a child showing that it had done what it was told, opened her mouth widely to show that she had emptied it.

"She must be given holy water to drink," Leofric said. "If she is possessed, the evil spirit will be thrown into a frenzy when it reaches him, and either she will vomit it up, or fall into a convulsion."

She took the chalice of water eagerly, and drank till the last traces of flour had been washed from her mouth. When she lowered it Morkere said, "All of it. No drop must be left." She raised the chalice to her mouth again and drank steadily and slowly, drinking as much water as she had had in two or three days during the bad times of their journey from the south.

"So be it," Morkere said. "She is not now possessed."

"Unless by a spirit of exceptional strength," Leofric said. "She must be cut above the breath, while she holds the cross to her heart to drive him out."

This time she began to shriek and struggle when the first man grasped her, holding her arms behind her while the second approached carrying a shining blade handled with a horn cross. She closed her eyes again and forced herself to be silent, in case they might think the cries were not hers, but came from some threatened spirit inside her ribs. She gave a small cry, though, when she felt a stinging pain across her forehead, and some heavy thing that was pressed between her breasts made her fear for a moment that she had been stabbed and was about to die. She opened her eyes when her arms were released, and saw that a few drops of blood had dropped onto the stuff of her Virgin-blue gown. She breathed deeply and found that she was whole, and knew that what she had felt at her breast was a metal cross. She put an exploring hand to her head. She had a small, painful cut above her left eye. She stared at her judges, wondering whether their tests were finished, or whether she was to be put to any further ordeals. They stared back at her, busy with the same questions. After a time they leaned together, quietly discussing what was to be done next. She waited, confidence growing in her. She had no way of knowing whether these three believed the tests were valid, or whether they used them only to frighten her into false admissions. But she had admitted nothing in spite of her fear, and she had begun to hope, and to feel a measure of triumph.

Canon Morkere broke off the muttered conference. It was plain to those who watched that they had failed to reach any agreement. "Your arguments," he said, turning to the Promoter.

The Promoter was taken by surprise and glanced down at the parchment in front of him, gathering his forces. "Many things have not yet been answered," he said. "To begin with, there is the charge of the woman's own priest that she is a poisoner."

"I think he made no such charge," Morkere said.

One of the scribes, feeling himself called on, shuffled the sheets in front of him and read, "'*Veneficam non retinebitis in vita.* Thou shalt not suffer a *poisoner* to live.' "

"He was translating," Morkere said impatiently, "not accusing."

"Nevertheless, it has yet to be answered why and for what purpose the woman fed specter-producing poisons to the people."

"What have you to say to that?" Morkere said.

"I was hungry," Clodagh said. "Messire, we had to eat the things that we could find. Until I had eaten the stuff, I did not know its strange properties."

"And having found them," Leofric said, "you forced the others to eat, engendering in them obscene fantasies and hallucinations."

"No," she said, "I did not give the stuff to anyone else. The Lady Eleanor gathered what there was."

"It is a common thing to seek safety by accusing someone else."

"I accuse nobody. The mushroom brought Magnus great relief when his pain was too big for him to bear. *I* did not give the stuff to him."

Morkere looked again at the Promoter, who was ready with his finger on the place. "There is the charge that she conjured away all game and water, so that the people were brought into her power by their weakness and thirst."

"We have the evidence of the native people that it is poor, bare country, and poorer and barer since the Moors laid it waste as they were driven out," Morkere said, dismissing this.

"That she did entice the man Gyll into unnatural acts."

"Unnatural, I do not think so," Father Guilliame said. "Young blood burns itself very hot."

"There remains the central matter of the boy," the Promoter said. He did not need high words to bring this back into their minds. The magicking of the boy into animal form and the eating of his conjured flesh was clearly the most consummate charge against her.

Canon Morkere sighed. He did not think there was any good answer to this question. The priest believed the boy had been eaten by beasts. The Lady Eleanor believed he had wandered away and, for all that anyone could tell, might find his way back in time to Christian people. The very mention of the boy terrified the accused, but Morkere thought her terror came from her pity rather than from her guilt. He himself was inclined to believe that that party had lived because the boy died, that he had been eaten and that his flesh had sustained them during the most crucial days. If that was so, then what more natural than that rough peasants, suspecting what had been done, should try to shift their guilt onto the shoulders of the one abstainer, as earlier they had tried to shift them to the goat? What should he do? No doubt he could rack a confession from the twins. If they confessed, they could die for it, and properly those who had eaten should lose their hands and their ears. Was he to order the lopping of the Lady Eleanor's hands, or have the ears cut from under Simon de Baude's crusading helmet? Justice, alas, was never such a simple matter. The temper of the army commanders in Porto was austere. God had prospered them. God had guided them to overcome the Saracen's evil brothers in Portugal. The fighting men believed that Bernard spoke the truth—they had lost the First War because of the profligacy and unworthiness of those who fought in it. They would win the Second, if their lives were pure. Neither the commanders nor the common

soldiers would easily accept any but condign punishment for a woman accused of witchcraft, for fear that
she might turn her bright eyes next on them. He did
not think she was a witch. He did not think she was a
good woman, and he thought acquittal would reinforce
her sinfulness and her weakness of faith. He sighed
again. Besides all this, he had the problem of reconciling the views of his fellow judges. Father Leofric was
an ascetic, a soldiers' priest, a man in whose heart there
blazed continually the vision of Jerusalem restored to
the true faith. He supposed Leofric to have his own
doubts about the culpability of the girl, but he thought
that Leofric would think her life a straw, if its snuffing
out would help Christian people to kneel once more in
the Sepulchre. As for the Portugee, Father Guilliame,
he thought him a simple fool, with his flesh insufficiently
subdued below the level of his priest's girdle. He did
not think the woman's tears would have influenced
Guilliame so much if they had slid over wrinkled skin,
out of a hag's eyes.

"For the last time," he said, addressing Clodagh, "I
beg you to put away your pride and seek to save your
soul from perdition by reconciling it with God. We
have great pity for you. Offer yourself on the altar of
your heart, put away from you all traffickings with God's
Ape, the Devil, remember that in purgatory there will
be nothing to feed the flames except your sins. If your
sins are small, the flames will burn your soul clean
again; if you persist in sin, those sins will feed the
flames through all eternity."

"When may I be brought to confession?" Clodagh
said.

"There will be a time for that," Morkere said. "Make
your heart small. Do you acknowledge the temporal

power of Holy Mother Church and submit yourself, without reservation, to her judgment?"

"Yes," Clodagh said faintly. It seemed the only answer. She was uncertain what he meant by the question.

Morkere looked from Leofric to Guilliame, and both nodded in agreement. He rose, and the others rose too, so that her three judges faced her, standing, across the table. "This is the sentence of the Church," Morkere said.

Clodagh stood quickly up. It did not seem good to her that she should hear it seated.

"For your sins," Morkere said, speaking slowly and heavily, "we do sentence you that you be taken from this place to a place in England which we will determine, and that you do live cloistered and enclosed there, under the rule of the nuns and without access to any person of the outside world, until God shall determine the end of your earthly life."

Clodagh stared at him, the horror of her sentence slowly working its way into her mind. She had lived the greater part of her life in the fear of convent walls, had known as a child that she was promised to this living death, had fought and wept and prayed and cajoled her mother until Blanchefleur, much regretting the promise made for her unborn child, had damned her own soul by breaking it. Now the convent was to get her back. She was to be shut away from the sun, from life, friends, happiness, the hope of children. And the shutting away would do nothing to reverse the fate Blanchefleur had accepted for her daughter's sake. "*No!*" she said, taking a pace forward towards the table. "It is not fair. It is not just. *No.* I will not. Rather I'll kill myself."

"We are trying to save your life," Morkere said.

"No," she said again. "Rather I'll die damned than

live safe, shut away. I am *eighteen*," she said, her voice
rising to a wail. "How is it pleasing to God, if I am
buried alive?" Tears overflowed her lids, ran down her
cheeks and dropped to darken the colour of her gown.
"I beg you, I beg you . . ." she said, "please listen . . .
I beg you . . . how is it just, when nothing has been
proved against me, when I have spoken the whole truth
to you, when the priest, and the Lady Eleanor . . ."

"You have sinned," Morkere said, "and the sin——"

"I have sinned neither greater nor worse than many
hundreds," she said, sobbing, "and they are not enclosed to die, lonely, in the dark, with no joy and no
happiness. . . ."

"You will have joy," Morkere said. "And happiness.
You will suffer greatly at the beginning, as is right. But
God does not turn his face forever from a penitent. You
will be reconciled. You will know true joy."

"I will die," she said. "I will kill myself, before this
cruelty can be done." Watching them through her tears,
she could see that this did not move them, that neither
her tears nor her threats would make them change their
minds. "Messire," she said to Morkere, concentrating
all her appeal on him. "Nothing has been proved against
me, *nothing*. Have pity on me. I do not want to live,
perpetually imprisoned. If my sins are so great that they
deserve this, give me the larger penalty. Take my life
now."

"The Church does not take life," Morkere said
firmly.

"But . . . if I had done these things, and confessed . . .
or had them proved against me?"

"The Church condemns, but it does not execute,"
Morkere said. "Had death been your proper penalty,
you would have been delivered to the secular arm. You

are fortunate that this does not arise. You will spend the rest of your life secure, disciplined and beyond harms."

"But I will not submit," she said desperately. "I withdraw my submission. Either I must be guilty, or I must be innocent. How is it right that I should be punished, without this being decided?"

"Let her be put to the ordeal," Leofric said.

"What ordeal?" she said, turning to him. "Already two ordeals have proved nothing against me."

"There are others, and more searching," Leofric said. "If she so much fears the cloister, it is a symptom," he said to Morkere. "In any case, reason and law allow her to demand proving, before punishment."

"But I will not be tortured?" Clodagh said, glancing fearfully behind her to the heap of instruments.

"No," Morkere said. Leofric, he thought, would not be averse to it to preserve the sanctity of the Crusading Armies, but Morkere's conscience would not allow it in the present case. "There are two ordeals. You may choose which."

"And if I prove my innocence by overcoming, do I go free?"

"I promise it," Morkere said.

A feeling of confidence made her lift her head and stand proudly facing them. The holy water had not thrown her into a fit, the smothering flour had not taken her life. She would survive a third ordeal. She would go free. She would be among friends again, under trees, in meadows that were full of flowers and bees and sunlight. "What ordeals?" she said confidently. "I don't fear them."

"First," Leofric said, "there is *Candentis ferri*, by which you must carry two handfuls of burning iron from the church door to the altar rail. If you are inno-

cent of the charges, the iron will be powerless to burn
your flesh."

Clodagh shook her head. Whatever the alternative
was, it must be preferable. She did not believe that all
the lemon trees of all the saints could stop red-hot iron
from burning hands, whether they were innocent or
guilty.

"Second, there is an ordeal by water," Leofric said.
Clodagh nodded. She did not fear water particularly. "A
witch's body will not sink in water," Leofric said, "but
her head will be held above it by the Devil."

A doubt began to creep into her mind. "I am innocent," she said. "So I will sink?"

"Yes," Leofric said, "if you speak truth."

"And so, being innocent, I will be drowned?"

"No," Leofric said. "If you are innocent the water
will accept you and close over you, and in a little while
it will carry you up, so that you float with your head in
the air again. There will be hands there, and ropes, to
bring you safely in."

"And I will go free?"

"It has been promised," Morkere said.

"May I make my confession first? To Father Nicholas?"

"We grant that," Morkere said, glad to be done with
the business. "You will be confessed tonight, and go to
trial early in the morning."

Alone in her room at the monastery, with the old
monk once more on guard outside her door, she was
happy for the first time in many days. Soon the priest
would come to her and she would confess and receive
Absolution. She didn't fear the water ordeal very much.
She had been through worse. The wild sea on the night

the *Grace Dieu* sank had been worse water than any they could throw her in, and though the waves had submerged her many times, each time she had come safely to the surface. In truth, that had been the only time in her life that she had been in water so wild and deep that she couldn't stand with her feet on the bottom and her head in the air. She supposed tomorrow's water would be deep, but it would be daylight when she went into it, and there would be others there to help her out. All she would need would be God's help, and a deep breath before she went in.

The priest came to her in the evening, and her confidence was a little shaken by his misery. He seemed to have aged more in the few hours since she had seen him from her peephole in the alcove, and his hands, when he took hers, were shaking as though he were palsied.

He had spent the intervening hours trying to pray, but his fear for her came between him and God. It seemed to him that even the Holy Grail, brought by Merlin in his crystal ark, could not survive were it thrown into water that was cunningly chosen. He thought the water *would* be cunningly chosen. He feared Leofric and the present temper of the Crusading Armies.

Clodagh's confident mood, the happiness of her greeting to him and her eagerness for him to hear her confession only deepened his despair. It seemed to him that God was mocking him. He had accepted as inevitable that he would be punished for his failure by being denied the satisfaction of reaching Porto and the end of the journey. That would have been just. But God had allowed him to reach the end, had comforted and restored him a little and now had turned to punishing him again. He had been forced into the sin of questioning God's judgment, and so must die heretic and damned. It

added to his self-contempt that he should be now so
tender for the fate of his own soul, when Clodagh's
should be his whole concern. "The last duty of every
Christian is to die patiently, and with humility," he
said.

"When the time comes," Clodagh said with a smile. "I
shall not die, Father Nicholas. This ordeal is no worse
than any other. They have tried and failed. They proved
nothing against me."

"I wish you had chosen the convent walls they offered."

"Why?" she said. "Because I was promised there, in
my childhood?"

"No, because there is great safety there. As for the
other, you are not responsible for the sin of your par-
ents, even though you were born because of it."

"This is a better way," she said, trying to comfort him.
"Today and tomorrow to suffer in, and the rest of my
life to live in my own way. I am very young, Father. The
rest of my life would be a very long time to live enclosed.
Tomorrow, afterwards, what will they do to those who
accused me wrongly?"

"Nothing," Father Nicholas said, out of conviction
that it would be so. "They are vile, rough people, impious and malicious. They could not bear the weight of
their own sins."

"But they are *Christians*," Clodagh said. "Surely they
have been taught, as we are all taught, that Jesus was the
scapegoat for our sins?"

"Eleven hundred years is a long time, and Calvary is
a long way away. It is more comfortable to have a scapegoat close to their hands. It is the common longing of all
men, and the cause of all the world's cruelties."

"Then they have failed, and their sins are still on

their own heads," Clodagh said cheerfully. Their behaviour was unexplainable. What the priest said did not
really make it any clearer to her, but she didn't see why
she should be bothered by it any longer. There was tomorrow to be got through, and after that a new life to
be lived. It would be without Apelfourde, and without
Gyll, without place and without honour for the time
being at least. But there was a whole lifetime of years
ahead. As a child she had felt that if the lien of the
convent could be broken, then something extraordinary
would happen, she would do something memorable in
her life. But, with the lien broken, all she had done was
to make an unexceptionable marriage. Now that was
gone. She was being given a second chance. Some mo-
mentous opportunity for splendour lay, she thought,
only a day ahead.

"Will you hear my confession, Father Nicholas?" she
said, anxious to be done with it, to be alone, to think and
sleep and dream.

"Yes," he said, "but first you are to be rebaptized."

"Rebaptized?" she said, startled. "Why?"

"It was ordered," he said, "by your judges. As a remedy
against error—"

"I am not in error, not in *their* error."

"—and to remove any of the mud that clings. Kneel,"
he said, and uncovered the stoup of holy water he had
brought. He dipped his finger and signed her on her
forehead and lips and on each wrist, and said, "I conjure
thee, Clodagh, being sick, but regenerate in the holy
water of baptism, by the living God, by the true God,
by the holy God, by the God which redeemed thee with
His precious blood, that thou mayst be made a conjured
woman, that every fantasy and wickedness of diabolical
deceit do avoid and depart from thee and that every un-

clean spirit be conjured through Him that shall come to judge the quick and the dead, and the world by fire. Amen."

When he had done, she got to her feet. She was angry. "That was not right," she said. "That should not have been done. Nothing is proved against me. I am not possessed."

"I do what I must do," the priest said. "What I am told to do. Besides which, there is no one of us alive into whom the Devil in all his feathers has not entered at some time. Kneel down again. I will confess you now."

While she confessed, she was shocked to find that Father Nicholas was weeping. "Are my sins so black?" she said, breaking off, the last of them driven out of her mind by the sight of his distress.

"No," he said, "no. Forgive me, child." She stared at him, forgetting her sins in her fear that there was more to come tomorrow than she knew, and that Father Nicholas wept because of his knowledge of it.

"Go on, go on," he said, letting the tears run unchecked down his face.

"I can't go on," she said fearfully, "not unless you tell me why you are so sad."

"I have failed you," the priest said. "Even now I am failing you, because I weep for myself and my own sins, when I should weep for you."

"No one should weep for me," Clodagh said, putting a hand out to him to comfort him. "I am safe. I am saved."

"I truly believe so," Father Nicholas said. He forgot the rest of her sins, and began the Absolution, and it seemed to her holier and more absolute because his breath caught in small sobs as he pronounced it.

When he was finished she only wanted him to be

gone. His admission that he wept for himself and not for her left her lonelier than she would be were she alone. "Dear soul," he said, "do not waste the whole of this night in sleep. Pray. Pray to Mary Virgin that She comfort and support and cherish you. Pray for me too, I beg you, pray a little for me." He gathered up his cloak and his stoup, moving slowly as though movement had become very difficult for him. Then he pressed his lips to her forehead in a farewell kiss and went out, taking his fears and his failings.

Alone, she was too lit up with hope and happiness to continue with her prayers. She would pray later. Now she went to the window, pressing her head against its bars in order to see out into the night. Light from torches and from cooking fires spilled down the steep slope of the opposite bank, and lay in bright reflected pools on the river's water. The sight of the water chilled her for a moment, but the water would not be dark in the morning, and it would not be so cold. Below, on the waste ground where children played in the daytime, she could see the glow of a fire where a group of soldiers, back from the fighting in the south, were celebrating their safety by getting drunk. They might, for all she knew, be Robert Apelfourde's men. They began to sing a ribald song, using Wenceslas's tune, and the words of it came to her clearly on the night air.

> *In the tavern's straw to die*
> *Is my resolution:*
> *Let wine to my lips be nigh*
> *At life's dissolution:*
> *That will make the angels cry,*
> *With glad elocution,*
> *"Grant this toper, God on high,*
> *Grace and absolution."*

It seemed to be the only song they knew, and they sang it over and over again, their voices louder and louder as they drank. Soon she was singing it with them, her face pressed to the window, her heart light with the knowledge that this was the gay and dirty world she would rejoin tomorrow. The sound of the door opening startled her. She had expected to be alone for the rest of the night. The door closed again as she turned to look, and Gyll was standing there, just inside it. "Gyll!" she said, and rushed to him, flinging herself into his arms. It was what she had most wanted without thinking of it— it was her proof that the world would right itself and be hers again. "Were you hurt, tortured?" she said.

"They didn't question me."

"But they said you swore against me. In the court they said——"

"They wouldn't hear me," Gyll said. "They didn't question me, they wouldn't hear me and they wouldn't let me go where the others were."

"Why did they let you come to me tonight?"

He held her in a painful hug against his chest, and she could feel the extra strength rest and food had given to his arms. "The Lady Eleanor arranged it," he said. "It cost her two rose nobles, and a jug of strong ale for the old monk outside the door. And she sent you this," he said, pulling two pieces of withered brown stuff from his belt-pouch.

"What is it?" she said, leaning to look.

"A little piece of the mushroom," he said. "She said you were to eat one tonight, so that you sleep, and one in the morning, so you're not afraid."

"I don't need it," she said, knocking his hand up so that the pieces flew over his head and fell to the floor. "I am drunk already with the joy of seeing you."

Gyll laughed and went down on his hands and knees, searching for the pieces.

"I am a little afraid of the water, all the same," she said.

"Don't be," Gyll said, putting the salvaged pieces of mushroom carefully in the middle of her table. "There isn't any need to be. How many times did I push your head under when we were at Aveiro, and you came to no harm."

"This will be deep water."

"It doesn't make any difference," he said. "Deep or shallow doesn't make any difference. You can drown in a bucket, if you have a mind to."

She laughed uncertainly. "Will you be there?"

He meant to be there. He didn't trust those bugger priests to be ready with a quick hand when her head rose above the water again. "If you want me to," he said.

"Oh yes, I want you to be there." She began to fiddle with the pieces of mushroom on the table. She didn't know what they were to do, what to talk about. She hadn't expected to see him again in this world. She didn't expect to see him again, after tomorrow. Soon she would be at home, and if she saw him there, he would be what he had been before—a tenant farmer, a nobody. But now, but now . . . and yet she had just confessed and been absolved, and she thought that she might float better in the morning if she went into the water with no new sins upon her. "He promised not to hurt you—Robert Apelfourde," she said.

"But my farm's gone," Gyll said. "He sent Daubeni to dismiss me."

"So you don't have to fight?"

"Not for him. I'll have to look for someone else to pay me."

"Why not go home?"

"To what?" he said. "I have no land."

"Go to the Lady Eleanor," she said, sick at the thought that he should lose everything when she was gaining so much. "She has brothers, and they have rich lands. She'll help you. She's our friend."

"Yours," he said. "She's from a family had their own boat at the Flood. Why should she bother with me?"

"Go to her all the same," Clodagh said urgently. The only alternative was to send him to Blanchefleur, and she didn't want him in her own neighbourhood when she was there again. "Tell her that I ask. She will do it for me. A small farm, a handful of coins to get you home again. Go to her. Promise me you'll go."

"I promise you," he said. He had his arms around her again, and he was nuzzling at the lobe of her ear. Tentatively she put a piece of the mushroom to her mouth, nibbled at it, waited for warmth and colour to flood in. "It's changed colour and got dry, and it doesn't work any more," she said. She bit off a little more and chewed and swallowed it, and then she put the rest into her mouth and pushed it into Gyll's mouth with her tongue, as she had done before. "We can't make love," she said. "I wouldn't dare."

"Not all of it," he said. "We can make a little bit," and he tried to draw her down onto the floor close to the fire. She broke away from him and ran through the doorway to fetch the fur coverlet from her bed. And when she walked slowly back carrying it in her arms, she felt the beginnings of the mushroom's spell, so that the skin of her arms seemed to feel the warmth and brownness of each single hair in the fur.

"It still works," she said, and saw by his smile that it was working for him. They spread the rug and lay down on it together, and at first all the pleasure that they needed came from their fingertips lightly stroking the other's face, and from the strange play of colours the light of the fire made on their half-closed lids.

"I mustn't sin," she said. "Just for tonight, I mustn't do any sin."

"There isn't any sin in touching," he said. His hands began to move softly over her body, and wherever he touched her the magical feeling of being transparent came.

"Everything inside me is pale violet, like gillyflowers on a windy day," she said, letting her hands stray lovingly down the length of his body. "You've still got it," she said, and laughed softly. "They said I magicked it away, and threw it into a tree."

"I got the tree back instead," he said boastfully. "But a tree needs roots. It won't grow forever if it isn't planted."

"I have to be watered first," she said, thinking of the next morning, and it seemed to them both that this was very funny, and they laughed. "Don't," she said after a moment, "don't laugh. It darkens the colours."

They lay for a little longer, touching and stroking, and the rest of the world dissolved and fell away. "Now everything inside me is burning crystal," she said, and the familiar heat seemed to burn away the last of her fears.

"I have to go," he said after a time, bending over her. "They said an hour. I have to go."

"And there wasn't any sin," she said without opening her eyes. "There wasn't, was there?"

"None," he said firmly, sitting up. He wanted to be gone now. She frightened him a little. He had wanted to see her, and not wanted to, expecting whimperings and tears and terrors. Those he would have understood. The lack of them, after the day she had spent, and the horrid thing she must face in the morning, abashed him, reminding him too painfully of their differences. He went to the table, and stood fingering the little piece of the mushroom that remained. "You will remember to eat it," he said. "Just a little bit, less than you had tonight. Just a little bit to make you happy while . . . on the way." He knew that there would be crowds and insults and things thrown. News had run through the town and the encampments that they were going to swim a witch tomorrow.

"I'll remember, and to breathe deep, and you *will* be there," she said, without opening her eyes. She had heard him move from the table towards the door, and she didn't want to see the last of him, or to lose the soft glow of colours inside her head.

"Yes," he said. "And afterwards? I will see you afterwards, again?"

"Of course, of course," she said, knowing it wasn't true.

The place they had chosen was at a distance from the town, and close to the sea. The tides had cut a deep basin there in the banks, and though the water was green with depth, you could see through it to clean sand on the basin's floor. They had brought her downriver in a rowing boat—Father Leofric, two foreign knights and three unknown English priests who kept their eyes turned always away from her. She was not very much afraid. She thought it one of the most beautiful, one of the most dazzling mornings she had seen. She had woken early and prayed for a long time, and then she had eaten a little shred of the mushroom to calm herself, and tucked the rest of it into the breast of her gown in case she should want it later. She had brushed her dark hair into a shining fall, and left it unbraided, so that it hung to her waist. There had been no sound as they came down the river, except for the noise of rowlocks and the water, and the soft murmur of Father Leofric's prayers from the stern of the boat. He was haggard and sleepless, and he looked like a man who had spent the night devouring his own heart.

When they came to the last bend in the river and the rowers began to pull towards the basin, Clodagh was dismayed to find that there was an excited crowd—soldiers and townspeople and their children and dogs—on the bank. The rowers brought the boat close inshore so that the people could see her, and then circled the basin, giving everyone a clear view of the boat and the people in it. The people shouted at her and shook their fists, and a rain of rubbish and fruit peelings and clods of earth began to fall on the boat and the water, making the priests throw up their arms to guard their faces. There was nothing she could do to protect herself. Her wrists had been lightly bound behind her back before they set out. She hoped it was only for the journey downriver, and that they would be unbound again before she went into the water. She sat upright, ignoring the shouts and the people, with her hair streaming softly out behind her in the breeze, and her eyes searching all the time for the sight of Gyll. She saw Father Nicholas at the edge of the water, kneeling in prayer. She thought she saw Godda and her sons in a noisy group of people, but she turned her eyes quickly away from them, looking for Gyll. Then a tall woman, standing with both arms raised as her mother had stood on the Dartmouth dock, caught her attention, and in the moment before she lost sight of her she was joyous with the hope that Blanchefleur was there, and that soon they would be together. Then she saw Gyll's head above the heads of the watchers, and lost it again. Again it appeared for an instant, level with the boat, and she knew that he was running behind the press of people, keeping abreast of the boat, keeping close to her, so that he would be near at hand to bring her out of the water. Now it was easier to ignore the crowd and their shouts. She watched for the brief appearances of his face, lifting her chin to him in acknowledgment every time he came into sight. As the boat finished its circuit and reached the outer edge of the basin once again a very great fear of what was to come overwhelmed her, and she closed her eyes, praying over and over again, "Dear God, make them untie me, make them untie me, God."

A change in the boat's direction made her open her eyes. It was pulling out from the bank now, towards the center of the basin. The early sun was striking bright dazzles from the wavelets made by the boat's motion. The water was a limpid and lovely green, and though it was very deep, she could see golden sand rippled into ridges on the bottom, marked with the pale moving shadows of the floating things the people had thrown.

The priests stood in the boat, and the two rowers uncovered their heads, holding the boat to its position by an occasional movement of the oars. Father Leofric began a Paternoster, and Clodagh stood too, her bare feet firmly planted to counter the slight rocking of the boat. The priest intoned a Confiteor and a Misereatur, using the Latin, and speaking quickly and quietly. He had no mind to prolong the business. The other judges had washed their hands of it, leaving the management of the ordeal to him. He had prayed unceasingly through the night, balancing the single sparrow against the whole of Christendom, God's reluctance to surrender His Sepulchre to the sinful against one straying lamb. He had prayed that the cup might pass from him, but it had not done so, and he feared that even that prayer might be a sort of sin. Perhaps the people on the banks could not hear his prayers, or perhaps their impatience overmastered them. In any case, they kept up their calls and their shouts of laughter while he prayed.

When he had done he and the other priests crossed themselves, and because the girl's hands were tied so that she couldn't make the sign herself, he signed the cross on her forehead with his finger. He took her by the shoulders and turned her so that he could check the binding of her wrists and then, at the last moment and to double assurance, he took from his robe a lead ball with a hook imbedded in it, put it between her cupped hands and pressed the hook into place over the wrist bindings. Two of the attendant priests seized her at a sign from Leofric. Clodagh looked upwards at the clear sky and drew an almighty breath into her lungs. Then she was thrown, head foremost, into the water. Her long dark hair floated out in a shining stream behind her, so that she seemed, in that last instant, to be winged.

And so it ended for her as it had begun—in sparkling water and bright sunlight, with an excited crowd watching as she went.